This book contains darker themes that may not be in everyone's comfort zones. Please review the list below prior to reading this book:

18+ Adult content

Detailed intimacy scenes

Detailed military chapters

DV, SA, CA

Kidnapping

Stalking

Car accidents

If I Have To Say Goodbye

Written by Allisa Rhipps

As always, this book is dedicated to my loved ones, which now includes my awesome team at Smiley's Unique Universe, and a friend of mine who is gone but never forgotten.

Thank you for believing in me, even when my impostor syndrome told you not to.

This book is also dedicated to those readers who have yet to see this page, because I like to believe someday you might, even if you never make it past this section. On November 27, 2024, at four in the evening, I was thinking about who you all might be, and it made my heart happy.

Chapter One

August 13, 2023

Delaney

I don't know what had felt worse as I stood beside the casket at my husband's funeral. The fact that I had hardly recognized anyone there, or the guilt I had for being angry at him for dying. It felt as if I was barely more than a shell, as I observed a sea of faces made up practically of strangers..

This wasn't what I thought my life was going to be like at twenty-five years old. Although, when Adam enlisted, I knew this was always a possibility. Every military member here had been a reminder of how naive I had been.

It didn't help that they also had the same look on their faces as they told me they were sorry for my loss, as if they were really saying "I told you so." Maybe I had missed the memo that declared pity was the required funeral attire for situations like mine. I should have been prepared for most of the people that showed up to pay their respects to be from his military world.

It would have made Adam proud, but to me, it was one more reminder of his sacrifice. I hated myself for the resentment I felt over his death. He was only months away from leaving the Army for good.

"We lost a good soldier, a good man. Please let me know if you need anything, Mrs. Anderson," Sergeant Jacobs offered gently as he shook my hand.

I nodded numbly. The phrase "good soldier" was repeated in the last hour so many times the words had lost their meaning. I could count on one hand how many people here had known him before the Army dictated every detail of our lives, before it made me a widow.

Kendric Tate walking in didn't change that. The air and conversation in the room, however, seemed to diminish the moment the doors slammed shut behind him. Oblivious to the disturbance, my husband's best friend bee lined in my direction.

The moment he clenched his jaw, I knew the look on his face hadn't been from grief. Anyone who didn't know the man wouldn't have been able to tell the difference. I unfortunately knew him well enough to know better; he was pissed and judging by the way he zeroed on me immediately, I was the target for his anger.

The sergeant had barely taken a step away from me when Kendric grabbed my arm. Whatever he had come to scold me about must have needed somewhere more private. Without a word, he pulled me into the doorway between the kitchenette and the viewing room.

“Tell me there was a typo,” he demanded low under his breath as we came to a stop.

I blinked back my confusion. Restraining himself, he took a deep breath.

“Interment will follow at Morley Oaks Cemetery,” he said verbatim as if reading it straight from the obituary. His voice was louder this time as he struggled with his rising anger.

I straightened. He couldn’t have been serious. This wasn’t his decision. In fact, it had been Adam’s, not that it had been any of Kendric’s business. Still, I was honestly surprised Adam had never mentioned it to him.

“Not here Kendric,” I dismissed.

We were headed toward a fight that I was desperately trying to avoid. I knew we weren’t completely out of earshot.

“Would you prefer we have this conversation at the gravesite?” He challenged me as I tried to walk away from him.

I gave an apologetic nod to the friends and family that had patiently waited to give more sincerities or support. This wasn’t the place or the time, but he didn’t seem to care. I braced myself for the argument Kendric was determined to have.

I turned to face my husband's closest friend, and I pointed to the kitchenette behind him, giving him a silent order I prayed he would follow. Clenching his jaw once more, he turned and waited for me to enter the room. The silent countdown began.

"What part of not here did you not understand?" I hissed under my breath as he shut the kitchenette door behind us.

The smell of the flowers faded into the overpowering smell of stale coffee, after he sealed us off from the rest of the building. The barley lived in furniture and the generic hospitality smell reminded me of a hospital waiting room. At least after Kendric informed me of all the ways I failed Adam as a wife I'd have the comfort of warm caffeine.

"The part where Adam deserved better than to end up back in the town we escaped from, for starters," He shot back as if the gravesite had been picked as a punishment.

I let out a humorless chuckle at his audacity. Who did he think he was? He had known me most of my life. Out of anyone here, he should have been the one other person who understood what it meant to Adam to be next to his mother.

"So let me clarify; you think I spitefully chose his resting place? Figured I was so mad he chose the Army over me that I would pick the one place I thought he'd hate?" I asked, failing to keep the anger from my voice.

“He should be in a VA gravesite. He earned it,” Kendric volleyed.

It was clear he had no idea that these plans had been made well before Adam died. If it had been up to me, I wouldn’t have made the decision alone. In our whole marriage, Kendric had probably spent more time with him than I had.

“That is not yours or your precious Army’s decision,” I snapped back, instead of providing any other explanation.

I wasn’t even aware Adam had made these decisions until I found the paperwork safely tucked away in a box of important documents we kept on top of the fridge. The fact he hadn’t even told his best friend left me with an uneasy feeling, but I couldn’t voice that. Not when Kendric was practically accusing me of using Adam’s interment to get back at my husband.

“Yeah, well it really shouldn’t have been yours either,” Kendric huffed under his breath, but I heard it.

It wasn’t the way he had said it that bothered me. It was the truth behind them. Until I heard it from his lips, I still held onto the hope that no one knew how strained my relationship had become.

“And I never wanted it to be,” I replied, barely audible.

Kendric's ice cold glare dropped to the floor at my words for a moment. I didn't care that I had just scratched at an old wound that never healed properly. It was an unspoken agreement between Kendric and I that was never to be mentioned, but in my self-hate, my filter broke.

"Be as angry as you like, but I am not one of your soldiers and this is not up for discussion," I finally spoke, breaking the silence that had grown between us after my last comment. Before he could fight it anymore, I pushed past him and opened the door.

Kendric reached out to grab my arm to stop me from leaving but I shrugged it off and looked up at him.

"Not. Here," I said through my teeth, solidifying my exit.

"We will talk more later," He threatened as I left the room, forcing the conversation from my mind so I could play my role as the grieving widow.

August 10, 2015

Kendric

On the first day of my senior year, I was up before my alarm clock blared the overplayed pop song. It felt like a sign that the song chosen for that particular morning had been stuck in my head for days. This was meant to be the last year I was trapped in my tiny hometown, and the song chosen was meant to symbolize the ability to be anything once the mindset set was in place.

"Turn that fucking thing off!" My father shouted above my symbol for hope.

Taking a deep breath, I reminded myself that I was going to be gone soon. Ten more months and I wouldn't have to deal with him or the alcohol that ate away any chance I had for a college fund. Less than a year, and I would finally be free.

My game plan had been to enlist the earliest I could. My eighteenth birthday was a month before we were supposed to graduate. One more sign I counted on like I needed oxygen. Some days, that timeline had been more of a lifeline than a goal.

I pulled a t-shirt off the back of a chair, giving it a sniff test before I recounted the game plan I had memorized for the last eight years. The minty smell of my toothpaste made it almost impossible to tell if the shirt was past its prime. Before I had too long to second guess the shirt itself, my phone buzzed on the shelf beside me, with the text I had been waiting for.

Adam: Ready for the SS?

SS stood, rightfully, for "Shit Show." My best friend's daily message hadn't changed since we were in the sixth grade. Still, it felt nice to have someone who represented some form of stability in my life.

I smirked at his reference. Mainly because his reasons for being annoyed at having to go to school were completely different from mine. He didn't have a family he needed to escape from and no substantial plans after high school. He was counting down days to graduation as if the diploma would show the world he was officially an adult.

Dodging my father's early morning temper, and my mother's tearful send off, I darted out the door. It was a thirty minute walk from my front door to the school, and I wanted that rare moment of peace to get my head straight. That half hour felt like ten minutes as I hummed the song that played through the alarm clock the whole way there.

Standing predictably at the entrance of Morley High, was Adam. It was no surprise he wore the same shirt he had sported most of that summer. The girl in front of him however had been a new development I wasn't prepared for.

She was someone who would have been worth remembering, but I didn't know her. It wasn't often we got new students in our tiny town, nor had it been like Adam to hit one up on the first day. I stayed back for a moment and watched their interaction.

It was like watching a rom-com play out in front of my eyes where the pretty new girl zeros in on a guy who thinks he's the outcast but is really a prince charming in disguise. That was Adam. He could have fit in with the jocks if he had wanted to, and he wasn't a "ladies man". He was the kind of guy who fit with a girl like her.

She seemed to fit that All-American girl aesthetic, which would have immediately placed her into that social crowd. Her high ponytail and smaller build screamed cheerleader material. I wondered what made her someone he was comfortable enough to talk to, like an old friend.

When curiosity got the better of me, I waved at my friend and closed the distance between us. When the girl turned to face me, it almost felt like someone had knocked me backwards. Her freckled cheeks and big green eyes were definitely something I wouldn't have forgotten.

It was no wonder my friend had been so captivated. She was gorgeous and the warmth of her smile answered every question I had about their interaction. The instant attraction left me mute as I stared at her in embarrassing awe.

"Oh! sorry! I didn't realize you were meeting someone, I should go find my first class," The girl said to Adam from over her shoulder, never breaking eye contact with me.

Waiting for any kind of greeting, she stood there watching me with a raised eyebrow. Out of the corner of my eye, I watch Adam's smile grow wider from my reaction. Weirded out by my silence, she turned to head through the doors of the school.

"New student?" was all I could choke out as I called after her.

I could have introduced myself, or offered to show her to her homeroom, but all intelligent words escaped me. It didn't help that Adam was fighting back his merciless taunt in the background.

I stood there preparing to die in that very spot when she turned and looked at me, unsure if I had shouted that at her or Adam. Hesitantly, she looked down the hall behind her before returning to Adam's side, pointing at her chest and tilting her head.

"I am?" She answered with a smirk as if amused by my awkwardness.

I went to respond but my brain was still fighting through the embarrassment from before. Adam, sensing my brain glitch, put his hand on the girl's shoulder, temporarily drawing her attention off of my failure to function.

"Welcome to Morley High. This ball of awkwardness that stands before you is Kendric Tate. Don't worry; he gets less awkward the longer you are around him," Adam said with a wolfish smile.

I cleared my throat from the tension and rubbed the back of my neck, unsure if I should shake her hand or defend myself. Not missing a beat, she faced me again with a smile from ear to ear and reached out her hand.

"Delaney Martin, you can call me Laney," she offered and I shook her hand, grateful she made the decision for me.

"Don't worry; awkward people are *my* kind of people," she said softly in an attempt to ease my embarrassment.

I could feel the heat creep over my cheeks as she said it. I knew at that moment that Delaney Martin would be trouble. Maybe it was the unearned jealousy I felt when Adam looked at her, or the way she seemed to fry my brain cells, but either way, I knew she could ruin me and the plan I had to escape Morley.

Chapter Two

August 20, 2023

Delaney

I walked into my house after a double shift and felt the weight of its emptiness. It was the first time it didn't feel like home since the men in uniform informed me about Adam's death. I threw my coat on the counter and sighed.

My mother kept reminding me that things would get easier. On one hand, I was sure she meant I would eventually stop feeling so broken, but the grief was a constant reminder of Adam. On the other hand, I wasn't sure what would be left of me when the pain faded. I had been the wife of a soldier for half a decade.

There were little moments when my brain would blissfully forget that he was gone. Moments where I caught myself missing him and had a small spark of hope he was almost home for good. They happened when I first woke in the mornings and until this shift, they had been when I first walked through the door.

Like clockwork, my phone rang. My mother's name filled the screen. I closed my eyes and gathered myself before I answered.

"Hi, mom," I repeated out of habit as I put the phone to my ear.

"Hi honey! How was your shift? Do they always work you these long hours?" She responded and I pinched the bridge of my nose to fight the defensiveness my brain instinctively adapted.

"Not always. They were short staffed last week while I was out," I replied.

I couldn't tell her I volunteered for more hours. It would have led to her worrying I wasn't making enough to live comfortably, or worse, I would be forced to tell her I had to save up to move off base within a year. In all honesty, I didn't mind the extra work because it kept me out of this empty house full of reminders.

"As long as this isn't something they expect of you all the time. Your mental wellness is really important right now," she lectured as I looked around the house distracted.

I spent the first week after Adam's death cleaning my house obsessively. At first I thought my unease had been the fact it wasn't pristine. It wasn't until after the funeral that I realized what made the whole house seem like it was taunting me.

All the decor, and furniture were things I had set up when we moved in only four months before his death. He had promised to add his flare when his contract was up and he was out for good. He was finishing his last deployment when the IED took him away from me.

I wiped away the tears that the reminder had summoned. For one blissful moment I had forgotten I was still on the phone.

"Honey?" My mother repeated in concern at my silence.

"I'm sorry, mom, I got distracted. Can you repeat that?" I asked, hating how exhausted my voice sounded.

"I asked if you had heard anything else about the investigation," My mother repeated and my heart rate increased.

It was uncanny how many times my mother had hit the nail on the head, about what thoughts clouded my mind. The problem was, she didn't understand that the civilian world and the military one were different. It didn't take a brilliant detective to figure out who had been responsible.

"It was an IED, mom. There wasn't a ton to investigate," I answered, bracing myself for the advice she was no doubt about to give me on how to get more answers I didn't need.

As she droned on about how she would handle the situation if she were in my shoes, I headed to the kitchen. The shift had been a crazy one, and I hadn't eaten since breakfast that morning. One look into my barren fridge reminded me I should have stopped for groceries.

Her rant faded into the background as I decided on an apple and some peanut butter. It was better than nothing. I threw out a few distracted "uh-huhs" as I reached for something to cut up my apple.

Before I could grab a hold of the knife to cut it, my phone buzzed against my ear. Pulling the device from my face, I placed it on speaker as my mother droned on none the wiser. It was just my luck to receive a message from the bane of my existence.

"Have you talked at all to Kendric?" She asked once again, enacting her clairvoyant powers.

"No mom, I haven't. I really have no desire right now," I said irritatedly as I read his text.

Kendric: You home? We need to finish that conversation.

I glared at my phone and tried to ignore his message. Leaving my mother on speaker, I pulled the knife from the drawer to resume preparing my dinner for champions.

"I think it'd be a good idea to lean on each other. You both lost someone important in your lives and regardless of your past..." Mom had started but I cut her off, unwilling to talk about the history I had with the man.

"I know mom. Adam was his best friend, but you don't know what he is like now," I argued.

She sighed heavily on the other line and it seemed to echo through the house.

"I'm just saying you aren't alone," she replied.

A knock at the door followed her statement as the universe had gotten with my mother for an unnecessary intervention. In my shock at the noise, my hand slipped, slicing open my finger instead of the apple.

“Mom, I need to go, someone is here,” I rushed out, purposely avoiding any mention of my new battle wound.

I quickly hung up the phone with my mother, and rinsed my fresh cut under the kitchen sink, peaking out of my window. An impatient knock sounded a second time through the house. Sure enough, parked across the street, was Kendric’s black worn down pickup truck.

August 17, 2015

Kendric

One week of Delaney Martin only solidified the theory that she would be trouble. At first glance, she might not have seemed like much of a threat, because in all honesty, she was like bottled sunshine with a ponytail. Part of me believed that was the whole reason she was an issue when it came to my future plans and the friendship between Adam and I.

We didn't make it four hours into that first school day before I noticed Adam was as addicted as I was at first sight. We couldn't help it. Delaney was intoxicating.

"Earth to Kendric, Aren't you late for P.E.?" Delaney asked as she waved her hand in front of my face.

I rolled my eyes and grabbed my bag off the ground beside me. I wanted to thank her or respond in some way that didn't make her feel like I disliked her. The indifference I wore like a mask was my only defense.

I would have needed to keep my distance regardless of how Adam felt about her. Every time she looked up at me with those big green eyes, I was reminded how easily falling for her could ruin any plan I had to join the Army. She needed someone who didn't leave her for months at a time, and I couldn't be that person.

"Of course, Del, Please excuse me while I rush off to the gym where an overweight and balding man can tell me I am not running fast enough," I grumbled as I pushed past her quick enough I could hate myself without seeing her face.

“That’s not my name,” she half-heartedly fought back.

She didn’t know it but that was the whole reason I called her that. Laney felt too comfortable and Delaney felt too formal. It was a way to keep my distance. I didn’t make it ten steps before Adam was on my heels.

“Hey, man!” He called after me as if he thought I would try to ignore him too.

I didn’t turn to face him, but I slowed my pace, allowing him to reach my side.

“You could be nicer to her,” he chided as we walked toward the old auditorium.

We both knew he was right, but I couldn’t agree with him and not give away why I had chosen to be rude. At least his plans for the future didn’t involve the military. If she picked either of us, it should be him.

“You are nice enough for the both of us,” I teased, but I could hear the jealousy in my words that I hoped he didn’t pick up on.

He blew the statement off as if hearing the lie for what it was. We walked in silence to the locker rooms. It didn't take me ten minutes to get dressed in my shorts and t-shirt, but I needed a moment to kick myself privately.

Today was the first round of tests where they judged how fast you could run a mile after a summer of assumed laziness. Something our school did to "compare" times to the one they did at the end of the year so they could brag at the improvements we made. I had half the mind to walk it.

"Dude, did you check out that new girl?" A familiar voice gossiped in a different row of lockers.

I knew the voice and knew whatever conversation I was about to overhear was nothing short of disgusting. Quietly, I shut the locker, and prepared to leave. The last thing I wanted to hear was Quinton Beck's opinion of the girl I was trying not to fall for.

"How could I not?" Quinton's right-hand stooge, Kevin Gear, replied in a brainless chuckle.

I clenched my jaw and headed toward the door as I tried to ignore them. It was none of my business.

Delaney wasn't exactly mine and their locker room talk was always reperformed publicly in front of their meathead friends.

"Bet I could get her number before the end of class," Kevin challenged as I paused in my steps.

These guys were not the same kind of jock that Adam was. Their bets never stayed at a reasonable level. Since the seventh grade, they had sent out nudes to the guys in our class from half the female students' population.

"Haha, dude, you keep that number. I'll have her cup size before you send your first text," Quinton challenged back and the three of us knew what this meant.

There was a group of five guys from the football team, including Quinton and Kevin, who ran in this tight circle of sleaze bags. All five had been known for their pranks. Quinton's signature involved seeing just how far he could get with anyone stupid enough to try to change him. He'd lead them on, push their boundaries until they broke, and then he'd send out the evidence.

White hot rage filled my chest as I imagined them using Del as their latest conquest. She had only been here a week, and had no idea how cruel they could be and that's what they counted on. I wasn't sure if she would accept it if I tried to warn her thanks to my self appointed behavior toward her.

I was so close to leaving the room my hand was on the doorknob, but I couldn't bring myself to open the door. The longer I stood there trying to convince myself this wasn't my fight, the angrier I got at the worst-case scenarios in my head if I stayed quiet. By the time their footsteps sounded off, I had decided.

The moment I turned to confront them, the two boys had already rounded the lockers and were in view. Quinton was making groping motions in the air and they were laughing, but I could hear them over the rising buzz of my fury.

When they saw me standing there, they slowed to a stop just out of arm's reach. Kevin's eyes widened as he took in my expression. Quinton's mischievous smile stayed firmly in place oblivious to the fact I was a possible threat.

"Oh, Sorry *Ricky*. Didn't realize you were still in here," Quinton said cheerfully as he began to register my stance on their topic.

Normally, I would have decked him for calling me the same name my father used. His dad wasn't much different than mine; the only separation had been the money our families had. He knew better than anyone why no one else called me that.

My conscience tried once more to reason with me to walk out the door. Delaney was intelligent. Even if she didn't believe me or Adam, surely she would find out from the other girls that these guys were a waste of oxygen.

"Just leaving," I replied

Forcing myself to follow through, I turned to leave. I thought if I said the words out loud that my logical side would win the argument, but as my hand hit the doorknob, everything in me rebelled.

"Wait," Quinton commanded as the slime practically dripped from his voice, "You are friends with Delaney Martin, right?"

"Enough to know the only cup size you'll get from her will be five years from now after you have prematurely peaked," I retorted as I turned to face them, ready for the fight I tried to avoid.

Any debate on doing the right thing disappeared from my mind the moment he asked the question. I wish I could have said it didn't matter who he had been asking about, but it did. She wasn't mine, and I had zero claim to her, but I was done hearing her name come out of their mouths.

I watched the humor drain from Quinton as Kevin suppressed a smirk. Half of the time that was how it was. Quinton was the star of the duo, and Kevin was the loyal friend who blindly agreed, regardless of his own feelings. I might have liked him, if he had enough of a spine to voice his own opinions.

Knowing we weren't far from blows, I scanned the area. Quinton's simmering rage seemed to be building as he worked hard to find a witty comeback. I knew I could take them individually, but I was doubtful I could take on both of them alone. Thankfully the bat rack wasn't too far from reach.

"The only reason I'd be behind her wouldn't involve soft drinks, but if you need proof, I am happy to videotape it," Quinton popped off as he elbowed his buddy as if his primitive and offensive comment had been some big inside joke.

Without warning, or ability to stop myself, I swung. My fist connected with Quinton's jaw, causing him to stagger backwards. Everything felt like it happened after that in slow motion. I dodged the punch his buddy threw and headed straight for the bats.

Quinton's shoulder slammed into my ribs just before I reached one, the impact forcing my torso to collide with the wooden frame of the rack. Shoving Quinton back with one hand, I grabbed a bat from the box.

Neither of them seemed to know I had grabbed it. As Kevin steadied Quinton, I resituated my grip on the weapon Quinton didn't see until it was too late to block my upward swing.

Once again, Kevin played catcher as he kept Quinton from losing his balance. The blood seeping from between Quinton's fingers was a satisfying confirmation of my hit.

"You broke my nose, you psycho," Quinton let out a muffled curse from behind his hand.

I glanced at Kevin who stood there almost panicked as he pulled on his buddy's shoulders. Despite Kevin's attempt to get Quinton to leave, neither of them moved. I raised the bat for round two.

I watched both of the jocks evaluate their chances. Spineless Kevin raised his hands in surrender as Quinton looked at me with pure hate. My teeth were clenched so tight it felt they might fracture from the pressure before either made a move.

“We got it dude,” Kevin tried to reassure as he shoved his friend toward the door.

Quinton didn’t budge except to spit blood onto the floor near my shoes. He didn’t seem to get the message. Part of me prayed for a second round.

“And just like that, you have made her my pet project,” Quinton challenged with promise in his eyes.

He didn’t get the whole sentence out before I charged him. Kevin ran for the door as I pinned Quinton to the lockers with the bat to his throat.

“Try it and you will be mine,” I threatened as I pressed more weight into the bat.

He wasn’t able to say anything back before the coach busted into the room, Kevin shortly behind.

“Break it up! Tate, principal's office, now! Kevin, take your friend to the nurse!” The coach demanded as his voice reverberated through the room.

I looked Quinton up and down before pushing off of him from the bat. He sank to the linoleum floor, choking for air as Kevin rushed to his side to help him up. I didn't bother to look at the couch as I tossed the bat to the locker room floor.

"Make sure you tell her it was your fault when her video goes viral," Quinton yelled after me as I walked out of the locker room and into the gym.

The room fell silent. As the runners slowed to a stop, I met Adam's questioning eyes from across the room. Feeling guilty, I dropped his stare and headed toward the principal's office.

When I passed Del, I pretended not to see her. Everything in me wanted to warn her about Quinton and Kevin's plan, but I knew it was only a matter of time before the fight got around the school. It was better to say nothing and let her come to her own conclusions instead of painting myself as her knight in shining armor.

Chapter Three

August 20,2023

Delaney

As Kendric's impatient knock echoed through my home, I ripped a paper-towel off the roll. I was too anxious to get rid of him or care as the quilted towels fell from my countertop and unraveled across the kitchen floor. It wasn't like he would be coming in to see my house, anyway.

I wrapped my finger in the makeshift bandage and I reached for the doorknob. Bracing myself for whatever he had come to scold me for this time, I opened my front door just in time to see him heading toward his truck. If I had known he was that impatient, I wouldn't have bothered.

The moment I thought about it, I regretted it. Driven by my stupid empathy, I called out to him. It hadn't been like him to give up so easily and the fact that he had made me annoyingly curious.

"I thought you were out," He said as he approached me, almost hesitant.

I didn't miss the way he said it looking at the ground instead of up at me. Everything about him seemed off, but I took the moment to hide my poorly wrapped finger from sight. I couldn't pry without expecting him to do the same, and I didn't want to give him an excuse to follow me into the house.

"I was just..." I paused, trying to sort through what to tell him.

He would have understood if I told him I had been on the phone with my mother. It would have been the truth, but something about that admission felt more personal than the small talk we normally had. The pause in my excuse made him look up at me as if he was preparing for a lie.

"Mom called. I was trying to get her off the phone," I admitted barely above a whisper.

He nodded once as if resisting the urge to call me out on it. The awkward silence grew between us as he stood uncomfortable on my doorstep. When that silence grew so big I thought it would swallow me whole, I broke it.

"Look, if you are here to argue more about that burial site, I just worked a double shift and I really don't—" I started in a tone somewhere between dismissive and defensive.

Kendric held up his hand to cut me off, and I paused. His blueish-green eyes stopped me in my tracks, or more the intensity of them. There had been more emotion behind them than I had seen in years.

"No, I…I came to apologize," He spoke as if the words felt bitter on his tongue.

I blinked back my surprise, but I must not have concealed the concern that still lingered from the way he acted. Our normal conversations had either been icy cold, or full of heated malice. I wasn't sure I had heard those words from his mouth since our graduation.

I waited for him to finish as I looked him over. Another thing that I hadn't done much of since we were teenagers. It was easier to get along with him that way, but Kendric had always been someone I didn't have to look deep into in order to understand him. It had always felt closer to trying to understand the meaning of a book after reading its pages.

"You were right. I shouldn't have lashed out at you in the funeral home," He finished, never actually saying the words "I'm sorry", but I wasn't concentrating on his words.

The wetness of the paper-towel and the difference in his demeanor distracted me. I didn't have to look to know I would have to clean the blood off my door when he left. I had been so caught up in answering the door, I hadn't even really bothered to look at the wound before I wrapped it.

His brows drew together in an expression I couldn't read as he watched me carefully. The self-consciousness I had felt when I hid my hand behind the door multiplied under his gaze. Kendric had been reading me too.

"It's fine," I finally choked out after I realized I never really acknowledged his attempt to make things right.

Everything in his expression told me he didn't believe me. Kendric took a step toward me and I tensed.

He studied me and for a moment, it was like we had been thrown back in time. Nostalgia crept over me as I remembered who he used to be before he enlisted.

"Can we go inside and talk?" he asked, as if trying to feel me out.

Internally I panicked. I knew what he would see when he walked into my house, but the worry had been linked to just how much Kenderic would observe. He already seemed to think I didn't care enough about Adam. How would he react when he saw nothing in the home that really reflected his best friend?

The guilt made my eyes fall to the floor before I could answer him. As I became overwhelmingly aware of his eyes on me, I swallowed hard to unstick the words from my throat. My pause in answering him, gave away so much more than any transparent lie would have.

"It's been a long day," I finally choked out.

My hand tightened around the door the moment I saw a familiar look on his face. He had full intention of calling my bluff. The sharp pain from the pressure made me wince and I grabbed my cut out of pure instinct.

“Del?” Kenderic asked as he came to my side with unfiltered concern in his voice.

The quickness of his movements told me he didn’t think before he made them. Something about that stirred old feelings I had thought were long dead. I swallowed them down out of self-preservation and focused on the only thing I could; mild irritation.

“That's not my name. Wait here,” I cursed through my teeth.

I had been right. The blood had completely soaked through the dressing. I stepped back into the house to find the roll of paper towels that I had left on the floor. As I should have expected, he ignored me and followed me inside.

“What the hell happened?” he demanded. The soft tone to his voice from before was completely gone, like he was actually angry I let myself get injured.

“I told you to wait outside,” I snapped as the panic rose in my throat like acid.

“While you were holding up your hand covered in blood, which I can help with if you’d just let me see your damn hand,” Kenderic shot back as he grabbed my wrist firmly and turned it so that he could see the cut.

Gingerly, he peeled back the soiled towel, and I shut my eyes. I wasn't sure if I closed them so tight to avoid seeing the cut or the look on his face when he did. Either way, they shot back open the moment I heard him curse under his breath.

"This needs stitches," he said as if he was speaking more to himself than to me.

I tried to pull my hand out of his grip but he firmly held me in place. As I accepted I couldn't overpower him, Kenderic shot me glare as if I was being a disobedient child.

"It's fine. I...I can go get it checked out," I lied but I knew it hadn't been convincing.

He looked down at my face for a moment, as if trying to decide if I would honestly take myself in. A deep breath later, he slowly grabbed the paper towel roll from where I cradled it to my side.

"Let me wrap this and I will take you in," he said, once again giving me no wiggle room for escape.

He ripped a sheet of the towels off with his teeth before letting the rest drop to the ground. Everything about him was starting to piss me off. I wasn't a child. It wasn't his place to handle me as if I couldn't, now that I didn't have a husband to dote on me halfway around the world.

“I’m a grown woman. I can take myself!” I snapped.

Shaking his head, Kendric focused back on the task at hand. Every time he tried to apply pressure, I winced. Watching his reaction felt like I was watching him remember I was attached to the wound he was trying to fix.

“I’m taking you in,” His voice a low commanding growl, as he secured the paper towel and released his grip on my wrist.

The moment he let go, I jerked my hand back, holding the freshly dressed wound securely to my chest. There was nothing he could say that would convince me to go anywhere with him; I wasn’t his puppet.

“Like hell you are!” I snapped but my words had more bite than my voice.

“Tell me one good reason why I shouldn’t? It’s bleeding like a stuck hog and pressure isn’t helping,” he sounded exasperated.

Maybe it was the tiredness. In all honesty though, it was probably the fear. Either way, before I could stop myself, I answered him.

“Any reason I can give you would just be another lie,” I whispered, and he straightened.

"Then you are coming in with me. Nothing good will come of you treating it here by yourself," he barked, and I took a step away from him.

"No, you are not. I'm not coming back to…this. I did it once already today and I don't have it in me to do it again," The words came out of my mouth before I could stop them.

The house always felt heavier and more empty anytime I walked through the door, even more so at night. The unwelcomed reason crashed down only hours before and I had no desire to relive it. It wasn't like I would bleed to death from a cut on my finger.

Looking at the concern that had been plastered all over Kendric's face, it was obvious he wasn't budging. He watched me for a moment before he looked back down at the paper towel that once again had soaked through.

"Fine, just hold pressure on it," he ordered as he grabbed his keys from his pocket. Without any explanation, he headed out the door.

I had expected more fight out of him, or for him to question my intelligence, but it felt as if he had given up far too easily. Before I knew what had hit me, I was watching my front door close behind him and I wasn't sure what was wrong with me. The last thing I had expected was how strongly I felt his absence.

My finger pulsed against my palm as I gave into his command. All the while trying to convince myself that the feelings I was having was due to the once again emptier house. The last thing I could accept was that I actually wanted him to be here.

As my body started to relax and my thoughts went back to normal, my front door opened and Kendric slipped in holding a duffle bag. I raised a brow and watched him as he set it at my feet and kneeled down to open it while I suppressed the relief I felt at his return.

"What are you—" I started as he pulled out a pair of pastel blue gloves and draped them across his knee.

The words died in my mouth as he pulled out a suture kit and balanced it on top of the gloves. Realization hit me as I took a shaky breath.

"You need stitches," He said, distracted, as he placed a roll of gauze on the pile and palmed a roll of medical tape before zipping up his bag.

I stared at him in disbelief. He couldn't be serious.

Kendric shot me an impatient look out of the corner of his eye. He definitely was 100% serious. He moved the items from my knee and set everything up on my counter as I watched in horror.

“You will have to hold still. Should take three, maybe four stitches tops,” he instructed when he was ready, not caring if I was or not.

I could have fought it or caved and went with him to the hospital but I didn’t. That part of me that feared coming home kept my feet firmly in place. Instead, I silently nodded, and he placed the heel of his dominant hand on my wrist to pin it to the counter as if worried I wouldn’t be able to hold still.

“You know it wasn’t my decision right,” I blurted when the nervousness got the best of me.

Not stopping, he brought the needle from his suture kit to the hand that was holding my wrist in place.

“What wasn’t?” he asked as he pinched my finger on either side of my wound, pushing it together.

“Where Adam was laid to rest,” I answered with a wince, “He didn’t even tell me that was where he wanted it to be, but there were forms. He made the decision without me,”

Kendric paused a moment, taking in my words or maybe just bracing himself for what he needed to do. Either way, when he spoke, his voice had an unexpected softness to it.

“Why didn’t you say that at the funeral home?” he asked as he sewed the first stitch in place.

My stomach turned from the pain and I bit back a verbal cry. Kendric tensed sensing my discomfort and gave me a moment to pull it together before he went in for another.

“Why did I have to?” I challenged back as he readied himself for the next stitch.

“You are right; you shouldn’t have had to,” He agreed as I fought the urge to vomit.

“If it’s any consolation, the moment I saw his mom’s headstone, I realized what an ass I was,” he added when I hadn’t replied.

“And I should have told you before we both made jerks of ourselves,” I said as my voice shook from the pain.

When he started the third stitch, I braced my other hand on his shoulder and he flinched slightly under my touch. At first I had thought it was from the surprise at my contact, but it wasn’t. Under my fingertips, I felt the uneven skin beneath his t-shirt.

Judging by the size and the indention, it felt like the kind of scar someone would have gotten if they had been shot. The feeling of it reminded me of a story Adam once told me about the first deployment they shared. As quickly as I placed my hand on Kendric, I jerked it back.

There was no amount of change in Kendric that my conscience would allow me to let on that I knew about that wound. I couldn't explain to him how I knew about the situation or why I had never brought it up, not without revealing my feelings when I heard. It wouldn't have mattered if by some miracle he became the guy he was before he left for basic.

November 13, 2015

Kendric

The last bell rang announcing the end of the school day as the classroom erupted into chaos. Everyone, including the science teacher, Mr. Gilliam, seemed in a rush to get home. Thanks to the last football game of the season, the normal mayhem paled in comparison.

I couldn't have cared less. Patiently, I waited for the class to file out so I could walk out with Del. By the time I saw her, we had been the only ones left in the room with Mr. Gilliam.

"Have a good weekend, Mr. Tate," Mr. Gilliam said impatiently as if trying to rush me out.

At first, I didn't think Del was in the room, but the longer he glared at me, the more nervous she was getting. When I heard the paper in her hand crinkle, I turned to see her anxiously folding the corner down. I knew as soon as I saw the hint of red ink, she had waited so late, because he had asked her to stay for a scolding.

Her big green eyes caught mine on my way out the door, and I paused. The anxiety in them left me with a bad feeling. Before I could say anything, Mr. Gilliam cleared his throat. I reminded myself I needed to keep my indifference.

The moment I shut the door I regretted it. Hard to believe rumors tugged at my decision to walk home so I leaned against the wall opposite of the classroom and waited for her. It wasn't like I had been in a rush to go home, and Delaney only lived a couple blocks away from me.

I watched the last bus leave the parking lot out of the big glass doors, trying not to watch the time. The longer I stood there, the more I justified walking her home. Six extra blocks would only extend my freedom, and I didn't have to be anything other than the Kendric she knew.

The classroom door swung open with a bang and startled me from my excuses to spend more time with her. Del walked past me, staring down at her feet as she rushed by, unaware of my existence. I had never seen her like that.

“Hey, Del, wait up,” I hollered after her as I sped up to catch her.

“Not now, Kendric,” she dismissed me.

Warning bells sounded off around me as I finally caught up. Before she could tell me to leave, I grabbed her arm gently, just above her elbow and slowed us to a stop. I came around to face her.

She wouldn’t look at me, but I didn’t need her to. Her cheeks were flushed and wet from crying. On pure instinct, I pulled her into me and I knew by the way she melted into my chest that I was done playing distant.

“What happened back there?” I asked just above a whisper.

As if my voice made her remember our fragile friendship, she pushed off me and wiped her face. I didn’t miss the way she hadn’t completely pulled out of my arms. Even though the voice in the back of my head told me to, I couldn’t let her go either.

“Nothing. *Nothing* happened,” she lied as her eyes stayed firmly on the sidewalk beneath our feet.

I lowered myself to try and get her eye contact, but the moment I did she looked away from me, embarrassed. For the first time since I met her, I wished I had done things differently. I wished I had let her in enough that she felt like she could be honest with me.

“We aren’t moving until you give me something more to go on,” I threatened. The soft tone to my voice had been sharpened by my concern for her.

She crossed her arms and looked up at the sky to prevent more tears from falling down her face, still avoiding me. She took a deep breath as I straightened. Finally, she looked at me.

“I can’t answer that and I’m not really sure myself. Just promise to never leave me alone with him again,” she spat out as if the words were bitter on her tongue.

I stilled. Mr. Gilliam had been hired at the end of the last school year. Where I had found him to be mind numbingly boring and strict, there had been a rumor right before school had let out. It didn’t sound any more believable than most of the high school rumors created by bored teens.

Without replying, I let her go and headed back toward the school. If there was any luck, I’d catch the bastard in his car. There were very few things I thought were worth losing my future on. This had been one of them.

“Kendric, stop! What do you think you are doing?” Del shouted after me, full of panic.

“Making up for leaving you with him,” I posited, even though I didn’t mean to answer her out loud.

She raced to cut me off. Her eyes once again brimmed with tears. This time however, the feelings behind those beautiful eyes had shifted. She looked desperate.

I paused, the plea in her addictingly green eyes made me feel like a monster. She had no doubt heard about the fight in the locker room, although no one seemed to know it was over Del. The last thing I wanted was for her to fear me and my reactions.

As desperately as I wanted to calm down, I couldn’t get the possible scenarios out of my head. The rumor had morphed into so many different versions, there was no telling which one had been the truth. There was still a chance they had nothing to do with what happened in that room when I left.

“Tell me he didn’t touch you,” I said through my teeth, needing confirmation.

Her eyes widened as the doors opened behind her. I couldn’t tell if it had been from my assumptions, or out of concern that I already knew. Either way, her gut reaction to my question made my heart race.

“W-what?” she asked as her voice shook and broke, adding one more stone to the pit of my stomach.

Mr. Gilliam walked out completely unaware we stood nearby. The countdown began. I looked back at her searching her face for any sign of truth to that rumor.

"Did.He.Touch.You?" I ground out, forcing down the unease as my peripherals tracked the teacher's lazy steps toward the parking lot.

"N-no! Just leave it be," she choked out as realization hit her.

There was no sign of her usual tells but something in the way she lowered her voice made me question if she was being completely honest. I heard a car door shut from the direction of the parking lot and I took a deep breath. I had missed my chance and scared her in the process.

"Can we go home now please?" she asked after a moment of intense silence.

I got the sense that she was doing so for my sake instead of hers. I nodded reluctantly. Something bugged me about the situation I couldn't quite put my finger on and I wasn't confident I got the truth from her.

We walked in silence for a few more minutes. The scenarios in my head of what happened in that classroom grew worse and worse as the doubt crept in. It didn't help that she was holding herself as if trying to appear smaller.

That was when it hit me. The thing I couldn't quite figure out about the whole interaction when she stopped me. I cleared my throat.

"You didn't ask me why I would ask that." I observed out loud, gauging her reaction.

I wasn't saying it as an accusation or a question. Something inside of me needed her to know I noticed it. She needed to know I knew her enough to know it was unusual.

She swallowed hard, as her face grew red. The few deep breaths she needed to take before she could answer told me she had hoped I wouldn't notice. That only validated my growing concern.

"Because I heard the rumors too," she said softly.

I tried to suppress a wince as I realized she probably thought less of me for letting her be there alone in the first place. At least that was how I had felt about myself. It didn't matter that at the time I thought the rumors were fake.

"I'm sorry. I should have stayed," I said, matching her tone.

Once again there were crickets as she processed my apology. After a few feet, her steps slowed angrily to a stop. I turned to face her and prepared for whatever punishment she felt I deserved.

"Why?" She finally snapped.

I closed my eyes trying to gather my thoughts. Something told me she only asked to see if I'd be truthful with her. If she had heard the rumors, then she knew what I had to be thinking.

"You're right. I do not know what happened. All I know is how destroyed you looked when I saw you after whatever went down. I'm sorry. I shouldn't have kept bringing it up, but damn it Laney; all I can hear is that rumor on repeat in my head," I nipped back.

She furrowed her brows, unaware of the events that supposedly happened the school year before. I had fallen for her bluff.

"You almost tanked your dreams of the military over a rumor?" she asked almost in disbelief.

"No, not over a rumor...over you. Because I let it happen and if I had just listened to those idiots..." I stopped myself.

All I could see was red, and she didn't need to hear my self-hate. She was the kind of person who'd carry the guilt for it. I turned away from her, and started toward my house, not wanting to make her day any worse than it already had been.

"What idiots? What rumor?" She questioned as she followed after me.

I could have blown off her questions. It would have been better for both of us if I had just kept walking, but I turned around. Something about the interaction made me believe it would have been easier for her to hear it from me.

"Last year, whispers started to spread across the school maybe two months before summer vacation. Mr. Gilliam was a new hire. Nobody seemed to like him, but Misty Harlow.

"She was a senior and for some reason, she was called to stay after hours on a weekly basis," I started, and she listened intently to every word.

"The rumor started small. Things were said about the extra attention he would show her, or the fact he only seemed to request her for these meetings on days she wore specific outfits, but by the time I had heard it, she stopped wearing them entirely. The sudden change in her fashion choices only fueled the rumor mill," I continued, and Delaney closed her eyes as if she knew where I was going with the story.

"Two weeks before school let out, Misty stopped showing up to school. I heard another student witness Mr. Gilliam threatened Misty that if she didn't... start acting more interested in his advancements, he'd fail her. From my understanding, most of the rumors end with a faculty member walking in on him trying to pin Misty against his desk." I continued.

Delaney's face paled as I talked, and I wished I had kept my mouth shut. It felt as if I could feel her distrust in me growing by the second. I just knew any minute she would be done with me, and decided to walk home.

As if sensing my regret, she slowly slipped her hand into mine. I stiffened at the unexpected touch, but I didn't fight it. I interlaced our fingers as my hand seemed to swallow hers.

"When she showed up to the graduation, Misty had told everyone she had been sick and Mr. Gilliam was never penalized. I chalked it up to the run of the mill drama, but when you shut down right after your meeting..." I trailed off, unable to finish telling her how badly I screwed up.

She squeezed my hand as we walked to her house in silence. When we were close enough to see her front door, I realized I wasn't ready to let go of her hand yet. We should have spent that whole walk home talking about anything else, but nothing about that day went as planned.

I broke my rule about keeping my distance too late, but I had been so good at it leading up to that point she couldn't talk to me. I ignored every gut check I had, and scared her in the process. It amazed me she let me walk her home, and held my hand.

When we got to where her pathway to her porch met the sidewalk, she stopped. Her fingers squeezed my hand a little tighter as she debated on letting me go. It put me a little at peace to know she wasn't ready for that either, even though I had given her every reason to.

"He came on to me. He graded a project I turned in last week with a note stating that he needed to see me after class to discuss the rough grade, but when you left, he didn't mention it. Instead, he rambled about an after school study program he offered.

"He didn't say it to my face. He said it to my chest and the tone of his voice made my skin crawl. I swear he never touched me," she admitted and fury clouded my vision.

"Laney," I started to apologize as I forced myself to bottle my rage, but she stopped me.

Not with words or placated statements about how my apology wasn't necessary. She leaned up on her tiptoes and softly kissed my cheek, knocking the air right out of my lungs. Any intelligent thought and all of the anger temporarily disappeared from my brain.

"Thank you for almost risking everything and if it's any consolation, I wouldn't have believed it either," she whispered in my ear before she let go of my hand and walked to her front door.

Chapter Four

September 13, 2023

Delaney

I was running late to a meeting I desperately didn't want to attend. Not that my disdain for the widow support group had anything to do with my tardiness. It seemed like for the last month, running behind had become a regular occurrence for me, thanks to the brain fog caused by the grief.

Grabbing my keys, I rushed out the door, barely remembering to lock it on the way out. I wasn't a fan of the new habit. It ate at my anxiety as I fumbled with my keys to start my car. The last thing I wanted was to hear the dreaded phrase, *If you are on time, you are late*.

Every time I heard it, I thought of Adam. Not that it was anything he would have said to me. If anything, he would have been proud of me for being so unorganized. It made me miss his teasing.

The thought of how he would react to who I had become occupied my mind the whole way to the meeting. I barely registered the radio. I was too distracted as my mind searched for the last time I remembered hearing his laugh.

After parking my car, I took my grief spiral with me as I climbed out of the driver's seat. A car door shutting nearby woke me from my thoughts. At least I wasn't the only one tardy to the meeting.

I looked over toward the sound to find a face I recognized. Just a few cars away stood Daniel Monroe. He and his wife lived across from us before Adam was re-stationed. I waved gingerly in his direction as the realization hit me; his wife deployed around the same time as Adam.

He waved back as he met my eyes and I immediately zeroed in on the hollowed expression he wore on his face. It was all the confirmation I needed. He walked over to me and joined as we walked into the church.

"Tell me you are here by some crazy mix up," he greeted as he slowed his pace to match mine.

I gave him a sad smile, unable to give him the answer he wanted. We both knew he only said it to be kind.

"I'm sorry Laney; Adam will surely be missed," he responded to my nonverbal reply.

"Same to you and same for Caroline," I started and kicked myself for my awkwardness before I tried again.

"I mean, she seemed like a great person too, and I am sorry for your loss," I corrected.

In response, he gave me a one-armed hug as we reached the doors leading down toward the basement. He opened one side and allowed me to walk in ahead of him. Two empty chairs set across from each other in the circle.

Everly Gore was in the middle of her story. She was recounting a happy memory as Jenelle, the group leader, glanced at me and Daniel with small hints of judgment in her eyes. When Everly finished, Jennelle cleared her throat.

"For those who have just joined us, today's topic for discussion are things we wished we had said," she looked between Daniel and me to make sure we were listening, "The rules are simple. You discuss your last memory you had with your partner, and how you would have said goodbye differently," she summarized as if it wasn't a heart breaking discussion.

I suppressed the urge to roll my eyes. Things like that had been why I didn't want to come in the first place. The exercises seemed to only cause more pain and everyone here except Daniel seemed to know it.

Janelle opened the floor for anyone else who wanted to share and the room filled with crickets. When no one volunteered, Janelle sighed. There was a tense moment as her eyes scanned the group as if debating on assigning the next speaker. Her eyes landed on Daniel.

"Okay, new plan. We have a new member starting this evening, as I am sure you all have noticed. I'd like us all to take a moment to introduce ourselves, and when we are done, if you are comfortable with it, I'd like you to return the favor," She said, aiming that last part toward our newbie.

Janelle directed introductions around the room. Mine was saved for last. She looked at me, waiting for the same song and dance the others had done: my name, who I had lost, Adam's rank, and how long ago I had lost him.

Nervously, I looked at Daniel, who raised his brow almost as if amused by the possibility.

"Delaney?" Janelle prompted when I missed my cue.

"Oh, sorry. He kind of already knows me. We were neighbors once," I answered, realizing that the rest of the group had no way of knowing that.

Janelle's face hardened before she spoke again, this time with less patience, "Go ahead and run through it, anyway."

I suppressed my desire to flip her off, or down right refuse. Part of me thought she was only urging me on for some sort of power trip, and I had enough of those lately for a lifetime. Swallowing hard, I glanced at Daniel, who gave me a supportive smile.

"As everyone here knows by now, my name is Delaney Anderson. I lost my husband, Adam, a little over a month ago," I answered as briefly as I could, but everyone waited for the rank.

I didn't provide it at my first meeting either. I wasn't going to sum up his life with a rank he wore when he died. Why did his rank matter when it came to my grief?

Janelle's stare lingered only for a moment. She knew if I challenged it, I would say exactly what was on my mind about the whole tradition. Neither of us wanted that.

Instead, she turned to the next in line and plastered a gentle smile on her face. It was Daniel's turn.

"Hi everyone. I'm Daniel Monroe, Delaney's old neighbor," he started, and the room lit up with small chuckles from his pointed joke.

I smiled softly and sank in my seat, uncomfortable from the attention.

"My wife, Caroline, was killed about a month ago when her convoy hit an IED," He finished and the room once again looked over in my direction.

I stilled, waiting for the whispers to erupt but no one said a word. Daniel glanced between the wide-eyed stares and my palling features.

His wife died in the same accident that took Adam. I knew that there had only been two fatalities from the explosion, but I had no idea the other had been Caroline. My brain dissociated before I heard anyone say her name. I never made it to the list of survivors, either.

Janelle shifted in her seat, moving the metal chair across the concrete floor. The loud screech drew the attention of everyone else in the room, except Daniel and I. She cleared her throat as I watched Daniel piece together the strange reaction from everyone around us.

“Let's go ahead and end tonight's group a little early. Your homework assignment is the same as last week. Think about what goodbye you wished you had,” Janelle dismissed the class and slowly everyone stood to put their chairs away.

My mind raced as I went through the motions on autopilot. The last thing I wanted to do was stay there a moment longer than I had to, but at the same time, the new information left me with questions I wasn't ready to voice out loud.

I got out of my chair on autopilot as I formulated my exit strategy. When Daniel realized why the meeting had shifted so suddenly, it was clear he didn't know Adam had been involved either. I hadn't processed the connection enough to discuss it.

Cutting my goodbye short, I headed out the door, making my way to my car. I had never been so thankful for that familiar sense of seclusion as I buckled myself in and started the engine. I let out the breath I didn't know I was holding as I left the parking lot.

The whole way home was a blur as my mind fought with what I heard. Pulling into my driveway, I almost missed Kendric's truck parked across the street. It was like he could sense when I was at my breaking point.

I got out of my car as Kendric stepped off the darkened porch. If he noticed my sour mood, he ignored it. I held my hand up, cutting him off before he started in on whatever tangent he came over for.

"Not tonight Kendric," I said flatly and he slowed while raising his eyebrow.

"I would have just texted you if this wasn't important," he started but I cut him off again in my growing irritation.

"Whatever it is, it will have to wait," I blew him off as I passed him, leaving little room for any argument.

I heard him follow me up the steps to my porch as I reached for my purse to fish out my keys. Just as I turned to tell him off, a car pulled in behind mine and I closed my eyes, taking in a calming breath, as I recognized the driver.

Daniel stepped out, closing his door behind him, and Kendric turned, his shoulders tensing at the sight of the newest unwelcome guest.

“I hope you don’t mind. I got your address from Janelle. I was hoping we could talk,” Daniel said nervously as he eyed Kendric standing in stoic silence.

I looked between the two men trying to decide how to say “go the hell away” nicely to both of them. Taking the moment of silence as an opportunity to make the situation lighter, Daniel extended his hand.

“Daniel Greene. I’m sorry to intrude. I’m a friend of Laney’s,” Daniel offered.

Kendric looked down at his hand as if debating on ignoring the gesture.

“Kendric Tate. I’m a friend of her husband’s,” Kendric replied in a low and territorial tone as he reluctantly shook Daniel's hand.

My growing irritation zeroed in on Kendric’s introduction. A “*friend”* of my husband’s, not claiming to be anything to me, or reference the years he and I had known each other. This was a reality check I didn’t know I needed.

Daniel withdrew his hand the moment Kendric let go, rubbing it with his other as if Kendric had squeezed it a little too hard.

For the first time in what seemed like forever, all I wanted to do was go into my house and lock the rest of the world out. After the last couple of hours, I needed the emptiness it offered.

Unwilling to stand there and watch whatever measuring contest Kendric was aiming to start, I looked through my purse for a pen. As quickly as I could, I jotted my number down on the back of a receipt and put the pen back in its rightful place.

"Right now isn't the best time. Here's my number. Text me tomorrow and we will set something up," I said to Daniel a little shorter than I intended to as I handed him my number.

"As for you, you have my number. Use it next time before you decide to waste a trip," I huffed at Kendric, less restrained.

Both men looked at each other before Daniel turned to leave. I started to unlock my door when Kendric's voice answered.

"Whatever you say, *Laney*." He mimicked as his footsteps departed.

I didn't look back as I walked inside and locked the door behind me. Closing my eyes, I took in the brief wave of peace as the quiet settled around me. When I opened them, the first thing I saw was the box of Adam's things his squad had sent to me.

It didn't have it in me to look through it as I had planned to do that evening. I ignored every impulse to cut through the tape as I hauled it off the counter and carried it to my bedroom. It didn't matter that it could have held the answers I needed.

I couldn't look at it and not shatter after everything I had learned. Especially when the new information made me question if I really knew my husband. I was going to put it away until I could look through it with a clearer head.

February 8, 2016

Kendric

I looked at my reflection in the bathroom mirror. The dark blue bruise around my eye seemed to mock me. There was no hiding it this time, and I was going to be late for school if I didn't leave soon.

Realizing I had zero chance at covering the monstrosity, I grabbed my backpack and headed out the door. If I had skipped school until the evidence of my father's temper faded, I would put my grades at risk.

Blaming it on my reputation would be better than the truth. It wouldn't have been the first time I had to hide behind it. I also knew it probably wouldn't be the last.

I had my father's drunken temper down to a science, but he had woken up uncharacteristically sober that evening. The only way I could keep him from hurting my mother was to become the target for his rage. I walked away with a bruised rib, and a black eye, but it was worth it.

Lost in my head, I didn't hear Laney come up behind me. I jerked and immediately winced the moment she laced her arm around mine. The smell of her vanilla perfume hit me seconds later, keeping me from launching into fight or flight.

"Someone should stop watching horror movies before bed," she teased as the sunshine almost radiated from her.

"Someone should warn a person instead of using their mini ninja skills," I grumbled as I kicked myself for jumping.

I prayed she didn't take it personally. I wasn't sure I could explain it if she did.

She moved in front of me to look at my face, trying to get to the bottom of my sour mood. I closed my eyes before I could see her reaction. This moment had been the one that made me debate on wearing concealer.

I heard her gasp as she grabbed my arm for support.

"Kendric..." she started, but I took her hand off of me as gently as I could, stopping whatever else she was about to say.

"We are going to be late," I barked out.

My self-consciousness and panic had gotten the best of me, and I wasn't ready to lie to her. She had been the only one that made me hesitant to blame my history of fights for the wounds. I didn't want her to think I was a monster.

Her face fell, heavy from all the unspoken questions and concerns. I tried to ignore the hurt that crept across her features, but the guilt it caused made that almost impossible. It wasn't a secret I kept because I didn't think she would understand. It wasn't her burden to absorb.

When Adam saw us, he reacted the way I knew he would. His anger was clearly reflected in his eyes, so dense it could have melted ice. He looked to Laney as if she had answers he knew I wouldn't give him.

"What set him off this time?" Adam asked instead of a greeting and I held my breath.

Laney's eyes grew wide from Adam's comment. The question "who?" hung between us without being vocalized. Adam stilled, seeing her confusion. He had assumed I had already told her about the abuse.

Adam had no idea he was the only one, outside of my home, who I told about the skeletons in the Tate family closet. It was better that way. I didn't want to be known as that poor abused kid.

Thankfully the first bell rang, cutting off any questions Laney wanted to ask. I headed to my homeroom without another word. I felt their eyes on my back as I left my friends behind.

I didn't see Adam until it was time for P.E.. This time there wasn't the anger I had seen in him before. He was back to pretending my black eye wasn't there. I only wished everyone else would have followed suit.

I didn't miss the whispers as I exited the locker room. Ignoring them, I found my assigned spot on the rubberized floor. Quinton and Kevin were already in place in a row directly in front of me.

It was no surprise that the two idiots were playing their favorite game. They took turns whispering about the girls who were coming out of their locker room one by one, rating them by "bang-ability." Our physical disagreement in the locker room had thankfully left Laney's name off their lips in my presence.

When they turned their heads to follow a cheerleader, Quinton's eyes locked with mine. A curious smirk spread across his face. He elbowed Kevin as Laney fell into her assigned spot close by.

I looked for Adam, preparing myself for the possibility that I would need backup. Adam had already noticed the possible conflict as he narrowed his glare on the jocks. Tension filled the room like oxygen as Quinton's smile only grew more dangerous.

"Looks like ol' Ricky here has been protecting Delaney's honor again," He mocked loud enough that half of the gym probably heard him.

Laney looked to me, searching for some kind of answer, and I stilled. The fight between Quinton, Kevin, and I hadn't been a secret, but none of us had fought the rumor that it happened over Chelsea Dole, not her.

It had been the most popular opinion because Chelsea was my ex from junior year. Our three-month relationship ended when I found out she and Quinton had slept together. I had only found out about the affair because Quinton couldn't stop bragging about it to anyone who would listen.

Chelsea's parents found out about the rumor, the week before I took a baseball bat to Quinton's nose. They transferred her out of Morley the same day as the fight. It didn't take much for the school to connect the events together.

"A little too caveman, if you ask me. What do you think, Delaney?" Quinton asked her, his face feigning interest in her answer.

She blinked back the confusion as she tried to process what he was saying. I clenched my jaw, fighting the urge to deck him where he stood. She, like everyone else, thought it had been over Chelsea, and I chose not to correct her assumption.

"Maybe if he aimed for your teeth instead of your nose you would have learned to keep your mouth shut," Adam snorted, coming to my defense.

Laney's eyes sparked with agitation as Adam answered for her. She was connecting the dots, and I was frozen in embarrassment. I never wanted her to find out that fight had anything to do with her.

"What do you mean, defending my honor?" she shot back, ignoring Adam's outburst as her eyes bounced between the four of us.

“It seems our buddy Kendric, here can’t handle the idea of you being with anyone else,” Kevin chimed in, but his witty response lacked all conviction as he looked to Quinton for approval.

“If you ask me, his violent reaction is a major red flag,” Quinton added with a shrug.

The paralysis lifted as I watched the blood drain from Laney’s face. I had kept her in the dark for so long, and time seemed to slow as I watched her connect the dots. The smile on Quinton’s face as he stood there, bringing my worst nightmare to life, made me snap out of it.

“You guys are leaving out the best part. Go ahead and tell her about the bet between the two of you that threw me into a jealous rage,” I mocked.

The smirks fell off their faces as they glared at me. The gym hushed into a deadly calm as everyone waited on their answer, fully aware of the bets the two of them often made. Laney looked to Adam in confusion as Adam’s face sombered from the whole interaction.

Before anything else could be said, the teacher walked in, blowing his whistle, signaling the end of the argument. Time itself slowed to a mind-numbing pace as I waited for the class to end. By the time the bell had rung for the next period, I was ready to bolt.

After a couple of hours of successfully dodging her, Laney waited at my table in the cafeteria. Adam made a convenient excuse to leave as I sat my tray down. I would have to talk to her eventually, and I weirdly missed her more than I wanted to avoid her.

She crossed her arms as I sat down in front of my tray. If she noticed the other people in the room staring, it didn't show. She was obviously on a mission.

"I can handle my own *honor*," she spat at me the moment I got situated.

I could tell by her flushed cheeks she was barely containing herself. Taking a deep breath, I prepared myself for her anger and prying questions. I could tell by her impatience, she wanted to get this argument over as quickly as possible.

"It wasn't about that," I tried to explain but she wasn't going to let it go that easily.

"Then explain it to me and while you are at it, why let everyone else think it was all over some ex? Why go that far to keep it from me?" she demanded.

I glanced around the room and took in the people trying to eavesdrop. The once- loud and static conversations that had filled the cafeteria when I had first entered were now barely audible, faded away into nothing more than whispers.

“Not here,” I said through the mouthful of fries and grabbed my tray, waiting for her to follow me.

Keeping an eye on me as if I was about to disappear she stayed close enough to grab me if I tried to run. I took her to an empty classroom not far from the cafeteria where we could speak in private. Her angry footsteps echoed behind me down the hall.

“The fight started because I overheard them taking bets on who could sleep with you first,” I started and Laney rolled her eyes.

“Do you really think I am that kind of girl? Swoon at the popular football players who notice me?” she accused, as I licked my incisor trying not to get defensive.

“You didn’t let me finish. All I knew were the two assholes in front of me and the lengths they go to one up one another; you and I barely knew each other. They saw a pretty new girl and made you their target,” I admitted, the irritation rising in my throat.

“*Wooow*. If you had bothered to say two words to me back, then you would have known they were wasting their time, but look at you! You don’t get to keep me at arms length and beat up anyone who shows interest in me like you are my brother.” Laney hammered home as she pointed to my black eye to emphasize her words.

"You seriously don't get it. I didn't get this because of you, and I wasn't behaving like your brother when I took that bat to Quinton's face," I cursed, unable to filter myself.

The moment I admitted it out loud, I regretted it. I had said too much. Laney looked at me, studying my face as if trying to figure out if I was telling her the truth.

I waited for her to ask me to expand on my statement or to explain it to her but she didn't. Flustered, she switched topics.

"Why not tell me? If I was their target and you were trying to protect me, why let me believe the rumor was all over some ex?" she fired off her next question. The hint of jealousy in her voice caught me off guard and I faltered.

"Because I thought I stopped their idiot plan and I didn't want you to know how they thought about you. I put this distance between us for a reason and I didn't want my actions to undermine it," I answered honestly.

She let out a humorless laugh as if what I said had been a bad joke.

"Right, because Heaven forbid that you come off warm and fuzzy. It'd ruin your ice cold reputation," she spoke sarcastically, calling me out for everything I didn't confess.

I winced. If I had been smarter, I would have left it at that. That distance would have survived another round of close calls, but I couldn't. The defensiveness overrode any chance I had at self-preservation.

"It's not that easy when it comes to you," I let out barely above a whisper and it dented her hostility toward me.

"Then why put walls up one moment and take a bat to Quinton's face the next? What about me is worth defending, but not worth lowering them to let the one you are protecting in?" She asked but her voice wasn't mad this time. There was a hint of something I couldn't quite put my finger on in her tone.

Before I could answer, she started toward the door. Her words echoed more like a goodbye in my head and I was sure if she walked out the door, she wouldn't come back. I panicked.

"I think you are someone I could fall for and the walls were meant to keep myself in check," the words fell from my lips before I could stop them.

She paused and I turned to look at me in the doorway.

"Laney, nothing I did had anything to do with your worth. I like you and I shouldn't because I'm signing my life away in a couple of months. I just couldn't listen to them talk about you like that, or lead you on when I knew I wasn't staying around," I finished my confession, and she looked at me in disbelief.

Not giving her a chance to leave, I walked toward her. Her gorgeous green eyes watched my every move, but she didn't try to leave. As I got closer and saw my words sink in, I couldn't stop myself.

I grabbed the sides of her face in my hands, and rested my thumbs along her jawline. Pausing, I waited for her to pull away now that she knew everything I had felt for her and why I never acted on it. But, Laney didn't move.

Crossing every line I had placed down to prevent this very moment, I bent down and I kissed her. Twice in twenty-four hours, I acted on impulse, ignoring the pain I knew my actions would cause. Both times, I knew without a doubt in my mind, they were worth it.

Chapter Five

February 17, 2024

Delaney

I used to change the channel anytime a crime documentary came on. Until I found myself alone almost every evening. Eventually, I watched whatever I could find, and unfortunately for me, crime shows were something I could always count on.

I used to categorize the documentaries as overly dramatized entertainment, no different from the wrestling shows my father used to watch. At least I had until a month ago when the texts started coming in late at night from Adam's number. Those shows felt more like research after that.

Like clockwork, the moment I settled into my bed one night, my phone buzzed. The loud vibration from my device I had placed on my night stand increased my pulse. The last thing I wanted to do was wake up to a message from that number.

Hesitantly, I reached for my phone, burying myself further under the safety of my covers as if that would keep the fear away. I exhaled in relief when I saw Kendric's name. It figured his number would only provide some relief, when it was only slightly better than a message from a poorly executed prank.

Kendric: "Be there in five."

Agitation quickly replaced the fear as I threw the covers off. I wasn't exactly dressed for company, but normally people didn't stop to pay me a visit after ten PM. A knock echoed as I shrugged on a pair of shorts. Not that they made much of a difference; Adam's T-shirt hid them from view.

The second knock came before I had a chance to get to the door. Frustrated, I threw it open to find Kendric there in his usual statue-like appearance. He looked me up and down as an amused smirk spread across his lips.

"What do you want?" I asked as I stepped aside to let him in.

"Hi to you too, Del," he greeted cheerfully just to piss me off.

I glared at him.

"That's not my name," I spat as I slammed the door shut behind him.

The smirk on his face spread to a smile. I wasn't in the mood for his games, but in the back of my head I knew it was because I was dreading the good night text I had been receiving from a stranger. I crossed my arms, pushing my fear far away from Kendric's mind reading capabilities.

“Did you get the box of his things yet?” Kendric asked, cutting straight to the point.

“I was heading to bed, Kendric. Why does it matter right now? It's late,” I wondered instead of immediately answering.

The box in question was sitting in my bedroom but hadn’t had the courage to open it. By the time I had been ready, the texts from Adam’s number started to come in. The last thing I wanted to do at that moment was open that damn box while the threat of the next message hung over me.

Sensing my hostility toward the topic, Kendric focused his eyes on my face. Once again, trying to read my mind through his harsh glare. I didn’t react. Instead, I waited for his answer as the silence grew between us.

“I was hoping to get a picture back that I had loaned him,” he finally blurted out when he realized I wasn’t going to give in to his normal intimidation.

“A picture?” I looked at him in disbelief.

He seriously stormed over here in the middle of the night for a picture? Taking a deep breath, I braced myself for his reaction, fully prepared to tell him to leave and come back another time. Before I could, I watched something in that stone-cold expression break.

"It's important to me," He spoke softer than I had been expecting, almost like a plea.

The vulnerability in his voice took me off-guard. My anger cracked as the note of veiled desperation filtered through his carefully constructed walls. The word "important" seemed to be an understatement to him.

Without saying a word, I nodded toward my bedroom. He followed me in silence into the room as I switched on the lamp at the bedside table. I used my body to block his view as I flipped my phone over in case the text came in while he was there.

Instead of walking over to the box, I gestured to it and sat down on the edge of the bed. A hint of a question sparked in his eyes before he followed the direction I was pointing, to the box of Adam's things across the room. Noticing it hadn't been opened, he glanced back at me before pulling his keys from his pocket and crouched down.

The sound of his keys ripping through the tape set my nerves on high alert. The strained energy between us crackled like my rising anxiety as I forced myself to stay seated. I didn't think I could handle looking at the last things Adam had kept to remind him of home, or the pieces of what his life had been over there.

Right on cue, my phone vibrated loudly from the nightstand. There had been no way Kendric didn't hear it, but to my relief he didn't say a word. The rustling of the box filled the room as I tried to control my urge to look at the text or move from my spot on the bed.

A second buzz, more amplified than the first, sounded off like Kendric's impatient knocking. I clenched my eyes shut tightly as my lungs began to constrict, hating myself for not carrying the damn box into another room.

"I guess someone else doesn't realize you operate on normal business hours," Kendric said, slightly distracted.

I didn't respond. Failing to fight the urge to look any longer, I picked up my phone. I tensed as Kendric's rustling filled the room, praying to anyone who would listen that someone else had messaged me. I knew before I saw the name that it had been a foolish hope.

Sure enough, Adam's number had sent me both messages. A photo and something that chilled me to my core.

Hubs: Why is HE there?

Above the words, the stranger had sent a photo taken from outside of my bedroom window. In it, Kendric was just inside the door looking at me, while I was flipping over my phone.

I stifled a gasp with my hand as I looked toward the window Kendric was now knelt in front of. Out of the corner of my eye, Kendric stuffed whatever he had been looking for in his pocket. I all but threw my phone back down on the table as Kendric turned to face me, ensuring it had landed face down.

Kendric stopped dead in his tracks and I knew my fear had been written all over my expression. I covered my face with my hands, trying to hide my thoughts from his uncanny powers of observation. The burn in my chest intensified as I felt the start of a panic attack forming.

I waited for his questions or for him to make a sarcastic comment but neither came. Without saying a word, I felt him sit down on the bed next to me and he pulled me into him in an uncharacteristic hug.

"I'm sorry," he whispered as he held me to his chest.

I couldn't understand his behavior, but I also couldn't get a handle on my own. Unable to stop myself, I let myself be vulnerable with him. He held me to his chest as I sobbed to relieve the pressure in my ribcage that kept me from taking a full breath.

When I finally stopped crying, he pulled away from me. Reality crashed into the room like a wave, because that wasn't who we were any more. Both of us had held onto our walls for so long, the whole situation felt slightly inappropriate.

“It’s late. I should probably head out,” he finally broke her silence, morphing back into that statue I knew and loved.

With the picture still fresh in my mind, I couldn’t let Kendric go out there. I wouldn’t have been able to live with myself if he had gotten hurt because of me, but I couldn’t bring myself to tell him about the messages or the creep that might have been waiting outside. He cleared his throat and stood, and I followed suit, hoping to find the words to keep him there.

“Don’t,” I rushed out before I had time to think of any reasonable argument to support my request.

His eyebrows shot up from the uncharacteristic plea. The shock in his face was quickly replaced by concern as he stared at me, waiting for me to explain my sudden request.

“I-It's late, you shouldn’t drive. I can make up the couch,” I said, giving up.

It had been a shitty and incomplete excuse. One I knew he could see through, but there must have been some reason he didn’t want to leave either. Instead of fighting it he looked toward the box as guilt flashed across his eyes.

“I don’t really want to be in this house alone tonight,” I softly confessed and I hated myself for every word.

“Okay,” he answered and nodded as he headed to my bedroom door.

Kendric paused in the doorway, looking me over once more as if trying to decide if he had made the right call. Before he had the chance to change his mind, I pushed past him to set up the couch. Thirty minutes later, we said our goodnights, and I headed back to my room.

I reached for my lamp to shut it off and stopped myself. My eyes landed on the opened box across the room. Something in me needed to know if his phone had been inside. I forced myself not to look out the window as I crept to it.

Just as I had expected, Adam’s phone hadn’t been inside. My mind raced as I tried to justify any reason how someone else would have it. He was allowed to use it under specific protocols. If it had been on him when he died, there wouldn’t have been much left of it.

I couldn’t shake the feeling I was still being watched. If having Kendric over so late had upset the person on the other line, I didn’t want to leave anything to question. I knew I wouldn’t be able to sleep without assistance.

I quietly opened the drawer of Adam’s bedside table, and sorted through the random odds and ins through tear blurred eyes. Toward the back of the drawer, I found the bottle. Taking a couple of his sleeping pills, I crawled into bed, leaving the lamp on to leave nothing to my stalker's imagination.

February 17,2024

Kendric

I stared down at the cardboard box in shock. The thin layer of dust that had settled on the top showed signs of not being touched in weeks. It was hard to believe she hadn't tried to at least peek inside and made the lies she told me about not having it painfully clear.

I glanced back at her, wanting to ask why, but the look on her face stopped me. She seemed to stare right through me and everything in her posture seemed on edge. It was easy to assume she hadn't opened it because of her grief.

Pulling the keys from my pocket, I tried to push down the prying questions I wanted to ask. The sound of the metal teeth tearing through the tape, seemed to rip the air from the room. I watched as Del's reflection slightly jumped from the noise.

As I opened the cardboard flaps, a buzz came from behind me. Her phone had vibrated against the table beside her bed, and the sound seemed to have caught us both off guard. I heard her let out a nervous breath.

“I guess someone else doesn’t realize you operate on normal business hours,” I commented and peered into my best friend’s time capsule.

I didn’t know what I would find when I opened it, but the amount of letters he held onto seemed unusual. Between various keepsakes, the letters were separated into two different stacks. I fought the intrusive thought to look through them as I moved things around to find the picture I was there for.

At the bottom of the box was a picture from our prom. It was the only one I knew of that had all three of us before everything changed. I couldn’t tell her that it was something I held on to like some people held onto hope.

In the photo, Del was posed in between us, smiling so big her eyes were shut as if soaking up the sun on her cheeks for later. Adam was making a goofy face oblivious to how Del and I leaned into each other. I couldn’t help but notice the smile didn’t reach my eyes as I had intended. As I reached to close the box, my eyes lingered on the way my hand in the photo had been wrapped around her waist.

Trying not to get caught up in the feelings that image stirred, I turned my focus back to the task in hand. I was pulling down the flap when I noticed the writing on a folded sheet of paper pinned to the front of one the stacks of letters.

Written in handwriting, that wasn't Del's, was Adam's name in feminine cursive. Curiosity got the best of me as I palmed the stack of letters, tucking it behind the photo. Another buzz sounded off behind me as I watched Del's reflection reach for her phone.

Worried she would catch me snooping, but unwilling to let the letters go, I stuffed the bundle into the pocket of my pants. I quickly planned out my excuse for a hasty exit and turned to leave, but the look on Del's face made my blood run cold.

All the warning signs I had missed during my intrusion screamed back at me as her face grew more and more pale. I wasn't sure if it had been the fact I had forced her to open the box before she was ready or if she had caught me trying to steal the letters. Then I saw Del's eyes well up with tears instead of anger.

It knocked the wind out of me the moment she covered her face in her hands, drawing her arms close to herself. We had grown so far apart over the years that I had forgotten how she could look so small and fragile. Just like when we were in high school, I lost all control over the distance that I had forced myself to place between us.

Acting on pure impulse, I sat down beside her on her bed and pulled her into me. I shouldn't have been so insistent on rummaging through the things she was obviously trying to avoid. It was selfish and thoughtless, and all I could think of was how I needed to fix it.

"I'm sorry," I whispered, unable to give the full apology she deserved.

I waited for her to fight me or push me away, but she didn't. Sobs shook her body as I held onto her tighter. I slowed my breath and just like she used to, she forced herself to match my pace. My reason for pushing her to that limit seemed more and more selfish as I waited for her to stop crying.

I knew her well enough to know she had masked her grief in the form of anger anytime I was around. I had often wondered if she let herself feel it when she was alone, but after months of the same mask, I didn't think I'd see her like this.

Before I could stop myself, I savored the feel of her back in my arms. This moment hadn't been one I prepared for, even though it had been everything to me. I felt the tension slowly ease from her body as the guilt filtered back into place.

Listening for her cries to fade, I braced myself for when I had to let her go. Worried the moment I did, she would fall in shattered pieces on the bed in front of me. When I was sure she was finally past the breaking point, I forced myself to let her go.

The moment I did, I was hit with the overwhelming desire to pull her back in and I didn't think either of us could handle it if I did. As quickly as it all had happened, I made myself stand and put some distance between us.

When she immediately stood to stop me, there was a moment when I could have sworn I saw panic behind her eyes. I watched her fumble for a lie, and fail to sell one, but part of the reasoning clicked as she mentioned not wanting to be alone. It hadn't been the first time she mentioned the unsettling feel of the house, but something about the way she said it felt different.

I couldn't bring myself to leave her after that. Del made up a spot for me in the living room and I watched her head back to her bedroom. I settled in on the couch that might as well have been solid concrete, wondering if I had made the right call for her or myself. All I could do was replay how off she seemed about everything tonight.

In an attempt to get comfortable, I rolled on my side and the crinkle of the paper in my pockets reminded me of the extra items I stole from the time capsule; those letters seemed to call my name.

I waited until the house fell unnervingly quiet. Making as little noise as possible, I reached for them, sitting up on my rock solid cot. Every crinkle of the envelopes seemed to echo around me as I tried to remove the first one from the stack.

Carefully I removed the letter and unfolded it, shifting toward the light coming from the hallway. Red flags sounded in the form of rustled paper as I began to read it:

"0345- Our spot-meet me there."

I stared at the invitation, unable to comprehend what I was reading. Folding it back up, I stuffed it back into the stack and grabbed another from the middle;

"Adam,

I am sorry I couldn't be there this morning and that I have to send this to you instead. Daniel called. He is really scaring me and I don't think he will take the divorce well. Have you said anything to Delaney? I know you wanted to wait, but I don't think I can handle being with him any longer than I have to be. He will know something is up. We can talk about it later when I see you, but maybe it would be better if we told her about us together.

Always,

Caroline"

In shock, I folded up the letter with shaking hands. I remembered how close they had been in country, but he swore it hadn't been what it looked like. I shouldn't have believed him. What the hell was I supposed to do with that information?

Chapter Six

February 18, 2024

Delaney

I woke up in a haze as my lungs cried out for air. At first, all I felt were his massive hands around my throat until the familiar stench of stale beer burned my nostrils. I knew immediately when I smelled it, Adam was having another PTSD episode in his sleep.

Desperate to get out of his choke hold, I used my knees to push him off of me. I didn't intend for my knee to collide with his groin during the struggle, but it was the only reason I escaped. When he collapsed onto the bed beside me, I took my chance.

My heart thrummed in my ears as I darted toward the door. He had promised me he wasn't going to take those pills anymore. They only made his night terrors more intense and when the sedative effects took over, he was almost impossible to wake up.

I could hear him behind me as I ran out of the room. If I could get to the car, I could hide out there until he woke up. All I had to do was get to it.

Without hesitation, I bolted toward the front door. Adam's footsteps ran after me as I turned out of the hallway. I barely felt the impact when I cut the corner too sharply. My shoulder bounced off the drywall but adrenaline propelled me forward.

After his second deployment, he'd have one of these a week as if settling back in triggered deep seeded fear. The episodes started with restless thrashing in his sleep. That was when the drinking started.

When I finally threatened to leave if he didn't get help, he brought home the first round of medications. We found out the hard way that his drinking habit didn't mix well with the pills and the combination made his nightmares more violent. He only got on a different kind after he almost killed me.

He woke up that following morning with his hands around my throat, but I had passed out already. He didn't touch a drop after that, but I don't think he kept eye contact any more after that. I almost didn't get him back after he shut down from the guilt.

This time had been eerily similar. The only difference had been the fact Adam was utterly silent aside from his movements. I let out a breath of relief as my front door came into view.

I tried to open it, but my stomach sank when I found it was locked. Before I could go for the deadbolt, Adam's arm snaked around my stomach, pulling me back. I held the doorknob tighter as he tried to pull me into him.

"You *are* home," I pleaded as I struggled to maintain my grip.

As I fought to keep my footing, I tried to turn the deadbolt with the tips of my fingers. In a stroke of luck, I heard the lock click open before he had the chance to overpower me. I was so close to safety, but Adam maintained his constricting hold on me.

When my grip started to slip, I tried to push down on his arms around my waist. The restraint he showed to firmly hold onto me, but not hurt me, seemed so different from only moments before when his hands were around my neck. As thankful as I was that he wasn't trying to kill me, it didn't make me feel any less helpless or safe.

Using his weight, Adam leaned us back, ripping my hold off the deadbolt, and sending me crashing into him. I felt his chest heave against my back as he held me there through my panic. I knew without a shadow of a doubt he would kill me if I didn't escape.

"Adam!" I cried out desperately, even though I knew it was a hail Mary.

At the sound of my voice, everything shifted. His hold on me laxed and his breathing became erratic. Shocked by some small sense of recognition, he stumbled backwards, jolting me slightly.

"What did you say?" Adam asked, but even in terrified haze, I heard the sleepdrunk tone to his voice.

For a moment, I really thought my voice had cut through his sedatives, but I was wrong. We were trapped inside his nightmare and fighting to survive each other. My will to fight for that survival kicked in before his and I pushed out of his arms.

The moment I broke free from him, I flung the door open. I didn't have time to dart out of it before he spun me around. With lightning quick reflexes, he pulled me into him and held me there as he slammed the door shut, cutting off my only exit as he pinned me between him and the wood.

I closed my eyes and braced my palms flat against his chest. Every time he took a breath against them, I tried to remember that he loved me and this wasn't him. I swallowed hard, forgiving him for everything he was about to do.

"You're home and you love me," I reminded, barely above a whisper as I prayed his subconscious could hear me.

"Laney!" he shouted as his voice morphed into Kendric's deeper one.

I stilled as I felt a hot breath against my tear soaked face. Hesitantly, I opened my eyes and the soft beams of early morning light burned as reality filtered in. I felt Kendric's chest rise against my palms as I realized I was still being restrained against my front door, but everything else seemed different, less clouded.

I looked up, only to find Kendric looking down at me. When my eyes met his and he realized I was fully present, I thought I felt his breath catch under my fingertips. The way he went from restraining me, to just holding me there, set off butterflies in the pit of my stomach.

Hesitantly, I pulled my hands away from him and he leaned back. Heat spread across my cheeks and the tops of my ears as I soaked everything in. My mind raced to put together exactly what had happened.

I must have grabbed the wrong sleep aid the night before, but Adam promised me he had flushed the ones that made his nightmares so violent. The irony that my monster had been the same Adam who took the pills didn't escape me.

Kendric just stood there, silently observing me. When my breathing calmed, he slowly let me go. I didn't miss the way he looked away from me ashamed. I flinched from his movements.

"Are you okay?" he asked as he took a small step back.

My mind filtered through the nightmare, retracing those last few moments. I couldn't figure out what had been in my dreamscape and what was real. Everything had felt so lucid and tangible.

"Del?" he asked when I didn't answer his question.

The air between us felt charged as I tried to calm my nerves. My fear was starting to fade, but the more I replayed that conversation, the quicker my heart seemed to beat.

"Don't call me that," I finished, hating the shake in my voice.

Awkwardly, I stepped around him, making my way into the kitchen. Kendric's lazy steps followed me as I walked over to the coffee maker. I couldn't look at him as I filled the reservoir tank.

"Do you do that often?" he wondered quietly as I reached for the coffee mugs.

"No, I just took the wrong sleep aid last night," I tried hoping I wouldn't need to tell him why I took one.

He shifted uncomfortably beside me as if he wanted to say something else, but didn't. Not immediately. I appreciated the small moment of silence he gave me.

"Laney, please talk to me," He pleaded barely above a whisper.

As my name came off his lips, it sent a shiver down my spine and I could almost feel the ghost of his arm around my waist. Distracted by the memory, I almost dropped the mug on the floor before I placed it on the counter.

"It was an intense nightmare due to a bad reaction, I'm fine," I dismissed firmly as I gathered myself and started the coffee maker.

When I reached for the second cup, I realized it had been a miracle Kendric had woken me up. My head still swam from the sedatives. It was a sobering realization as it reminded me of every time I couldn't do that for my husband.

"You called me Adam," He said with a steely edge to his voice, reading my mind. His words snapped me out of my thoughts so quickly my head spun.

I put the second cup down and braced myself against the laminate countertop. The way he said it confirmed he knew who I was fighting in my sleep. The sharpness to his voice had been unmistakable when he said my husband's name.

"Kendric, it's not what you are thinking…" I started, but stopped myself when I realized none of my answers would give him comfort.

I turned to face him, but his invisible wall of armor hid his emotions. He shifted his eyes from mine as if unable to look at me. The smell of fresh coffee filled the space as neither of us said a word.

I filled our mugs, and handed him his, as I tried to ignore the awkwardness filling the space between us. I didn't understand the total flip in his demeanor after our veiled confessions. He had been so adamant in interrogating me but I got the impression he hoped he was wrong about the monster.

"I'm just glad you are okay. You could have been seriously hurt," he answered and walked across the room to the sugar canister. It felt like he wanted to say more, but he didn't as he searched the drawers for a spoon.

He wasn't wrong, but the way he scolded me like a child irritated me. I was embarrassed enough as it was. I knew from experience that the danger of night terrors wasn't just to the person who was dreaming.

"*You* could have been hurt," I challenged back as I fished a spoon out of the dish drainer before setting it down on the counter by his coffee mug.

He stopped his pursuit and raised a brow at me in question before he slowly closed the drawer he had opened. Grabbing the spoon, he gave me a sideways glance.

“How’s your shoulder?” He volleyed back in irritation at my argument.

I flinched at his reference. My shoulder was fine, but his words were proof of some of what I felt actually happened. I focused on the defensive anger to keep my mind off of which parts of my dream had really felt Kendric instead of Adam.

“I was fighting against a drug induced hallucination. I wasn’t the one willingly struggling against someone I cared about,” I replied through my teeth.

He didn’t see what I had been seeing. He definitely wasn’t here when Adam’s PTSD became violent and what I had to do to survive my husband’s reaction to the same medication. Whatever his intentions had been when he grabbed me, he had no right to criticize which one of us was in more danger.

Kendric’s knuckles went white around the handle of his coffee mug. When I stole a glance at his face, I didn’t see the walls I expected. I found the same look he used to get when anyone mentioned his father.

Without thinking, I reached my hand out and gently touched his wrist. I had done it so many times when we were younger. I acted out of old habits. It hit me then that he wasn’t closing himself off over judgment; he was realizing why Adam played the role he did in my nightmare.

"It wasn't like that," I repeated in a whisper as he filtered back in.

He calmly placed his coffee cup back down on the counter as he collected his composure. His eyes found mine as his emotionless shield came back up. Everything in me started to worry he thought I was lying to him.

"So Adam never drank himself to sleep? Woke you up in the middle of the night screaming? Never laid a hand on you?" he interrogated, pinning me down with an intimidating gaze.

My body filled with a jolt of adrenaline as he put me on the spot. He knew the answer before he had asked it, but I didn't have the heart to tell him he was right. I barely registered my ringtone faintly coming from the bedroom as my voice died in my throat.

I watched his chest rise and fall a little faster with every passing second. My silence seemed to be enough of an answer for the both of us. He bit his bottom lip before grabbing his cup to leave.

I had to say something, anything to keep him from comparing Adam to his father. My husband might have shared similar demons, but he didn't hurt me willingly.

"Kendric!" I called out anxiously after Kendric, as I followed him into the hallway.

Both of us paused, as he stopped to face me. The familiar setting made my breath catch as memories of the dream filtered in. Before I could say anything else, a knock echoed through the entryway.

Kendric's attention shifted to the door as my phone rang louder from the bedroom. Torn between who I needed to answer first, Kendric turned back around and headed toward the living room with a shrug. Remembering my secret stalker, I chose not to run to my phone.

The second knock sounded as I peered through the peephole, trying to figure out who was stopping by the house so early. I knew by the slightly golden light that filtered through my windows it couldn't have been later than seven in the morning.

As I hesitantly opened the door, I was greeted by Daniel's friendly smile. His nervous expression shifted to shock as his eyes drifted to the hem of Adam's old t-shirt and then to my exposed legs.

"Good morning?" I greeted as I shifted uncomfortably where I stood, trying to ignore his lingering stare.

The reminder of my poor choice in sleepwear made me self conscious and I tugged the shirt down as far as I could. Realizing he had been caught, Daniel's eyes returned to mine. Clearing his throat, he reapplied his smile.

"Good morning! I was hoping you'd-" He started, but his anxious greeting was quickly cut off.

In slow motion, I watched Daniel's eyes land on something over my shoulder. Kendric's steps echoed behind me as I suddenly wished I hadn't answered the door.

"Oh," Daniel let out as I felt Kendric place his hand on my shoulder, almost possessively.

I could see the assumption and disappointment register in Daniel's eyes as Kendric stood too close behind me. It didn't help that I answered the door in a man's t-shirt. I could only imagine the smirk Kendric wore as Daniel's opinion of me plummeted.

"Daniel, right?" Kendric greeted the visitor with an icy tone.

Daniel nodded, too distracted by the scene laid out in front of him to notice Kendric slipping my cell phone into my hand. I let out a shaky breath as I worried what he saw when he grabbed it off my bedside table. This officially had been the morning from hell.

March 14, 2016

Kendric

The Senior Spring Fling was a Morley High tradition that every kid looked forward to. It was a night that promised absolute freedom, and every year the adults tried to shut it down. The rite of passage eventually escalated to the seniors' annual spy games.

By our senior year, a secret society had been formed to select the host to orchestrate the event. Whoever had been selected for ours had already made their first move. Emails were sent at random from an anonymous number.

When I received mine, it contained a set of instructions I had to follow if I wanted to earn my invitation:

Unknown:

Once during the week of March 21st, you will gossip near an adult or a narc. In that gossip, provide a false but credible location for the fling.

A specific task will be sent to you via text message. You will record yourself fulfilling the task verbatim. If you do not stray from the instructions and submit the video to the school's newsletter, you will receive a confirmation text that you have earned your invitation

If you earn your invitation, you will be sent directions leading to the fling. If the fling is shut down, all videos will be uploaded for the public to see.

Two weeks in, ten different addresses had spread like wildfire through the school. Nine other students had earned their acceptance into the party. Out of the nine tasks fulfilled, most of them had been innocent pranks.

“I think it's so they know whoever shows up won’t snitch,” Adam said through a mouthful of pizza.

Laney rolled her eyes. She didn’t know how these parties could get, so she didn’t understand why everyone was bending over backwards to get into this one. She had only decided to go because Adam made her promise to.

“Snitch? On loud music and teenage stupidity? Seems a bit extreme to make us prove ourselves,” Laney responded flatly.

Adam paused his chewing to glance in my direction. It was a nonverbal agreement that we’d warn her later about what she would be walking into. Breaking various laws wasn’t exactly Laney’s thing.

“Have you gotten an assignment yet?” I asked Adam, trying to avoid the lecture I could see gathering behind his eyes.

He swallowed the impressively large bite and looked around us for prying eyes.

“Yea, I got it this morning,” He answered.

Laney perked up. I didn’t expect her to take a serious interest in the topic.

“Don’t be near the gym at three today okay?” Adam winced as he spoke directly to Laney.

“But-” she started to argue and Adam’s face grew red.

He leaned in closer to us, almost bending across the table. His voice was barely above a whisper, “I have to streak across the gym with the words ‘MHS Basement’ written on my chest and stomach in red lipstick…”

“Avoiding the gym; got it,” Laney reassured as her eyes grew wide.

Something about his confession must have sent Laney spiraling through her mind, as she sat through the rest of the lunch distracted. As I walked her to her class, she moved as if on autopilot.

“We don’t have to go,” I tried, worried that her quietness had been linked to Adam’s confession.

“We promised him,” she softly recalled as she squeezed her arms closer to her chest.

I tucked her under my arm, trying to swallow down my unreasonable jealousy.

“Harmless pranks, right?” She asked nervously as if needing to hear my reassurance.

“Harmless,” I repeated to give her what she needed, but the word tasted bitter in my mouth.

I pulled her into me and kissed her forehead before she went to take her seat in Mr. Gilliam's class.

The look on Laney’s face before I left her and thinking about Adam’s prank distracted me from my English class. Mrs. Nelson lectured on the importance of a good resume but I barely caught what she was saying. It felt like hours had passed by the time the bell rang.

I stood from my chair the fastest and headed toward the door. I barely registered the static that cut through the room as the TVs flipped on. An announcement was getting broadcasted across the school.

“Attention all Seniors,” Principle Patton’s voice rang out through the building in a chorus from the school’s TVs.

I stood in the doorway impatiently. The more I thought about her reaction to Adam, the more I worried Laney had received her instructions as well. It had been the only thing I could think of that kept the green-eyed monster at bay.

“Rumors of the Spring Fling have grown to concerning levels. In order to ensure your safety, this event must be disbanded,” the principal continued as groans from other students sounded off.

Just before Principle Patton could issue the traditional threat of expulsion, the broadcast glitched into black background. The words “STAND BY” scrolled across the screen in big red block letters.

After a moment, everyone decided it was time to go about their business. The door to Mr. Gilliam’s class room was just in sight when a small hand reached out and grabbed my wrist. I let out a breath of relief as I assumed it had been Laney.

I turned to ask her if she had gotten her text, but it wasn’t my girlfriend. Instead, I found Chelsea. She nodded toward the library and pulled me in the opposite direction.

We made it to the doorway by the time my anxiety glued my feet to the ground. If I went any further I wouldn’t have an eyeline on Mr. Gilliam’s door. When I refused to budge, she let me go with a satisfied huff.

“Okay, mission almost complete,” she whispered as she looked around the empty space.

I glanced at her as her words sparked suspicion. Taking my eyes off of the classroom, I turned to look at her. My eyes narrowed as everything wrong about this situation became painfully clear.

“What do you mean mission? What are you even doing here?” I hissed at her as the hallways started to clear.

I hadn’t seen Laney exit the room. Stupidly, I had just dropped my eye from the ball, realizing that I was part of Chelsea’s mission. Laney probably thought I walked to my next class without her.

“It's the Spring Fling, Ricky,” she finally said.

I hated that nickname but she was the only one I ever let openly call me that. She had only been allowed to because I had felt she was way out of her league, and she’d look up at me when she called me that with doe eyes.

“You don’t go here anymore, and my name is Kendric,” I shot back as my unease grew restless.

I tried to leave but she pulled me backwards by my shirt.

“I didn’t leave by choice and earned the right to an invitation. The only way I can get in is if I complete the mission. You can't go anywhere yet," She rushed out as if pleading for me to listen.

Heat spread across my face and my ears as dread flooded my core. Why would the host include holding me hostage in her task? It had been too early for this to have anything to do with Adam's.

"They sent me your instructions, too," she offered as she dug her cell phone from her pocket before holding it up enough for me to read.

I took a step toward her to grab the phone, but she artfully kept the distance between us until she was blocking my exit. I glared at the screen as Chelsea prepared to move in case I wasn't done chasing her.

Anonymous:

To Kendric Tate: you have two options, Kiss your ex and leave, or wait for the signal. Your task will affect the other students at play. Any deviation from these options will result in loss of admission for yourself, Delaney, and Chelsea. Choose wisely or the choice may be chosen for you. Stand by.

"Just stay here for a bit longer," Chelsea urged as I looked up at her and straightened.

The look of desperation hung heavy in her face. It pulled at my guilt as Chelsea's expression reminded me of Laney's words, "We promised him."

"Something isn't right here, Chels," I tried to reason with her.

She shook her head as her nervous demeanor shifted into something similar to self-preservation. Pulling her phone back closer to her chest, she raised her chin.

"I was supposed to have a prom and walk with my classmates that had known me since I was five. This is the only Morley High tradition I have a chance to be a part of, and I won't let you ruin this for me," she scolded me through her teeth.

I shook my head and threw my hands palms up. The dread that had been building was to the point it hurt to breathe. I would choose Laney every time regardless of the fallout. Call it a sixth sense, but something had me crawling out of my skin at her name being on my instructions.

"I'm sorry, Chels. I can't," I feigned empathy for ruining her teenage dreams.

I walked around Chelsea slowly as I kept my eyes on her. Just before I walked through the doorway, she turned around so she wouldn't see me leave. Until that moment, I hadn't really cared what my actions would do to her and I paused.

"Maybe Adam and I can sneak you into the prom," I offered as she raised her arms and hung her head. I thought she had placed her face in her hands to cry.

"My parents would never let me go. Besides," she started in a mocked sad tone before turning to face me.

The front of her uniform was now unbuttoned to where her shirt was still tucked under her skirt. Her breasts looked barely contained as the black bra she had under shirt was on full display. She dropped to her knees in front of me before I knew what was going on.

I tried to back away but she had already grabbed ahold of my belt. I pried at her fingers as she unbuckled my belt, spread it apart, and pulled me in closer to her.

"What are you doing?!" I yelled at her as I forcefully pulled myself back, but the restraint I kept so I wouldn't hold her made me too slow.

She licked her lips as she angled her phone to capture both of our faces for a selfie. I stumbled back from her as the flash almost blinded me.

I scrambled out of the library, buckling my belt. I bumped into Adam as Chelsea yelled after me.

“Thanks for getting my invitation. Don’t worry; I won’t tell her about this,” Her words echoed past me and my stunned best friend.

Before I could dodge Adam’s protests, The TV in a nearby empty class room caught my eye. The stand by screen flipped to what looked like a recording from a hidden camera positioned in the back of Mr. Gilliam’s classroom.

I froze the moment I saw Laney leaning near the teacher’s desk. She was nervously messing with her hands, staring at the floor in front of her. Mr. Gilliam stood to her side, his legs plastered to the side of one of her thighs as he leaned over to touch her face.

I saw Adam straighten my peripherals. If he felt half as strongly as I did, he would gladly be my alibi. The more I watched the screen, the control I had over my anger was slowly becoming non-existent. I tried to do what Laney would have wanted me to do and let her handle it, but I didn’t know how long I could stand there.

“Let’s talk about extra credit,” Mr. Gilliam purred, leaning next to her ear, “ Maybe we can think of something to make up for that grade. I’d hate to see you fail your senior year.”

He barely got the last sentence out before I bolted from the classroom. I had skipped right past seeing red to white hot rage as I stormed into Mr. Gilliam's classroom. The whole room was empty.

"What part of this is getting your rocks off?" Laney's voice sounded through speakers. "Is it because manipulating a naive girl makes you feel pathetically powerful or do you have a dominance kink?"

I turned to find the TV mounted to the wall of his classroom. After I realized it was a recording, I started to take in more details about the video. If I hadn't initially panicked, I would have noticed she wasn't dressed the same.

I watched as Mr. Gilliam tensed and unglued himself from her side. Panic and anger bled into his features as his face morphed into an intimidating scowl. Straightening her spine, she refused to back down.

"Don't test me, young lady," He hissed as he grabbed her arm so hard her skin buckled around his fingers.

"And don't act like you are the only one with power in this room, Mr. Gilliam," she challenged as she ripped her arm from his grasp.

Her defiance only made him more desperate as he snapped his hand up and gripped her chin, forcing her to face him.

Slowly the realization started to hit me when this footage had been taken. She lied to me. I held my breath, waiting for the recording to end, trying not to drown in my feeling of helplessness.

“Say a word about this to anyone and you will wish you had just shut up and did what you were told. I will make your life a living Hell,” he threatened before letting her go with so much force she stumbled back into a desk.

She left the room and Mr. Gilliam watched her leave. The amount of deadly desperation in his body language sent a shiver down my spine.

A few moments after Laney ran out of the room, my voice echoed from the hall, “Hey, Del! Wait up.”

The TV shut off as I stood there numbly. That footage had been taken the first day I walked her home. She had promised me he didn’t touch her, and for some reason, whoever was hosting the fling, wanted me to see she had been lying.

“Where the fuck are they?” Adam’s voice broke through my disassociation as he yelled at me from the doorway.

If I hadn’t been so raw from everything leading up to that moment, I might have appreciated his protectiveness. Having no other outlet to release my irritation, I turned it on him to keep my head from going under.

“Not here,” I barked out as I left the room, giving up on finding Laney.

Chapter Seven

February 18,2024

Delaney

As I stood there watching everything unfold, Kendric seemed to be the only one unphased by the interaction between him, Daniel, and myself. I watched in frozen panic as I tried to grasp why Kendric reacted the way he did. It felt more like a jealous boyfriend than a suspicious friend.

I watched as Daniel's face grew red from the intimidation antics. It was clear that Kendric had meant it to be transparent when he didn't budge from the umbrella-like stance behind me. I just couldn't question Kendric's actions until I figured out what brought Daniel here at the crack of dawn.

"I-I'm sorry, Daniel, you were needing something?" I asked as I tried to gather my bearings.

Daniel tried his best to keep my eye contact as my shadow stood there like my personal bodyguard. I couldn't blame him as I was having a hard enough time keeping my focus on the situation. The phone in my hand kept bringing my thoughts to the stalker and the morning I had.

"It's okay. I can see you are busy," Daniel dismissed. He glanced at Kendric before turning to leave as if he didn't want Kendric to over hear.

The moment Daniel's feet hit the bottom step, Kendric stepped back, leaving an odd sense of coldness in his wake. I shook the strange feeling of disappointment toward Kendric's movement and called out to my old neighbor.

"Daniel, wait!" I called after him before shooting Kendric with a look that said "stay."

When I turned back to face my friend, I didn't miss the way his eyes kept dropping to my bare legs. He wasn't staring at them the same way he had when I answered the door. Instead of the shyness from before, all I could see was the possible judgment.

"It's Adam's. Sometimes it helps me sleep better and I needed that last night," I softly admitted as I looked back down at the faded black t-shirt that seemed to swallow me whole.

Daniel's face softened at my unprompted confession. Unable to stop myself, I tried to reassure him that any assumptions he had made about Kendric and I were incorrect.

"Kendric stopped by to look at some of Adam's things they sent back," I tried to explain, but even mentioning the box made my words catch in my throat.

Daniel perked up at the half-assed explanation. He didn't seem relieved but whatever I had said seemed to distract him for a moment.

"So...not that busy," he nervously chuckled as he glanced back at Kendric who hadn't moved.

I smiled politely, not sure how to respond.

"I just got Caroline's a couple of days ago. There was some mix up at the post office," He added, sinking back into his distraction.

I didn't want to talk about the boxes and instantly kicked myself for bringing Adam's up. There had been more than enough emotional destruction before my day had even really started. I had no desire to add anymore if I could avoid it.

"I just made a pot of coffee. Would you like a cup?" I offered to try to change the topic.

Daniel glanced back at Kendric and immediately I saw the unease in his expression. He shook his head before gesturing toward his car.

"Maybe some other time. I was just about to hit the morning meeting, I figured I'd check out another group leader, Janelle is...intense," he rattled as he searched in his front pocket for his keys.

"You'll have to tell me what you think," I said with a smile.

Daniel nodded as if I had given him an answer, but he hadn't asked me to go. Even if he did, I couldn't rush Kendric out if I was going to give him an explanation about Adam's night terrors. As much as I loved the idea of escaping, I had to stay and clean the mess I had caused.

"I gave you my number, right?" I asked, remembering I hadn't gotten any calls or texts from him.

Daniel nodded and left without another word. I watched as he climbed into his vehicle and drove away as my last attempt to postpone the conversation I needed to have left.

"So, he's not staying for coffee?" Kendric asked as I pushed past him to go back into the house.

I shot him a glare as I found the mug I had abandoned.

"He probably thought you'd poison it," I teased as I took a sip of the barley warm liquid and winced.

“I’m sorry. I didn’t realize I should be warm and welcoming to the man who looks at my best friend’s wife like he’s praying for x-ray vision,” Kendric mocked as he walked to the couch.

I followed him as his words sparked at the dying embers of my irritation. What exactly was his problem? Nothing about the interaction I had with Daniel felt like he was interested in me like that, and even if he had been, Kendric should have known it wouldn’t have mattered.

“His wife died in the same accident. I don’t expect you to ever be warm and welcoming, but the intimidation tactics were a bit much,” I defensively spat out before the full meaning of Kendric’s words sank in.

Kendric’s eyes widened and his shoulder’s tensed.

“That means his wife was…” he started but paused as he looked down toward the coffee table in front of him.

“Yea, she was, and I don’t think your whole ‘Protective Bestie’ routine came across the way you were hoping it would. Do you know what it looked like when you came up behind me like that? And I’m...” I started to scold him, but my words lost their bite as I realized the role I played in that image.

Kendric’s eyes lingered on my bare skin for only a moment before he stood and grabbed his keys from the table. He seemed too distracted by his thoughts to prevent the guilt that was written across his face.

"You're right, I should probably go," he forced out as he walked past me toward the door.

Once again, I had managed to say the wrong thing. Everything that had happened that morning stampeded through my head as I tried to find the words that would make him stay. I didn't want him to leave before I could clear up everything that had happened that morning.

"That wasn't what I meant," I tried as his hand landed on the doorknob.

"It's fine. Call your mom back," He answered as he opened the door.

I froze, remembering the way he put my phone in my hand earlier. He glanced back at me when I didn't reply, as if making sure I had heard him. I searched his face for any evidence that he had seen anything else on my phone, temporarily forgetting the reason I had been trying to stop him.

"I'll be back later," Kendric hesitantly reassured as he shut the door behind him, leaving no room for argument.

I watched him leave from the kitchen window before I let myself check my phone. Sure enough, I had two missed calls from my mother, but my breath caught as I saw the other notification waiting for me.

I had one new text from Adam's number.

April, 09, 2016

Kendric

I listened intently in my bedroom, waiting to make sure my mother's sobbing had stopped. It was twenty minutes past the time I was supposed to meet Laney and Adam at the bench in front of the school. I just couldn't bring myself to leave until I was sure my mother was okay.

It was supposed to be the one day my mother was guaranteed peace. My father's old war buddies met up annually and thanks to where it took place, he wouldn't return until the next day. He only attended for the free alcohol, but it was twenty-four whole hours my mother and I didn't have to worry about walking on eggshells.

Back when things were good, she used to cook breakfast for the three of us. Eventually, he started only taking his breakfast in liquid form. That particular morning, she had accidentally burnt the bacon she was making for me.

She had been flipping the last piece of bacon in the skillet when the grease sloshed onto the burner, causing a cloud of black smoke to fill the kitchen. Before either of us could stop it, the smoke detector emitted a high-pitch alarm that seemed to echo through the house. In slow motion I watched as the noise woke my father up from his favorite recliner.

There was a small period of time where I had convinced myself that my father's abuse had been purely the result of his PTSD. I didn't want to believe that he chose to be cruel and hurt us. It was moments like that morning where he often proved that hope wrong.

Just seeing his face as he walked into the kitchen made the hairs on the back of my neck stand on end. It was obvious he was pissed by the wild rage behind his eyes. There wasn't a hint of concern at the smoke that filled the room as he scanned it.

I waited for his anger to land on me, as it often did. When he stared through me as if I was invisible, a chill went up my spine. I watched in horror as his villainous glare landed on my mother, swatting the smoke away from the alarm, trying to shut off the high-pitched sound.

"It was me," I felt myself yell out as I darted to get between them trying to prevent the inevitable.

I held my palms out to put as much space between the two of them that I physically could. Closing my eyes, I braced for impact.

"*You* are telling *me* that my lazy ass son is cooking for *himself*?" my father drunkenly slurred, amusement laced in his voice as he questioned my mother.

I opened my eyes at the sound of his voice in confusion. A smirk creeped across his unruly beard as the smell of burning grease filled the air. My mother stilled.

When neither myself or my mother answered, his smile only widened. He backed up slowly toward the stove and pulled the skillet from the smoking burner, putting the burnt bacon on display.

"Lila, dearest, please come here," My father ordered in a saccharine sweet tone.

We knew those calm words were merely bait in his trap. He didn't have a quick release button to his emotions and his smile had been too forced and unhinged. He just wanted her in a reachable distance.

My mother hesitated. The fear radiated off of her like a shockwave. I motioned for her to stay there, but my father clenched his jaw at my attempt to save her. The moment she saw the muscles flex, she started toward him.

Helplessly, I watched her walk to him with shaking legs. When she stopped in front of him, he grabbed the pan and moved it to where I could see the charred piece of meat. When I close my eyes, I can still see the way she flinched at his sudden movements.

"It's important for him to know what he did wrong here," My father hissed in a manic tone before he threw the pan on the floor.

The contents of the pan hadn't settled on the floor before he lashed out and grabbed my mother's wrist. When I took a step toward them, he forced her hand toward the burner. I froze when I saw the way the coils were still red from the heat.

"Ricky, please!" My mother begged. Her voice breaking over the sound of my pulse in my ears.

His hand shook as she fought to pull away from him. In response to our defiance, he brought her hand close enough to the burner, the glow from the coils illuminating her palm. She stifled a yelp as she glanced back toward me, as if she had quieted herself down for my sake.

I knew what that look on her face was meant to tell me. She was begging me to let her take the fall this time, but it was the defeat I saw behind her eyes that gave me back my ability to move. I rushed toward them without a second thought.

My father's attention wasn't on me anymore, as he focused on forcing mother's hand down toward the stove. By the time he knew I had moved, my shoulder slammed into his chest. Knocking him off balance, my father fell into a chair, narrowly missing the table.

Before he could get back on his feet, I had already positioned myself between him and my mother. She turned the burner off with shaky fingers before she braced herself against the kitchen counter. My father grunted while he struggled to steady himself.

As I hoped, when he finally straightened, he narrowed his eyes on me. I squared my shoulders and prepared myself for round two. It dawned on me then that it didn't matter who won this fight; there would be more as long as we stayed, and as much as I tried, she wasn't going to leave him.

"We can either end this here or we can fight this out," I started, but he only snarled in response before he raised his fist to give me his answer.

I knew before I said it; he wasn't going to walk away from the fight. He was as addicted to our fear as he was to his booze. I just had to be smarter.

“But what do you think the school counselor will think when I show up again with more bruises? People are starting to talk and I am done giving excuses for your inability to hold your liquor,” I said as I latched onto his sense of self-preservation.

Once again, he clenched his jaw but hesitated. My phone loudly rang on the table beside him, interrupting his inner debate. My grandmother’s photo lit up the screen as he glanced down at my device before lowering his fists.

“I’ve got better things to do today than to teach you how to be a man. Stick to the bitch work. It suits you,” He spat out as he stormed out of the kitchen.

I sent a silent “Thank you” to the universe for the phone call before turning to face my mother. She rushed over to me and wrapped me up in a hug before I could look at her hand. When my father slammed our front door behind him, my mother dissolved into sobs on my shoulder.

When her death grip slacked around me, I helped her to her bedroom and checked her hand for burn marks. We sat in complete silence as I wrapped the hand in gauze she kept at her bedside.

As if she was waiting to hear my bedroom door close, she finally broke down. The closed doors didn’t stop her crying from echoing through the wall. Something in her sobs told me she had realized the same thing I did this morning; my father's temper would kill one of us if the alcohol didn't kill him first. I couldn't bring myself to leave until I knew she was going to be okay, Spring fling be damned.

By the time I had gotten to the bench, Adam was long gone. Laney, however, was waiting for me. It wasn't until I got to her that I realized she was lost in her own thoughts. When I sat down beside her, I thought she had been upset because I was late.

"I'm sorry I'm late. I- I couldn't leave," I apologized as the guilt weighed on me. My words rushed out of my mouth before I could take in Laney's body language.

At the sound of my voice, Laney crumbled into her hands sobbing. The stark difference between the anger I had been expecting and the utter devastation I was seeing shifted my focus from my troubled thoughts. I wrapped my arms around her and pulled her into me.

She curled into my chest and tried to pull herself together, but she had already gotten to the point of hyperventilation. Nothing else mattered in that moment as I tried to slow my own breath in hope she would try to copy it. The harder she fell apart, the tighter I held onto her.

"Talk to me," I gently ordered after she finally caught her breath and wiped her eyes.

"Mom gave dad an ultimatum today. His-his recruiting contract is up and he's been talking about signing another. She told him to retire or she'd leave him. Dad picked the divorce," she sniffled as I could feel her breath quickening again.

I laced my hand in her hair at the base of her skull and pressed her closer to my chest. It felt as if I could feel her breaking in my arms and I had nothing to say to make her feel better. All I could do was hold her.

"My mother is making us move to Northbrook, Wisconsin so she can be closer to my grandparents, and dad is staying with one of his friends, so we don't have to leave until the end of the school year. She says we are moving right after graduation," she sobbed and my heart rate sped up at the unspoken meaning.

I was scheduled to swear in at the end of July. The time I had left with her didn't feel like it was ever going to be enough. Selfishly all I could think about was what little time we did have was just shortened by months.

"It'll be okay. We will figure it out," I lied in an upbeat voice, attempting to reassure her that it wasn't a deal breaker.

"How?" she questioned as she wiped her face again and pushed off of me to look at my face.

“I don’t know, but if all else fails, we can start our letters earlier. I’ll be leaving a few months later, and Adam is going to college nearby there in the fall. Even in the worst case scenario, you won’t have to be in Wisconsin alone for very long and that could turn out better in the long haul,” I reassured her and she softened.

It wasn’t the solution she wanted to hear, but it was enough to stop her tears. I watched her as she wiped her face and straightened herself before she stood up from the bench. She looked down at me and forced a small smile, as if to reassure me she was alright.

“Speaking of Adam, we should get going. He’s waiting on us,” Laney said, determined to move on from the pity party.

I stood and held my hand out for Laney. She laced her fingers between mine and kissed me softly. The whole way to the party, I couldn’t shake the feeling my horrible day wasn’t over.

When we finally reached the location, I squeezed her hand tighter. In all the years I imagined what the fling would be like, I had always pictured an abandoned house or a vacant vacation home. I didn’t expect it to be held in a junkyard where stacks of crushed cars served as privacy walls.

In terms of a secluded place, this lot had crossed off every requirement for the party. It was just outside of town, enough that neighbors wouldn't call it in, and cars could be spotted for miles if the cops were called to check the place out. The overgrown vegetation along the mangled vehicles gave the place an eerie long forgotten look.

One of the football players stood at the entrance, sporting a clipboard as he searched for our names. I tried not to let my paranoia get the best of me as he repeated our names to his lackey unlike he did when the person in front us entered. The way said lackey pulled out his phone and typed something in only increased my heightened suspicion.

"Make sure Adam or me are with you the whole time," I warned my girlfriend as she pulled me inside, now excited.

"And don't take any drinks from strangers, even if they offer candy," she giggled as if I had been overly cautious.

Her light hearted demeanor dampened the moment we turned the corner past a stack of mangled metal. Music drummed loudly as groups huddled in various corners and couples acted like they were behind closed doors. She looked up at me with wide eyes as we passed a group of our classmates taking body shots.

"Ok, okay, now I get it," she said , stunned as we made our way through a cloud of skunky smoke.

When we found Adam, he was flirting with a girl I didn't recognize. Not wanting to interrupt, Laney and I kept our distance for a moment. I wish now we wouldn't have been so polite.

"Ricky! You made it!" Chelsea greeted as she came bouncing up to us.

Laney raised her brow at me as she registered the nickname. Chelsea's loud announcement drew Adam's attention. I thought when he walked over, he was coming to my rescue.

"Why don't we go get you a drink," Adam asked Laney as she shot me a questioning look.

She looked between Chelsea and I for a moment, as if waiting for me to stop her or maybe waiting for an introduction. I understood why Adam offered. He wasn't aware of the task drama and didn't know how uncomfortable whatever conversation with Chelsea would be. All he knew was that her and I didn't end on the best of terms.

When I didn't respond, Laney hesitantly took him up on the offer. I had hoped he would fill her in on the missing pieces and she would understand. Where Adam didn't know the whole story, he was right about me needing to talk to Chelsea alone.

"I told you, it's Kendric and whatever *this* is, I want no part in it," I warned in a low tone.

Chelsea's face fell at my words, as if expecting I would have a different response. If she hadn't pulled what she did in the library, I might have been warmer; I didn't hold anything against her for sleeping with Quinton anymore.

"I just thought…" her face fell.

The uneasy feeling inside of me started to rebel as my patience thinned. Chelsea was selfish and acted on impulse, but she wasn't stupid. I glanced around the party for Adam, knowing I would spot him over the crowd easiest given he was one of the tallest there.

"Save it Chelsea. Who put you up to coming over here?" I demanded, cutting off whatever lie she was about to tell me.

Chelsea's innocent behavior shifted back to the calculated girl I knew as she huffed and crossed her arms. I wasn't sure she was going to answer me, but she didn't budge.

"Look, I didn't know he was hosting this thing," she said, barely loud enough for me to hear her.

The guilt in her words stopped me cold. I stopped looking for Adam and pinned Chelsea down with a glare.

"Please tell me you do not mean Quinton," I hissed, as Chelsea dodged looking me in the face.

I knew the answer before she nodded.

"Did you send that picture to him?" I rushed out as the panic rose in my throat like acid.

The moment she confirmed it, I all but ran through the crowd in search of Laney. I knew then why our arrival seemed so off and why the host wanted to keep me in place while Laney played the video of Mr. Gilliam to the show with strict instructions not to tell me about it beforehand. Quinton was setting up his revenge.

I weaved through the sea of faceless people until I spotted my best friend. The moment his eyes met mine, I knew I had been too late. The anger in his face had been unmistakable.

"What the hell, Kendric? Chelsea, seriously?" he accused as I got close enough to hear him.

Laney was nowhere in sight. I spun to try and locate her only to find Quinton staring at me with a wolfish smile. I saw red as he winked at me and showed me his phone before returning to the conversation he was having with a group of random girls.

"I'm going to kill him," I growled as I took a step in his direction, but Adam grabbed my shoulder to stop me.

"This isn't on him. How the hell could you do that to her?!" Adam scolded.

I couldn't see Laney anywhere and his words only intensified the worry. Whatever Quinton implied when he showed them the photo made her leave the safety of Adam's side.

"Nothing happened, but I know it's hard to believe me if you saw the photo. I can explain more later, but I have to talk to Laney first," I rushed out as I started to realize the missing piece to Quinton's plan.

"She isn't here," Adam answered, still hesitant to tell me anything else.

I glanced back to Quinton before scanning the crowd once more. Someone else was missing from the party.

"Adam, I'm serious. I don't care which one of us finds her, but we have to get to her *now*," I reinforced as I started toward the exit.

"Kevin took her home. If I wasn't two cups in, I would have taken her myself. You should probably give her some time, Ricky," Quinton chimed in as he walked up to me and my best friend.

Just like that, it felt as if all the air had been knocked out of me. Without thinking, I decked him right in the jaw. Shooting a glare at my best friend, I watched as Adam put it all together; that this had been a set up from the very beginning.

Chapter Eight

February 18, 2024

Delaney

For what felt like the fifth time, I checked the clock on my nightstand. It was almost nine at night and there was no sign of Kendric. The text this morning from Adam's number still played on repeat through my mind. I couldn't help but wonder if he lied when he promised me he would be back.

I wouldn't have blamed him. It was one thing if the text had been sent from an unknown number, but it was another to see it come from his best friend's phone. The message read like something from a jealous lover and I wasn't sure how I would tell Kendric they had been coming in for a while now.

Hubs:

How does Kendric like his coffee?

It was an odd message. No stranger than receiving a text from my dead husband's line, but there had been a clue behind it. Kendric had been the one who had gotten Adam hooked on coffee when they deployed together. He even drank his coffee the same way Kendric did after that.

Anyone who really knew Adam knew that story. It told me whoever was behind the messages knew who Kendric was and had been using my husband's death to add to the terror. The realization sent a shiver up my spine.

The problem was the line the person was texting from had been from a burner phone Adam purchased for his deployment. It wasn't something I had the ability to cancel or gather any specific information about the new owner. The only thing I hadn't done was search the box for the device itself, but it wasn't like the ghost of my husband had been using it.

I stared at the box while I slipped on a pair of black shorts. My pjs had been specifically picked to avoid a repeat this morning. Even though my shorts weren't any longer than the ones I had on this morning, my tank top didn't swallow me to the point it looked like the only thing I had been wearing.

My phone vibrated on my nightstand and I froze. In the wait for Kendric and the worry he had seen the text from this morning. Unable to make myself check the newest message, I forced myself to go through the box I had been avoiding.

I knelt down in front of the box and my brain desperately tried to find another excuse not to open it. The text could have been from Kendric, but I wasn't sure I wanted to see that either. Between our confessions this morning and the concern that he discovered that I potentially had a stalker, my grief seemed easier to tackle.

The last thing I wanted to do was voice any of the messages to him. I didn't know where to start other than to confirm Adam's cell phone wasn't sent with the rest of his belongings. Keeping that thought in mind, I set back to the task at hand.

Gingerly, I opened the box only to be hit with the familiar scent of Adam's body wash. The smell of him hit with zero warning as it made me tear up from the unwelcomed reminder. Memories of the nightmare filtered in against my will before the memories of Adam took over.

Taking a deep breath to calm myself, I opened the box the rest of the way and stared down at Adam's things as my grief started to burn its way up my throat. I don't know why I had convinced myself that it would be filled with things he collected like souvenirs. It wasn't like he was there on vacation, but I didn't expect to see the life I never witnessed so neatly packed away, covered in fine white dust.

Half used bottles of body wash and shampoo sat in a slotted tray next to his worn down toothbrush and almost empty toothpaste. Letters I had sent him were bundled in rubber bands, as if he was trying to make sure they stayed together. I lightly reached out to trace the edges of the envelopes as my heart plummeted.

Tucked in the middle was a letter from his mother that she had sent him while he was at basic. The paper was so folded and worn that I felt like I would tear it while I gently pulled it out. The blue ink had faded behind the stains the paper had collected over the four years.

I held the letter to my chest and breathed him in. My chest hurt from all the tears I was trying to hold back, but they were coming whether I wanted them too or not. It had been the last thing he got from her. Cancer had taken her before he was able to get back home.

Adding insult to injury, my phone vibrated again loudly against the wood behind me. For a moment, I allowed myself to recognize that the only ghost of my husband was tucked inside of this box. Nothing else mattered.

I tuned the rest of the world out as I sat the envelope down beside me. Moving his toiletries and letters aside, I dug through the box forgetting the pointless search for his phone. My breath caught as I moved a hand drawn sketch and found a photo of Adam and me.

I wasn't ready for this. Taking the photo from the box and his mother's letter, I stood to place them in the case where Adam's flag was displayed on our dresser. I almost jumped out of my skin as I turned to find Kendric, silently standing in the doorway.

"I sent you a text," he said flatly as if that was an excuse to let himself in.

“How the hell did you get in here?” I asked as I glared at him, thankful I had chosen different pjs.

“Adam gave me his key before he left…just in case…” He started, but trailed off as he noticed the letter in my hands.

“In case you ever wanted to stop in to terrorize me?” I mockingly finished his sentence, ignoring the look of recognition on his face.

Kendric’s eyes shot back up to mine as if he had forgotten he had been saying anything. He didn’t hide the look of concern and confusion still plastered on his face.

“What?” he replied as the fatigue set into his features.

My defenses softened at his out of character demeanor. Taking the photograph and letter to the display case, I faced my back toward him. I set the items down gently and used both hands to unlatch the bronze painted latch at the top of the triangular case.

I felt Kendric walk up behind me before his fingers plucked the photograph from the top of the letter.

“Normally friends try to knock first,” I added, trying to drown out the familiar buzz underneath my skin at his closeness.

This morning, I blamed it on the emotional start we had and how balanced it made us. As much as I tried to repeat the excuse in my mind, blaming the box; it felt like I was lying to myself. There had always been this pull to him, but it was far easier to ignore it when he pretended that he hated me.

“Are we friends, Laney?” he asked so quietly I thought I had imagined it.

I turned to glance at him from over my shoulder and grabbed the envelope that rested on my dresser. It didn’t look like he wasn’t even aware that he had spoken the question out loud.

“When was this?” he asked in a more present voice the moment he realized I was watching him.

There was no reasoning behind the embarrassment I felt when he asked about that photo. I took my eyes off of him and tucked the envelope beneath the flag in the frame. It felt silly not to answer his question, but I couldn’t look at him as I did.

“A month or so after we got married,” I answered, before turning to take the photo from his hand.

He didn’t let it go immediately. Something like torment flickered in his eyes before he released his hold on the photograph. His eyes stayed fixed on our faces in the frozen scene.

I felt him let out a hot breath of air as I finished tucking the photograph behind the glass and closed the display case.

Only Adam's smiling face and the top of my head were visible behind the wooden frame. Kendric cleared his throat at the sombering sight.

Without thought, I turned around and hugged him. He froze as my arms wrapped around his neck. When I tried to pull away, regretting the impulsive action, he enveloped his arms around me in return, pulling me closer into him.

"I don't know what we are, but if this is the only way I can keep you in my life, then I will take it," I whispered before he let me let me out of his hold.

I hadn't meant for it to sound as intimate as the way the words came out, but it wasn't a lie. It didn't matter what I was to the man. He was the one person in my life who knew me better than I did at times and I was alone here without him.

Still, my statement made me feel dirty, like I had betrayed my husband. It felt almost unfair to Adam and his memory. Even if the thought behind my words were innocent.

"And for my next emotional trick, I'd like to show you into the kitchen where I keep the strongest alcohol," I forced out with a light-hearted chuckle.

"You want to follow that with alcohol?" he chimed in with amusement a few moments later as he followed me into the kitchen.

He watched me with a raised eyebrow as I pulled two shot glasses from the cabinet. Enthusiastically, I nodded as I walked over to the fridge and opened the freezer. I didn't drink enough for my usual drinks to be stocked in the house, but Adam kept a mason jar of apple pie moonshine on hand at all times.

"Well, I need to clear up some things we discussed this morning and I don't think I can do it effectively sober, so it's up to you but…" I explained.

My words trailed off as I poured myself a shot and downed it. Without a word, Kendric took the mason jar from my hand and poured himself a glass. Shaking his head in disbelief, he downed his own and the next phase of my emotional destruction began.

The End of Spring Fling

Kendric

Adam followed me to the exit as he tried to convince me to leave it alone for the night. If she had left with anyone else I might have considered it, but I couldn't. I didn't realize

Quinton was following us until he yelled after me as I got to the bouncer stationed out front.

“You should have just done your part for your invitation. Delaney did hers and that asshole was fired,” Quinton shouted.

His words finally filled in the missing holes in Adam’s mind. Finally understanding, Quinton was playing wingman, Adam turned on him. I heard the impact of Adam’s fist colliding with Quinton’s face as I ran out of the junkyard and toward Laney’s house.

As the school came into view, I felt my phone vibrate in my pocket. Fishing it out of my pocket, I prayed it had been her, but it wasn’t. Adam had sent a warning.

Adam:

Someone said she had been drinking. They were seen leaving with a six pack.

“Laney doesn’t drink,” I said out loud as I read his text.

I sent back instructions to keep Quinton occupied. The last thing I needed was my archnemesis coming to Kevin’s aid. Doubt crept in as I tried to hold out hope that her drinking had been another baseless rumor.

All the scenarios in my head ended in me tanking my enlistment. Both sleazebags had been known to feed alcohol to their victims and Laney's tolerance would have been next to nothing. The more I thought about it, the angrier I got.

Quickly, I texted Adam back and told him to leave as I formulated my revenge. To hell with the consequences. If Quinton wanted war, I would fight fire with napalm.

I didn't give myself time to second guess my plan as I typed in the number to the local police station. The moment Adam verified he had left, I made the call. I told them I was Kevin and that I had lent him my phone to make the call, naming Quinton as the ringleader before I disconnected the line.

I put my phone into my pocket as Laney's voice cut through the air. As our bench came into view, I saw them. All rational thought left my mind as I noticed the empty beer cans at Kevin's feet.

Chapter Nine

February 18, 2024

Delaney

The second shot of apple pie flavored moonshine burned down my esophagus all the way down to my stomach. Kendric cradled his glass in his hand as he watched me. If he knew the can of worms I was about to open, he wouldn't have hesitated.

I readied myself for a third as I reached for the mason jar on the counter between us. Even while his episodes were happening, Adam and I had never directly discussed them. I never imagined I would end up talking to anyone else about them. Adam's PTSD had been filed away under the things that didn't exist unless I had no choice to acknowledge it.

"We don't have to talk about it," Kendric offered with a concerned furrowed brow as I raised the third shot to my lips.

I took a steading breath as the fumes hit the back of my throat. As much as I wanted to take him up on the offer, I knew if I didn't then, I never would. I needed him to know Adam wasn't a monster anywhere but in that nightmare.

"No, no, we need to. I know how your brain works," I argued.

The cinnamon flavored aftertaste made me crinkle my nose. The added burn from the spice left my mouth on fire.

“He wasn't..he wasn't the same when the night terrors hit..” I started as I held my glass to my stomach as if trying to ease the slight nausea.

Kendric's amused face melted into the stone I knew, and yeah may have found a little appealing, my words. I wondered if he had done that for my sake or to protect his inner thoughts from me. It didn't really matter, but I found a strange comfort in it.

“He didn't know it was me,” I tried again as the traumatic events filtered in like unwelcomed home videos in my head.

Kendric downed his second shot and reached for the jar. I tried to think of the least troubling example to ease his mind.

“How bad did it get?” He asked after wincing from the mouthful of moonshine.

Unsure of how to answer, I took the jar back long enough to take another swig. His jaw clenched in response to my reaction.

“That doesn't matter. What matters is that you don't think he was like your dad,” I answered, no longer in control of my filter.

Once again, it was like Kendric was hearing things I hadn't said. The statue-like expression on his face began to crack as hints of his anger peaked through. His once laid back body language hardened as he straightened his spine.

"You never met my father before he was at his worst," He answered as I watched a familiar haunted expression behind his eyes.

"You didn't see Adam when he woke up. He wasn't taking anything out on me, and he started drinking to numb the guilt," I countered, but no signs of relief or reassurance came from Kendric.

He turned to the side, leaning against my kitchen counter to avoid my inquisitive stare. He wouldn't look at me. Instead, he trained his stare on the wall across from us.

"That's the problem, Laney; I did see it. It was maybe two months before we came home from our last deployment and he had stumbled into our bunk after I fell asleep. I thought it was a fluke…" he began before taking the jar from me and poured himself another.

I listened intently as the room began to sway. Drinking wasn't something I did often enough to think clearly after two shots, let alone four. I tried to process what he was saying, but Adam blamed the first episode after the medicine. I couldn't get past the lie as I tried to process Kendric's words.

"A couple of hours later, I woke up to what I thought was an intruder, but when I finally saw his face he looked right through me. He came at me with a knife and it took me fighting back to wake him up. I should have reported it but he promised he was going to get help when he got home," He finished as he glanced toward me to gauge my reaction.

The guilt in his face mixed with the scent of alcohol on his breath and the meaning behind his words sank in.

"So he had them before he came home…" I said under my breath as I realized Adam had lied to both of us.

"And apparently after," Kendric added as he filled our shot glasses and sat the jar on the counter behind him and out of my reach.

"He promised you he would get help?" I asked before I could stop myself.

Memories of the fight Adam and I had before his last deployment played in my mind. His PTSD had gotten worse before the deployment and the bruises had still been fresh on my neck from where he had pinned me to the wall the night before. It was something I hated myself for and it never should have gotten to that point.

It wasn't that I didn't want him to be in the Army. The military had become everything to my husband, something he was proud of. It was the fact I had spent the last few years watching it eat away at everything he had been before he signed on. I begged him to seek help and take the discharge. We even compromised on him finishing out his contract.

“He lied…” Kendric all but growled as he downed his last shot of moonshine.

I just nodded, finally feeling the numbing effects I had broken the jar out for. I swallowed my last shot before I could spill the extent of the lies Adam fooled us both with. The alcohol threatened to come back up as it hit my stomach, telling me Kendric was right to move the jar away.

“Jeez, Laney! If I had known…” He said as he sank back into the counter from the weight of my admission.

Maybe it had been the liquor talking, but the way he said my name again stood out like a neon sign. He couldn’t say it without revealing some emotion he was trying to hide. All I could hear in his voice was guilt he wasn’t responsible for.

“You can’t do that…” I hoped he believed me.

Adam had fooled the both of us. I couldn’t help but hate the way Kendric had been a little right about the situation. PTSD or not, it was hard to ignore the similarities between his father and my husband.

"He should have gotten help," I added as I steadied myself against the counter beside Kendric.

He leaned into me. Both of us didn't say anything for a moment.

"I should have reported it. I only made him promise because if they sent him home, you'd have to deal with it on your own. If I had known..." He started again and it was my turn to lean into him.

"You know how it goes; the Army came first. It would have been like this either way," I reasoned, barely above a whisper.

I pushed off of the counter and stumbled slightly as I adjusted to the spinning of the room. Kendric's strong and warm hand reached out to catch my arm as if he was worried I was about to topple over. When he didn't let go, I looked at him.

The stony expression was gone, carried away by the apple pie flavored reprieve. Something desperate and guilt-ridden took over as he searched my face for some level of understanding.

"It shouldn't come before everything," he said, matching my whispered tone and something about the way he said it brought back the same feelings I had been trying to ignore.

What was I doing? If it hadn't been for our past, I would reason it away by blaming my grief, but I knew better. Kendric had always felt like unfinished business, but I had forced the feelings down for so long. I felt as if I was losing my control.

"Annnnnd...we are officially cut off. Come on, let's go make up the couch. You aren't driving home like this," I said with an amused chuckle, trying to avoid any alcohol driven impulses.

His hand dropped from my arm before he wrapped them around my shoulders and guided me to the living room. We said our goodnights before I snuggled up in my comforter and waited for sleep. Just as I was about to doze off, my phone vibrated on the nightstand.

Not wanting to wake up to anything terrifying, I unlocked my phone to find I had missed three messages. One from Kendric, saying that he was here, and two more from my stalker.

Hubs:

I liked it better when you kept the curtains open.

Hubs:

Does your boyfriend know you're mine?

I stared at the phone. The liquid courage dampened the fear I normally would have had at the sight. I didn't know who had Adam's phone, but I was getting sick of them using his number for their twisted game and sick fantasies. Against my better judgment and in moonshine infused anger, I sent a text back.

Me:

Is your problem the fact that Kendric is here or the fact you weren't invited?

I slammed my phone back on the nightstand and closed my eyes. The buzz of my stalker's reply barely registered before the world fell away. Whatever they had sent back was now sober Delaney's problem.

April 9, 2016

Kendric

"See they get better the more you drink them," I heard Kevin offer softly as I watched Laney forcefully chug the drink in her hand.

Kevin laced his arm around my girlfriend's waist as he pulled her closer to him. She didn't seem bothered by the contact, but that registered after I noticed he didn't have a drink of his own. I wondered how many of the empty cans she had drank before I got there.

I started in their direction, fully intending to shove her beer can down his throat. In my head, I was mentally choreographing the fight when Laney's voice made me falter.

"I don't care how it tastes, I just want to close my eyes and not see *them*...like that..." she slurred, but the alcohol didn't distort the heartbreak in her voice.

"It was a stupid task. There's no way that went anywhere beyond a photo. Kendric's too...rigid," Kevin reassured, once again taking the steam out of my original mission.

For a moment, I wondered how much of Quinton's plan he had been a part of. I was feeling guilty for naming Kevin in the police report until he reached down and pulled another beer out to hand to her. Regardless of his intention, I was at least right about the fact he was trying to get her wasted.

"It didn't," I confirmed as I got closer to them.

I winced when Laney jumped at the sound of my voice. Maybe I should have listened to Adam, but I couldn't stop myself. There had been too much risk to her safety and even though I was doubting Kevin's involvement, he was putting her in a compromising position.

Kevin quickly stood from the bench, putting space between Laney and himself. His eyes widened as he put his palms up to me like I had done to my father that morning. To show I meant him no harm, I put my hands in the pockets of my jeans.

"I just wanted to make sure she got home safe." He started defensively as he took a couple more steps back from her.

"Thanks," I dismissed him, turning my attention to Laney.

She wouldn't look at me as her eyes stayed firmly planted on the sidewalk in front of her. She hugged her knees to her chest with one hand and wiped the tears from her cheek with the other. Kevin didn't stick around to listen to her reply, before bolting.

"Save your breath Kendric. I'm not interested in whatever charming lie you have prepared to make me swoon. I think you reached your limit on girls to con this week," she spat in my direction.

I swallowed every instinct I had to let it rest, wishing she would look at me. Waiting a moment to respond, I debated on stopping Kevin from returning to the party. The only thing that stopped me was the sight of the alcohol he had left behind in his cowardly escape.

“I’d never do that to you,” I tried when Kevin’s footsteps faded away, a tense silence between us.

“It's not like there was photographic evidence or anything,” she volleyed back as I took a seat on the bench beside her.

I expected her to scoot away from me or to ask me to leave, but she didn’t. When she didn’t try to get away from me, I continued.

“Her task was to distract me from leaving while that video played, and mine was supposed to stay distracted until it was over, but I couldn’t. I thought what was happening on that TV screen was being filmed live and Chelsea took the photo when she realized I was going to leave,” I started, but I couldn’t find the right words to explain it.

I had planned to tell Laney everything that happened with Chelsea after I had made sure she was okay, that day the video played for the school. I rehearsed every word as I searched the halls for her, but when I found her hiding out on this same exact bench, she was a mess.

Before I could say anything to her, Laney came clean about how playing that video had been her task, but the only thing I could focus on in those moments that had followed was everything she hadn't told me about the day Mr. Gilliam held her over from class. The lie she told me to stop me from confronting him consumed everything in its wake.

The more Laney fell apart that day, the less important it seemed to start a fight over it all. It was over and done with, and Chelsea had been forgotten. I didn't know how I could convince Laney I didn't keep it from her on purpose.

"Glad to know you thought about me while your ex was on her knees," she snorted as she went to stand up from the bench.

"Just what every girl dreams of; second best," she muttered to herself as she wobbled.

"She wasn't...jeez...Quinton set the whole thing up. What you saw as the second option she was given because he knew I wouldn't stay put as I was told," I snipped and Laney stopped.

"Give me one reason I should believe you." she asked hesitantly. Anger wavered in her voice as she finally looked at me.

"Chelsea and I broke up when she slept with him last year. Quinton knew I let you believe I took a bat to his face, over her, and knew how desperately she wanted to attend that stupid party. I wasn't just risking mine and Chelsea's admission when I left. They threatened yours too, but he knew it didn't matter. He sent her over tonight so he could sell it when he showed you the picture," I replied.

I heard her take a sharp breath. "So you never got the signal? Why would he let us in if you didn't follow through?" She was still trying to fill in the gaps.

"No, I left because I watched Mr. Gilliam touch you," I answered as the irritation flooded back in.

"And if I had to guess, we didn't get rejected because the big reveal was planned before the tasks were even sent out so he could finish that stupid bet," I added, ignoring the way her eyes widened at the words.

Laney sank back down on the bench beside me.

"I don't understand why she felt that desperate," she stated as she tried to fight through the beer fog.

"It's a rite of passage here that she felt cheated out of. By the time Chelsea pulled me into the library, I didn't care if it meant ditching this stupid party. Quinton relied on her feelings like she didn't have a choice," I explained and she nodded slowly at the reasoning.

"I told you I took care of it," she quietly defended.

"You also told me he didn't touch you," I countered as the rage I had been bottling up shone through my failing attempt to fix things.

"I wasn't going to let you ruin your plans to enlist by fighting a battle I had already won," she replied as she wiped more tears away from her cheeks.

"It would have been worth it," I pulled her into me, the truth ringing around us.

Sirens sang out in the distance as we sat there like that for a while. The longer I held her, the less I wanted to stop. I could have held her like that for hours.

In a couple of months, we wouldn't be able to do that anymore. Everything that made me want to stay would soon be moved to Wisconsin. Holding her made everything feel less temporary.

When it was time to walk her home, we walked in silence until we reached the walkway that led to the stairs of her front porch. As I went to unlace my fingers from hers, Laney held onto them tightly and pulled me toward the front door.

"I should go. I don't want to wake up your mother," I whispered as I suppressed a chuckle.

“Mom is out with her friends tonight. I was going to mention it earlier but…” Her words trailed off as she opened the storm door to her house.

“Oh,” I replied as I looked into her hazy eyes still buzzing from the alcohol.

“Stay here tonight,” she offered as she bit her bottom lip nervously.

As much as I wanted to stay, the last thing I wanted to do tonight was take advantage of her drunken state. The more she did things, like bite her bottom lip, the less likely I would be to hold on to that resolve. Instead, I kissed her softly and let go of her hand.

“I can’t,” I answered, unsure of my decision.

Laney tried to hide her disappointment as she nodded and checked the handle of her door to make sure it was unlocked. I didn’t want to leave us like that after the day we had. Gently, I took her face in my hands and made her look at me.

“But, I’ll see you first thing in the morning. Never for a second think you are second best to me,” I said softly before I kissed her more passionately than before.

She melted into me. Her lips tasted like beer and salt. Laney pulled away and hit me with her big green doe eyes.

“Okay, but you will have to make this up to me,” She teased after we broke the kiss and I took a step back to leave for real this time.

“Name it,” I answered happily as she stepped into the entryway.

“You, me, and Adam, The Spring Festival opening day?” she suggested with a mischievous smirk.

“It’s a date,” I answered before leaving her smiling.

On the walk back home, I came to terms with the fact Laney wasn’t temporary for me. I loved her and at the moment, I thought I had lost her forever; I realized there was no version of my life that I didn’t want her beside me.

I was going to use the military to get us out of there, but I wasn’t joining to escape anymore. I was joining to make a better life for us. It didn’t matter that we were kids. I could feel it in my bones; Laney was the one I was meant to grow old with.

Chapter Ten

February 19, 2024

Delaney

My alarm woke me from the vivid dreams of Kendric. I hit the snooze button as the ghost of his hands faded from my thighs. Even though I knew I should have gotten up, I laid my head back on my pillows, letting the guilt consume me.

I didn't know why I was feeling anything for Kendric more than friendship. We had tried that before. Granted, it had been several years since he and I were anything but distant. Growing up didn't make us any more compatible and the last thing I wanted for my future was to be tied down once again by the military lifestyle.

Still, sporadic images of the erotic dreams played through my head, taunting me. They fought and fueled my self-loathing as if the two conflicting feelings played tug-of-war in my head. For every thought of Adam, a moonshine soak scene from my dreams played so vividly I could almost taste the cinnamon.

I tried to picture how Adam would feel about it all, but in response to my conscience, I'd remember how Kendric's hand pinned me to the wall by my throat in the dream. I'd degrade myself for not being cold and numb to the idea of another man. Only to replay Kendric's hand sliding slowly up my thighs, as he raised my skirt higher...

Groaning, I threw the covers off of myself. I needed a cold shower. All I had to do was make it to the bathroom without running into the real-life version of Kendric. When I didn't hear any movement, I darted into the bathroom and I cursed as I realized I had forgotten to grab any clothing.

I stood frozen for a moment as I debated turning around to get them, but the fear of waking Kendric and having to look at his face stopped me. Unless he was in the hallway, I could make it to my bedroom quick enough to avoid an awkward towel run in. I decided it wasn't worth the risk.

Without second guessing my decision, I turned on the shower. I was going to start it off hot and make sure it was cool enough to wash the smut-like thoughts and the ghost of Kendric off my body. I closed my eyes and let the water fall down over me as the fan overhead drowned out the rest of the world.

The faint ringing of my alarm cut the peaceful moment short. In my rush to shake my regrettable impulses, I had forgotten I had only snoozed the alarm. I shut off the tepid water and grabbed my towel, cursing at the mistakes I made while I was distracted.

Pausing, I wrapped my towel around myself. Even though I knew I had heard it, it was like the alarm had stopped the moment the water had been shut off. I tiptoed to the bedroom only to find Kendric sitting on my bed, my phone in his hands.

I inwardly cursed again at the fact my alarm had woken him up. At least that was the first thing that I could think of as I looked at him and registered the anger written all over his features.

"I'm sorry if that woke you," I sheepishly apologized.

I felt his eyes land on me as I kept my eyes anywhere, but on him. He took a ragged breath as he set my device on the bed beside him. When I finally forced myself to look at him, I couldn't help but notice the rage that poured off of him as if it seeped out of every pore.

"How. Long?" He asked me through clenched teeth.

My eyes shot up to his instantly in confusion. How long what? I cocked my head to the side, trying to figure out what he was talking about, but nothing came to mind.

When I didn't respond, he stood up, grabbing my phone from where he had set it, and pointed it at me as his cold eyes burned through me. As I stared at my phone, hazy memories from the night before flooded in.

I sucked in a breath as I remembered messaging my stalker. That breath seized in my throat as I realized Kendric must have seen them. I had hoped the message I remembered sending was just another messed up dream, but I could tell by the look on Kendric's face that it hadn't been.

"Kendric I—" I started, but he licked his bottom lip before he pulled it between his teeth in frustration.

My words were cut off as he threw the phone back on my bed and pushed past me. I kicked myself for not telling him about the stalker as I followed him. I wasn't sure what to say to fix it, but I didn't know what all he had read.

"I didn't know how to tell you," I called out after him as he snatched his keys from the coffee table.

He let out a humorless laugh and shook his head before he turned around to face me.

"How about, 'Gee Kendric, I know my husband just sacrificed himself for the country, but I have found a new boyfriend,'" he snapped out in a sarcastic tone.

I flinched at his words as the feelings I had towards him reminded me that his statement wasn't completely false. The guilt delayed the full meaning behind his words. It wasn't until he reached my front door that it registered that he didn't realize all the texts were from Adam's number.

"You think I'd save a new guy's number under Hubs?" I blurted out in vexation as I spun him back around to face me by the arm.

"Honestly, Del, I have no idea who you are anymore," He said in a raised voice and I stilled.

What the hell did he mean he didn't know me? Aside from the time between him leaving for basic and Adam being assigned to his squad, Kendric had been in my life since I was seventeen. There wasn't another person alive who knew me better than he did.

"I have known you for almost a decade. How can you possibly still think of me as a stranger?" I challenged as I narrowed my eyes on him.

He matched my glare as his fingers let go of the doorknob. For a moment, I felt relieved that maybe I was getting it through to him. The second his restraint slipped and I saw the doubt behind his eyes, I knew I was mistaken.

He had been trying to use the statued appearance and I had been mistaking his anger for something else, like jealousy. The only thing he had restrained was the betrayal that now showed through, as if highlighted in neon lights behind his blue-gray eyes.

"The girl I knew didn't keep moonshine in her freezer, had men showing up and texting at all hours, and she sure as hell would have told me her husband was an abusive alcoholic before I had to witness her relive it through a PTSD episode. But, then again, I didn't even know my best friend had been involved in an open-relationship. So, no Del, I don't know you at all and I don't really care to," He snapped out as he waited for me to argue with him.

Even if I wanted to fight it, I couldn't. I couldn't breathe as my mind caught on the words 'abusive' and 'open relationship.' The more I tried to, the further up my throat the breath seemed to get stuck.

When he saw my reaction, something inside of him flipped. He closed his eyes and stepped toward me, but I was already turning around. Unable to be near him, I went to the only place I knew would hold some kind of answer to those words.

I already knew why he referred to the nights when Adam's night terrors got the best of him as the abuse. In a way, it might have been, but I knew now more than ever Adam had been sick. Hell, Adam didn't even know he was home in those moments.

My brain repeated the one phrase over and over in my head like psychological torture. Adam and I had never had an open relationship. As much as I tried to convince myself that

Kendric had jumped to that conclusion after meeting Daniel and reading the messages, it didn't really make sense.

The only thing I could think of that would give me any kind of understanding was the text thread between me and the person who was impersonating my husband. The closer I got to the bedroom, the less oxygen seemed to be left in the house.

I didn't register Kendric's footsteps behind me as my pulse pounded too loudly in my ears. All hope of breathing ceased as I reached for my phone and unlocked it. Sure enough, on my screen were messages I prayed Kendric would never know about.

I scanned the messages, but when I found the reply my stalker had returned to my act of stupid, drunken bravery. I sank to the edge of the bed. Kendric hadn't scrolled up the screen to see all the messages I never returned. I didn't find the answer to the cryptic words, but I understood now how he thought the conversation had been consensual.

There wasn't any room left in me to fill with the panic of that last message sent; the weight of everything else had killed my ability to be any more terrified. I sat there, staring at the last message, unaware Kendric had been watching me silently from the doorway.

Hubs:

Keep trying to make me jealous and show you… Or better yet, maybe I'll just wait till he leaves.

May 8, 2016

Kendric

I waited anxiously on the bench next to the high school for Adam. He was running ten minutes behind and it was cutting it close to when Laney was supposed to join us. I must have checked my watch for the hundredth time as I stood to relieve my lungs from the growing unease under my ribcage.

The sound of a car door being slammed shut pulled me from my panicked thoughts. To my relief, Adam rounded the back end of a car down the street. Finally, it felt like I could breathe.

"Shit, I'm sorry," he rushed out as he reached me.

His punctuality wasn't an issue anymore. All that mattered was that he got there before she did.

"No worries. You got it?" I asked hesitantly in response as that nervous energy crawled up my spine like thorny vines.

My question sent him into spy mode as he glanced around for any prying eyes before he rummaged through the pocket of his jeans. Paranoid, I glanced back to make sure Laney wasn't in view and held out my hand. He had been holding on to something for me since the day after the Spring Fling.

"Are you sure about this?" He questioned with a hint of doubt embedded in his question.

I let out a shaky breath before nodding, worried that the actual words would show the hesitation. He searched my face for any signs of cold feet before he placed my grandmother's ring on top of my palm.

I looked down at it, trying to convince myself this was really going to happen. The closer we got to graduation, the quicker it became apparent that I didn't have a choice if I wanted to keep Laney in my life. She was moving out of state in two weeks and my swear in date had been moved up to the day after she left the state.

"I didn't think you wanted to put anyone through the Army wife's life," Adam asked with concern.

I couldn't figure out if he was worried I hadn't thought this through or if he didn't think Laney could handle it, but it didn't matter. It was something I felt I had to do, and I had a limited time to do it. All I knew was that Laney was it for me.

"If anyone can handle it, it's Laney," I frustratedly blurted, redirecting my own doubts into defensive anger.

I wasn't mad at him for what he had said or for the concern that coated every part of his statement. The pressure of it all had eaten away at my nerves, leaving me raw and with little patience.

Offended by my tone, I watched his face grow red with irritation. I could practically see his defensiveness raise around him like armor.

"And what if she doesn't want it? The Army life? She shouldn't have to *handle* it because you can't *handle* the long distance dating first," Adam volleyed back.

"I'll lose her," I replied, even though I knew it was a stupid reason.

It was moments like these I realized just how similar I was to my father. As hard as I tried, I couldn't find the right words, the shame only reflected in hard words I didn't fully mean. I should have told him exactly how I felt about her.

"So you think your only options are a painful breakup or forcing her into the military world?" Judgment laced his words.

I couldn't look at him as I debated on lying. How was I supposed to defend myself when he wasn't exactly wrong? Instead, I looked back and watched for her.

“That’s life, Adam. At least this career can help me build a better life for us. It's not like I have a college fund waiting for me,” I replied, waiting for more anger that I rightfully earned.

“That’s the problem Kendric. You aren’t *thinking* about anything other than escaping. Marriage isn’t something you do to solve a problem and I don’t believe for a freaking second you are doing this for her,” he spoke in a deadly calm.

I looked back at him, readying to defend myself. Clenching my jaw, I bit back my gut reaction to his words. She was all I could think about and I already knew my motivations were centered on my insecurity, but I couldn’t lose Laney.

“Maybe it’s selfish, but I am doing this to keep her in my life and yes, I think it’s a far better option,” I hissed as I pushed down all the things I wanted to say.

“Every time you tell yourself this was the better choice, I want you to remember that instead of mourning you and moving on if something happens, you want her to play second to your precious career,” Adam warned as he nodded behind me and turned to leave.

I didn’t have to turn around to know what he was gesturing too. As I watched Adam leave, Laney bounded up behind me. I barely stuffed the ring in my pocket before she covered my eyes with the palms of her hands.

“Good morning….Staff Sergeant Gray?,” I teased, forcing out a feigned cheerful tone.

She dropped her hands and huffed at the mention of my recruiter’s name. Even though she knew I had figured out it was her before her fingers covered my eyes.

“Did Adam give it away? Where is he going, anyway? We have to be at the ticket booth in fifteen minutes,” she asked as she looked around.

I forced a smile as I rattled off the excuse he and I had prepared the week before. Even though Adam had promised he would come with us to the Spring Festival, he and I had made other arrangements for my proposal. The closer we got to the ticket booth, the quicker my heart beats and Adam’s words grew alongside my doubts.

“So…I wanted to tell you something later tonight, but…” she started as her voice grew more and more nervous and her steps slowed us to almost a stop.

Nervousness choked me as I watched her try not to look down at the pavement. Whatever she was about to confess left me feeling more unsure about my decision than Adam’s lecture.

“Is everything okay?” I blurted out as my heart dropped into the pit, forming at the base of my stomach.

She paused at my panicked reaction as she registered my tone. Removing the cloak of disappointment from her face, she beamed up at me in reassurance. It only made me feel more apprehensive.

“I pushed my classes back. Your swear in is still a couple months out and the thought of you being here while I was all the way in…” Her words trailed off as she caught the look on my face.

“You pushed your start date back?” I asked her as the swelling fears morphed my voice into less of a question and more an accusation.

“I thought you’d be happy. It means we can get more time together before—” she started again before my aggressive reaction fully registered.

“I won’t be here,” I snapped with so much coldness that I barely recognized my voice.

She stepped away from me, her confusion taking over any anger she might have had toward my response. The fear I saw in her face would forever haunt me as if she knew what was coming before I did.

“I leave after graduation,” I forced out, trying to fix the damage I had caused.

I wanted to tell her it wasn't her, that my poor attitude was from something else entirely and that I hated myself for ruining her summer plans. For a moment, I could see what our lives would have been like if I didn't enlist.

I shut my eyes and existed in that dream, trying to calm down, but all I could do was sit in the realization that the dream would be nothing more than that. I would hate myself for never signing and she would resent me for the life she would have if I stayed.

Needing to feel the ring in my hand to find strength in my decision, I wrapped my fingers around the cool metal in my pocket. I held onto that golden band like a lifeline as I opened my eyes to look at her. As the garnet dug into my skin, I used the pain as my link to rationality.

"I can't do this," I thought out loud as her face flushed with emotion.

It was my last chance to take back what I had finally decided. The side of me so desperate to keep Laney ate away at my resolve. My heart spoke over my doubts and personal needs as I replayed Adam's words in my mind.

"You can't do what Kendric?" Laney asked as if she didn't want to know the answer.

I sucked in a deep breath as I clung to the ring for my last bit of strength.

“You are no one’s second choice, Laney,” I started as I watched her heart break alongside mine.

“Just yours, right?” she accused as she backed away further away from me and tried to storm off before I could answer.

I fought back everything in me that screamed at me to go after her. The words to take it all back gathered along the sides of my tongue, desperate to escape and take everything back. The reality that she would end up getting notification officers at our door kept those words from falling out of my mouth.

“The Army is my…future,” I spat out as I delivered the final blow.

She paused as the words hit her square between her shoulders. I knew I would not keep up the act if she called my bluff and turned around. Part of me wordlessly begged for her to, but she kept walking just like the unselfish part of me kept my lips sealed shut, and not an ounce of sunshine radiated off of her.

I waited on the bench in case she came back, but she never did. Walking home, I came to terms with my decision. This was always how it was supposed to be. It was the reason I tried to shut her out after we met, but I didn’t regret loving her one bit.

Laney deserved better than a life filled with worry as I fought half a world away. All I wanted was for her to be happy and it took that fight with Adam to realize I couldn't provide that for her. Still, it didn’t change the fact Laney was it for me.

Chapter Eleven

February 19, 2024

Delaney

I stared at the words on my phone until I couldn't see them anymore. My breaths sounded like hiccups as I sat there, completely defeated. It would have been hard for the stalker to get to me before I died from lack of oxygen.

The other part of me wondered if that would be easier. If there was any point in feeling afraid of Kendric walking out that door. I was tired of living through the grief and the fear of who was on the other end of Adam's phone.

Out of the corner of my eye, I registered movement, but Kendric might as well have been on another planet. His voice sounded through my fog, but I couldn't understand him; it was too hazy and distant. My head dipped below the surface of my overwhelming guilt.

"Breathe, Laney. You have to take a breath and explain to me what the hell is going on right now," He ordered in an urgent, but soft tone.

Even if I wanted to, I couldn't respond. The edges of my vision seemed to swim as I couldn't get the oxygen past my throat. My chest ached louder than my desire to exist. He moved out of view as I ignored his command.

I didn't want to breathe or talk to him. It wasn't like he would believe a word that I would say and I didn't exactly blame him. Talking just felt as useless as breathing.

The bed beside me moved as he sat down beside me. I didn't understand why he hadn't left me yet. Just the fact that he stayed planted the tiniest seed of hope that I couldn't explain.

He had every reason to go. I knew he meant everything he yelled at me and my actions probably came off as a manipulation tactic. I had no right to hope he stayed for me.

Without asking or warning, he wrapped his powerful arms around me and pulled me into his chest like he had a couple of nights ago. My hands fell to my lap, dropping my phone. I didn't even bother to catch it as it slid off my lap or registered that he caught it.

I tensed in his arms as the ringing sounded through the air. My gasping breaths halted as I registered the noise, realizing he had called Adam's number for the answers I wouldn't give.

Kendric tensed around me, refusing to let me go even though he was waiting to hear someone answer the call. He felt like he was holding his breath, too. I didn't know what would have been worse; if my stalker answered or if it went to Adam's voicemail.

"You have reached Staff Sergeant Anderson's personal line. If you leave a message, I will get back to you." Adam's voice box message played over the speaker phone.

Kendric's grip loosened as soon as Adam's voice cut through the room. I closed my eyes as I waited for the last of my husband's sign off.

"If this is Sunshine, I miss you..." Adam's voicemail message ended.

Kendric flew off the bed as he hurriedly hung up the call. He stared at the name that stayed on the screen as if he was seeing those messages for the first time.

I knew the moment he read the last response all over again by the way his eyes shot up to me. He gripped my phone in his hand so tightly I watched his knuckles turn paper white. Without saying a word, he searched for the phone in the box of Adam's things like I had.

Angrily, he flipped the box over, spilling its contents out onto the carpet. I couldn't take my eyes off of him as he desperately searched through the wreckage on my bedroom floor. He would not find the answers in there either.

I braced myself for his questions that I already knew I would have no answers to. The edges of my vision turned black from lack of proper oxygen.

When Kendric realized Adam's phone wasn't in the box, he sat down on the floor beside its contents. He didn't look at me when he spoke, his eyes trained back on the screen of my mobile device still in his hand.

"Why didn't you tell me about this?" He asked with a raw and scary quietness.

It wasn't said as an accusation, but I wasn't expecting that to be his first question. When I couldn't find the words, he glanced up in my direction, as if remembering my previous state. He only looked at me long enough to see if I was still conscious.

"How was I supposed to tell you I was being texted by a ghost?" I forced out, but I couldn't raise my voice above a whisper as it came out broken and wheezy.

"Come on, Del. We both know this wasn't a ghost," he replied in irritation and I winced at his nickname.

I knew he called me by that name when he put distance between us. Most of the time, all it did was get under my skin, but I don't think he realized I knew why he called me that. I didn't think there was any room for another wall to come between us.

"I think you should leave," I choked out as I felt another wave of devastation catch in my lungs.

I was done having an audience while I shattered and he didn't want to be here. It was a blinking reminder that I didn't belong in his world. I was done proving him right. Stalker or not, I was going to be kicked off the base soon. If Kendric was determined to believe I was bringing this on myself, then there was no point in trying to sort anything out.

Kendric looked up at me in disbelief as I refused to repeat myself. He stood and took a step toward me before stopping himself.

"You saw this psycho's last message. What if he shows up here?" he questioned in disbelief.

"You made it perfectly clear that's my problem to handle alone. You don't want to be here and I don't *want* you here. Leave," I forced out as I turned my face away from him so he wouldn't see my heart break.

"How can you ask me to go now that I know what's happening?" Kendric let out a growl, boiling in frustration at my demand.

The irritation in his voice only triggered the replay of his earlier words through my ears. I pushed down the urge to fall apart and calmed my breathing the best I could. I was done being vulnerable in front of him.

I didn't answer him as I laid down and turned away from his prying eyes. There wasn't much time before my tears would start to fall. If he couldn't see my face, he couldn't watch me shatter. I took a moment to be sure my voice wouldn't give me away.

"We both know you'd only be staying out of a sense of obligation, but that loyalty belongs to the Delaney you used to know. You don't know a damn thing about me, remember?" I choked out to seal my point.

There was nothing that would have convinced me that Kendric would have stayed for anyone, but Adam. I wasn't a deathbed promise he needed to keep. Even when he loved me, he didn't love me enough to fight for it. Somehow, his insistence to stay on my late husband's behalf only added insult to injury.

May 08, 2018

Kendric

Laney,

I must have written this a hundred times. We have been nothing to each other for longer than we were dating, but there isn't a day that goes by that you do not cross my mind.

I need you to know what I wanted to say the day we broke up. Which writing it out now seems like a stupid thing to do. Especially since there is no guarantee that you have even thought about me over the two years, but I have regretted that day every day since.

The longer I am here, the more I wished I had picked a different path. I think about how strong you were and how you were at peace for me and how I never realized it. I know it is a selfish thought, but now and then I try to convince myself that you could have handled this.

If I had asked you to marry me then, like I had originally planned, you would have been perfectly capable of taking on the role as an Army wife. I held on to that regret for a long time, but this wasn't the life you deserved.

Until I got back home from my first leave, that hung over my head like a storm cloud. It influenced every move I made, because I had convinced myself that on that first trip back, I'd find you and beg for your forgiveness. Unfortunately, life had other plans.

We get assigned these partners over here. We call them battle buddies. You go nowhere alone. One of mine was

Corporal Stevens. He gave me a letter for his wife in case anything was to happen to him and I ended up delivering that letter to her, within hours after landing back in the states.

Watching that woman break to pieces in front of me made me realize two things. At first it showed me I was right to walk away. I had always thought the worst thing that could happen was I would become like my father. That the PTSD would swallow me alive and you'd be stuck just like my mother, but that wasn't the only thing that could put you in danger of the crossfire.

I couldn't bring myself to find you after that. There was nothing in this world that could convince me you wouldn't end up miserable and alone. It wasn't until days later that the second realization hit me.

When I went to check on her, she was surrounded by loved ones, but his wife pulled me aside. I apologized for her loss and told her Steven's was a great soldier. She dismissed it before thanking me for allowing her husband to give her one last goodbye.

I know this letter may only bring you heartache and where part of me hates myself for doing this, the other part of me won't let it rest. That second realization as this letter may be the only way I can make sure you understand what you are to me.

Laney, you are it for me and if I lose the fight over here, I died loving you even though I know I probably haven't crossed your mind once since you moved on. When things get rough here and every soldier dreams of what they are fighting for, you are my reason.

You are the positivity behind my mindset of doing the job and getting as many of us home as possible. The demons in my mind that tell me I should give up every day, but they are no match for your voice that I imagine, telling me to keep my head up.

So, I realized as I stood there next to my fallen comrade's wife, that if there was anyone on this Earth that I would want to say goodbye to, it's you. I needed to thank you for your influence, for keeping me sane while I was here even though you never knew it. I loved you more after I walked away than I could ever imagine and I am trying to get back to you even if we never reconnect.

I walked away because I thought I could save you from me and I know now you deserve more than whatever piece of me makes it home. I hope that you never have to read this. I hope I prove myself wrong and eventually deserve you.

You were never second best, Laney; you are who I needed to fight for and if you ever do read this, just know I died trying to prevent the need for you to.

Forever yours,

Kendric Tate

I folded the letter and stuffed it inside of an envelope as footsteps sounded from outside of my bunk. Muffled voices filtered through the walls as I hid the envelope under my cot. I barely had enough time to straighten before Sergeant Stanton knocked on the door seconds before he walked inside.

He wasn't alone, but blocked the view of the person behind him. Then again, Stanton had been built like a Greek god. Just him being in my bunk made it feel microscopic. He cleared his throat as I waited for him to introduce me to my new bunkmate.

"PFC Tate, I'd like to introduce you to one of the newest additions to our squad. Although, from my understanding, you may already be acquainted," He reported, as his serious face spread into a rare and kind smile.

I tried looking past Officer Stanton in curiosity as a familiar face stepped around the bulky sergeant. A mixture of confusion and excitement flooded me as I took in the man who stood there dressed in ACUs.

“Corporal Adam Anderson,” Stanton finished as Adam’s eyes met mine and held them.

All the air left my lungs as I realized what this meant. My best friend was now in the war with me and it explained why we had gone months not talking. I had thought very little about it until that moment.

As I scanned him over, trying to wrap my brain around this new reality, I couldn’t help but notice the one item he wore that was not military issued. Around his ring finger, he was wearing a black silicone wedding band.

Chapter Twelve

February 19, 2024

Delaney

I listened for Kendric's steps to slowly fade as I laid there, regretting my words. The longer I waited to hear him leave, the more I convinced myself that I hadn't heard the door shut over the pounding heartbeat in my ears. The more I believed that, the more I feared I wouldn't hear my stalker if he followed through with the threat.

Quietly, I got out of bed. We were not allowed to have a personal firearm, since we lived in base housing, but Adam never liked the idea of leaving me alone without an adequate weapon. I slid the aluminum baseball bat out from under the bed as silently as I could. Adam had modified it so that it held a more significant amount of danger.

I choked up seeing the bat, memories of the way Adam had made me practice for a more efficient swing. I shook my head to stare down at it. The sand Adam had funneled into the hollowed metal, made it harder to handle. That or maybe the fact it had laid under the bed gathering dust for years. Either way, the weight in my hands made me empowered and a little silly.

The sound of dishes clattering sounded off from further in the house. Taking a shaky breath, I geared myself up for a fight. The stalker had picked the wrong person to mess with and I had plenty of pent up aggression to channel into my blow.

I took calculated footsteps toward my bedroom door as I re-familiarized myself with the weapon. My brain grasped at the distant memory that was left of Adam's "training" sessions. The closer I got to the noises, the more my gut recoiled.

It sounded as if they were playing house. I rested my back on the wall that separated my kitchen from the entryway as I listened to the footsteps pace around my tile floors. The faucet turned on over the sink and I took advantage of the louder noise.

The running water masked the sound of my footsteps as I charged into the kitchen and swung at the figure standing over my kitchen sink. The impact of the bat hitting flesh echoed as time stilled. By the time I had landed the swing, I had barely connected the person I just assaulted wasn't some cracked out intruder.

Mainly, because Kendric spun on me before I could fully register who I had attacked. He turned on me and grabbed a hold of the aluminum so fast I barely saw him move. Jerking the bat forward, he propelled me into his hold. Before I knew what was happening, he whirled me around and had me facing him and leaning over the counter, his fingers wrapped around my throat.

His wild steely blue eyes widened on my face as he registered I wasn't the threat he had been expecting. We stood like that for a moment. Neither of us said a word. I watched his fight or flight die down as both of us stood there, slightly out of breath.

I didn't move or try to get out of the grasp he still desperately held. The heat of his ragged exhales traced my cheeks as he stood looming over me. As much as I wanted to apologize, I couldn't move. His desperation only reminded me of the dreams I didn't want to remember.

"What the fuck, Laney!" he cursed under his breath, slowly ungluing his fingers from my skin.

He had found his control only moments before I found mine, but I couldn't bring myself to budge. His palms rested on the counter beside me, casing me in between him and the speckled laminate. The bat rested at our feet as I hesitantly brought my hands away from his chest, unaware I had placed them there in the struggle.

"I-I'm sorry. I thought.." I started, still slightly in shock as my eyes drifted to his shoulder.

He was standing so close to me it was hard not to notice how my voice seemed to relax the tension in him.

"You thought I was the stalker?" He asked, not really needing the answer.

The guilt in his voice only confirmed my suspicion.

"I thought you left," I admitted sheepishly as I pushed myself through Kendric's strange embracing stance to put some space between us.

I didn't mean for there to be so much snippiness in my voice as I said it. The whole argument earlier was still too fresh. I hated myself the moment I said it.

"Do you really think I could have left after…all that?" he asked as if I should have known better.

It wasn't until he said it that I realized the thought of him running away seemed ridiculous. Kendric wasn't the kind of person who could leave anyone in danger, despite everything he had accused me of. Still, the realization he stayed specifically to keep me safe felt foreign.

"It doesn't matter, but I am sorry I hit you," I answered, unable to voice my honest feelings or my embarrassment.

His warm fingers laced around the bend of my elbow as I turned away from him to leave the kitchen. I hated myself for the way I jerked in response to the sudden contact, but he didn't move his fingers away. He simply held his grip and ignored my triggered response.

"It matters to me," he answered feebly, stepping closer.

He was so close to me I could almost feel him breathing. I cursed at the way my body reacted to him so automatically before I could shut the feelings down.

"I wasn't thinking," I lied, almost breathless as his closeness clouded my ability to think.

"If something would have happened to you..." He tried to continue, but it was like his words got caught on his tongue.

I shook my head, trying to convince myself to move away from him. He was acting on guilt or the feeling of responsibility. I reminded myself Kendric was the same man who slut shamed me only hours before.

He might have been wrong about me sleeping around, but he hadn't been wrong about my weakness for someone other than my husband. If he could really read my mind, he would have known that. He also would have realized he occupied more of my thoughts than I would ever admit to.

Every time I thought I was strong enough to move away, I'd feel his breath on my ear and the back of my neck. It felt bitter and intoxicating, like a forbidden guilty pleasure. I closed my eyes and forced myself to replay the memory of that fight to hold onto my anger.

"Look, I get it. You have an amazing sense of personal duty, but I can take care of myself. You don't have to stay," I hid my x-rated thoughts and tried to release him from any promises he might have made with Adam.

Something in my words provoked him. His hand dropped from my arm and wrapped around my waist. Once again, Kendric spun me to face him, his eyes wild like before but there had been a kindness behind them that he didn't have the last time when he responded out of pure instinct. Keeping one hand on my hip, he tilted my chin up to look at him.

He searched my eyes for any sign of seriousness at what I said. The hope I saw in his expression threatened to melt my newly reinforced agitation. What was he doing?

"Whoever has his phone threatened to come inside if I left. I wasn't going to allow that to happen," he clarified carefully as he waited for proof that his words had sunk in.

"This isn't your battle, Kendric. Whoever this is has some vendetta against me, and the longer you stay, the more they will use you in their twisted games, just like they are using Adam's phone," I argued.

Kendric's brows furrowed at my words as he continued to stare me down. It felt as if he was trying to read my mind. I wasn't going to let him in so easily this time.

"Unless I don't leave," He countered, trying to find a compromise.

I scoffed. How could he think more of his presence would be a good thing? Not all that long ago he had jumped down my throat as he confessed he didn't know me. It was obvious; neither of us wanted him here.

"No, nope, absolutely not. You can prove your loyalty to Adam some other way," I replied as I tried to push off Kendric's chest and out of his hold, but he held me there, his grip gentle, but firm.

Something dark filtered through Kendric's expression. He kept me pinned there as all instinct to fight and get away from him died down in the silence between us. Instead of letting me go, he pulled me closer to him just long enough to push us off the counter, giving me the chance to push him away if I wanted to.

"I'm not going anywhere," he let out in a heated breath as his expression told me he thought I would reject him.

I closed my eyes to escape his stare, resting my palm on his chest. My fingers were beginning to feel at home under his collarbone as I held my balance against my palms. Kenderic's heart beat so hard beneath my hand, it was almost thudding loudly against my ribcage.

Against all self-preservation, I felt myself lean into him. We were playing a dangerous game I wasn't sure we could get back from.

"Why?" I whispered, but I hadn't meant to say it out loud.

I felt his breath catch. His composure shattered slightly as he bent to rest his chin against the top of my head. Kenderic reached up and tucked a flyaway strand of my hair behind my ear before he cupped the side of my face so gently it was as if he thought I was made of glass.

"Because I couldn't live with myself if I lost you," he whispered.

Maybe it was the night of dreams where he and I were more, maybe it was our past, but something in the way he said it caused a reaction I had no control over. Without thinking, or the ability to stop myself, I kissed him. For a few moments, I lost myself in the feeling of his lips against mine and the hunger I felt behind them.

It wasn't until I pulled away I realized what I had done. He looked away from me the second I opened my eyes, but I caught the way his jaw flexed as he did so. He rubbed his face with his hand, then placed both of them on the counter for support.

The purple of his fresh bruise all but glowed in the evening light from the kitchen window. If it hurt at all, Kenderic wasn't paying any attention to it. The urge to apologize to him choked me down as I watched him stand there in complete silence.

I forced myself to look away from him as I glanced at the clock. I had missed the new support group meeting I had set the alarm for, but another class was due to start in thirty minutes. If I rushed to get ready, I could make it.

I wasn't about to discuss Adam in a room of strangers after kissing his best friend, but I had to get out. The day had felt too heavy and the house made me feel claustrophobic. I didn't give Kendric time to answer or judge me before I bolted toward my bedroom.

Ten minutes later, I was dressed. I knew if I had taken the time to paint my face and do my hair, Kendric would have convinced me to stay. I shot him a text as I grabbed my keys and headed out the door.

Kendric watched me from the front porch as my phone connected to my car. I ignored the betrayed look in Kendric's eyes as I pulled out onto the road. The ringing of my cell phone filled the confined space before Adam's voicemail played through the car speakers.

I knew my stalker wouldn't answer. I didn't dial the number hoping to gain any more clues. After everything, I just needed to hear Adam's voice, even if all it did was punish me for my mistake.

Drowning in my self-hate, I waited for his voicemail. Logically, I knew I wasn't cheating on my husband, but it had only been six months since he died.

Kendric was an amazing person. He was loyal, honorable, and everything that made for the perfect soldier, but I wasn't sure this life was one I wanted anymore. Everything about that kiss felt disrespectful toward him and to our Adam.

May 15, 2018

Kendric

Adam spent the next week dodging questions I had that involved his marriage. The most information I could get out of him before we were interrupted was the fact that he and his wife had been married less than a month before he enlisted. His unit was deployed not long after the training.

I couldn't sleep the night he arrived at the base. Adam and my relationship had been pretty strained since the day I was supposed to propose, but chickened out. It had been more on my part than on his.

At first, I had only inquired about his wife to make up for the space I had put between us. I would have dropped the questions entirely the first time he avoided giving an actual answer, but Adam always had a tell when he was trying to blow someone off. After the second time I asked him about her, I saw it wasn't just in my head. I had planned to call him out on it, but I was interrupted before I could.

"So you grew up with Sticks here?" Friedman, another soldier from our squad, questioned Adam.

Adam didn't look up at the man as he continued to secure his rucksack. When he finished, he glanced up at me before acknowledging the guy.

"Damn right. Need leverage?" Adam joked as he walked past me, smacking my shoulder.

"Man, I always need leverage," Friedman replied as he threw his bag on.

"And you are not even questioning the nickname?" I laughed as the three of us joined the rest of our group.

Adam looked over at Friedman, and both men raised a brow and chuckled in my direction.

“It will take more than a couple of quiet years for me not to understand that term of endearment, my friend,” Adam answered, and I smirked.

“Endearment, right, nothing to do with the stick Kendric seems to have permanently stuck up his…” Friedman added. I glared at him, cutting his insult off prematurely.

“Ah man, that’s nothing. You should have seen him when he was dating Laney…” Adam began, but as he mentioned her name, his eyes widened, as if it had slipped out before he could stop himself.

My eyes snapped to Adam’s face. There was something in the way he said her name that made my blood turn cold.

“Ohhh, Laney, as in your…?” Friedman started, his eyes growing twice their size before Adam halted him.

“We better get a move on,” Adam interrupted nervously.

Once again, I spotted the way he swallowed hard, like he did when I asked about his wife. It might as well have been a confession, but I needed to hear him say it. Friedman looked between the two of us before quickly finding someone else to talk to.

“Laney, is your what?” I asked as I pulled Adam to the side while everyone else piled into an armored vehicle. I needed to hear him say it

“I know I’m relatively new to this, but I got the impression this isn’t something we should delay,” He tried to deflect.

“Only one person at a time can really get in right now. Just say it Adam,” I demanded, refusing to let him avoid the question this time.

Everything in me told me to listen to him. We weren’t in the time or place where we could make our own selfish decisions; I couldn’t move until I heard it. I needed that confirmation.

“Kendric, this isn’t how… I was going to tell you. I just couldn’t find the right time…”

“When would it have been a better time to tell me you married *her*?” It escaped before I could filter out my possessiveness.

“There isn’t one. I get why you didn’t before graduation, but our circumstances aren’t the same,” Adam snapped.

“That’s funny, because the whole reason I didn’t that day was because you convinced me it was selfish to put her in the same position you are right now,” I shot back, as I walked away to join the rest of our squad.

The eerie quiet filled the space as we waited for our roles in the mission to play out. Half an hour later, we had made it safely to our destination and radioed our arrival. Oblivious to the tension, our sergeant assigned Adam to be my battle buddy.

I had been so focused on him and his confession, I had almost missed the little girl who came out from the side of a building as we approached it. She was small, maybe eight years old. Her long dark hair was matted in places and moondust was caked to her legs and face. I saw the tears in her frightened eyes before I noticed the metal object she was clutching.

Immediately, my weapon went up as Adam hesitated for half a second. He raised his following suit with mine, but I could tell it was against his basic instinct. It didn't matter how hard they drilled it in our heads in the training exercises; the first time you were actually faced with this situation, it messed with your head. He wasn't the first to hesitate and it wouldn't be the last child he would need to see the threat first before the age or gender.

I shouted at the child to stop, warning that I was preparing to fire. She stared at me for a moment with wide and terrified eyes. I prayed that she listened.

Hearing my command while walking to their assigned post, Friedman and his shadow came running. Weapons raised, they stopped a few yards from the potential threat. The little girl glanced between Adam and I. My chest tightened as I watched her little body shake from terror, I hoped that she would comply.

She opened her mouth to say something, but before she could get it out, she raised the object in her hands. I barely caught sight of the wires before I fired multiple times. Her body crumpled to the ground as the gunfire triggered my tinnitus.

No one moved for what felt like hours as we confirmed she was dead. Numbly, I radioed the incident in and called for the Explosive Ordnance Disposal team. Adam just stared at her body as he processed what had just happened.

“She was just a little girl…” Adam muttered to himself and I noticed his hands were shaking.

“Yea, just a little girl, holding a not so little threat,” Friedman dismissed as he and his partner turned to go back to their assigned area.

Adam scoffed in disgust when we were able to continue our task. We had been sent there that morning to deliver supplies to a clinic. I think that was the first time Adam realized we signed up to sacrifice more than our lives. From the moment we were deployed, we sacrificed our peace of mind.

"She was a victim chosen to prey on our compassion. Hesitation will cost you your life and possibly your whole squad. Shoot first and hate yourself later, and if you can't for your own life, then do it for Laney's," I advised, trying to do so gently, but he needed to understand the cost he would pay for his compassion.

Adam hung his head. Our training seemed more like the textbook version of the real thing. Where so many things were drilled into our heads, there was only so much the Army could prepare us for; this was one of them.

When we got back to the base and were dismissed for the day, I pulled Adam back to our bunk. Shut behind the privacy of our door, I pulled a bottle of mouthwash I had used to smuggle in vodka. I stole an empty water bottle from the side of my bed and filled it up halfway before handing it to him.

"I didn't figure you'd want to be drinking buddies anytime soon after our conversation earlier," He said dryly as he brought the bottle to his lips.

I took a long drink from the bottle and tried to focus more on the burn from the rotgut than the reminder of his marriage.

"Think of it more like a forgetting ritual than a drink between friends," I corrected without looking at him.

Adam choked on the cheap alcohol, looking surprised by the taste, similar to fuel than something actually ingestible. I chuckled and shook my head.

“One shot for any lives lost, one shot for the nightmares to come, and one shot for the scar no one will see,” I repeated to myself, remembering the mantra Steven’s used to say after a horrible assignment.

By the time Adam had finished the bottle, the emotions hit him at full blast. I watched him sink down onto his bunk as he cradled his face in his hands.

“How do I tell her we killed a kid today?” He asked, barely above a whisper.

“Some things it’s better not to,” I stayed cool headed for him.

I didn’t want to talk about her. It felt out of line to give the man advice given the history between his wife and I. At the same time, I knew he was asking me because I was the only other person here who knew her, or at least used to.

He said nothing for a moment, as if contemplating my suggestion to shut her out for peace of mind. When he finally spoke again, the buzz from the vodka was thick in his voice.

“What if we have a little girl?” I feel he meant to speak out loud.

"Laney?" I spat out, but the last thing I wanted to know was their plans on having children. The sting of his confession and the mission had already messed me up enough that day.

"Maybe you're right, but there's no way she'd stay if she knew. God! I messed up," Adam groaned and laid back on his mattress.

"You didn't give that girl a fucking bomb. People die over here," I tried to reassure him, but the more we talked about his wife, the more I wanted to drink.

There wasn't enough left in the bottle to convince me it could numb the anger I felt at everything. I reached for the cap to screw it back on before I could talk myself into finishing it.

"She is supposed to find out what we are having next week and I don't know how I will face her," he confessed, barely loud enough for me to hear.

Dropping the cap back down on the bed. I knew then what had made his decision to marry her so different from the one I made a lifetime ago; he had gotten her pregnant.

Thankfully, I had been wrong about how much it'd take for me to forget about that day and put me to sleep. The hangover I would have the following day would, no doubt, be worth it.

Chapter Thirteen

February 19, 2024

Delaney

I pulled up in front of my old high school and put my car into park, thankful it was the weekend and the building sat abandoned. The game plan was to drive and clear my head, but the moment I had left the base, it was like I had been on autopilot. I took in a deep breath from the comfort of my car before I climbed out.

Obeying my feet, I headed toward the bench where Kendric, Adam, and I used to meet. My fingers traced the worn wood that seemed to store all those memories from a better time in my life. If only the old Laney could see me now.

Following the motions, I sat down on the bench and pulled my knees to my chest. My toes hung over the edge, anchored by my heels planted firmly on the seat. I rested my head on my knees and closed my eyes, melting into the sounds of home.

“Laney?” a familiar voice called out my name a few moments later.

I lifted my head to look for the source. I spotted Daniel across the street. Beaming with a questioning smile, he headed in my direction. The stalker had wormed their way into my head as I studied the way Daniel seemed to “run into me” a little too frequently. I forced down the paranoia as I feigned a smile for him.

“Hi, Daniel,” I greeted as he stopped a couple feet away.

I uncurled my legs and scooted over so that he could take a seat beside me. His expression dropped as he absorbed my face.

“Is everything okay? What are you doing in Morley?”

I kept the fake smile glued to my face to cover my real emotions as he waited for my answer. If Kendric could shield his thoughts, maybe I could too.

“Yea, I just…” I started, but paused as I realized I couldn’t tell this man how I ended up on the bench. My mind raced through reasons that would sound anywhere close to the truth.

“Visiting Adam?” He finished for me, giving me the out I desperately needed.

I blinked up at him at the mention of my husband’s name and swallowed hard. Alarm bells sounded, wondering how he knew where my husband had been buried.

"I just needed to clear my head," I answered partly honestly. I couldn't make myself fully lie to him even if his presence sent me on high alert.

Daniel looked me over before settling into the bench. It wasn't until I looked at him to make sure he believed me I realized he was holding a small box. His wife's name was written in black marker across the top.

"Are *you* okay?" I pointed toward the box, deflecting the attention from me.

Daniel looked down at it as if he had forgotten the box existed for a moment. His fingers absentmindedly traced the "C" in Caroline's name.

"Yea, Just a misplaced package. Did they misplace any of Adam's things?" he asked and I froze.

"What do you mean?" I probed as I tried to hide the fear from my voice.

"Well, apparently some of my wife's things were sent to a house here in town. She moved in with family not long before she enlisted and someone made a mistake and sent her boxes to that address instead. Some sort of computer glitch," He rambled as I stared at the box.

"I thought you said you got her things," I continued, unable to process what he was saying.

"Well, I got one box. I guess this one got lost originally, I'm not sure, but her family still lives there and called when this one showed up."

Daniel looked at me and his brows furrowed in concern.

"Seriously, Laney, what's up? You look like you have been crying," he asked and something about the way he looked at me brought heat to my cheeks.

"Oh no. I just had some trouble sleeping," I lied.

He looked at me skeptically for a moment before he forced a gentle smile. My body relaxed in response as he checked his watch for the time.

"As much as I hate to, I should probably get going," He rattled off as if the two minutes he stopped had put him behind schedule.

We said our goodbyes and I had to admit, I was happy to see him leave. Instead of finding answers here, all I had found was more questions. I watched him as my brain ran with the information he had just given me; if Caroline's things were sent to the wrong address, what were the chances so was Adam's?

I waited until Daniel was completely out of sight before I headed back to my car. Half of my brain played back the timeline for Daniel's random run-ins to the messages. The other half went through a list of all of the places any other boxes could have been delivered to.

If the system had sent Caroline's things to the address she listed prior to going to basic, I knew exactly where to start looking. The problem was, our first apartment was hours away. Leaving to get some air after my reckless actions were one thing, but I couldn't just disappear on Kendric.

I was halfway home when my phone rang through the car's speaker system, announcing my mother's call. I fumbled for the button next to my radio to answer it.

"Hello?" I greeted

My mother let out an exaggerated sigh of relief at my voice before her lecturing tone cut through the tiny space, "Oh, thank god you are okay. Kendric called me absolutely in a panic and all I could picture was you laying in a ditch somewhere."

I winced at Kendric's name.

"I highly doubt he was panicked, mama," I replied as I tried to ignore the guilt I felt for leaving Kendric the way I had this morning.

"Well, he was worried enough to call me and considering that man hasn't had my number since before we left Missouri, I highly doubt it was anything less. Now, quit giving me the runaround and tell me what the hell is going on. Are you alright?" She scolded as I sank into my driver seat a little further.

I fought to keep my focus on the road, instead of the awe I felt, that he was worried enough to call her. Him and my mother lost touch when we moved, but it didn't change the fact that she loved him the most out of all of my ex-boyfriends. It wasn't that she disliked my husband, but a shotgun wedding hadn't been the dream she had when she pictured my wedding.

"I'm fine, really, it was just an overwhelming morning. I needed to get some air and some space," I pray Kendric hadn't given my mother any details about my stalker.

"Young lady, if you need space, you ask your guest to leave. You don't charge out of your house, leaving them there to disappear to God knows where, and stop answering your phone," She chided.

"The house just hasn't felt like home since Adam died, mama. I'll apologize to Kendric when I get back, I promise. You know as well as I do, he will need to see me in person," I was wishing she would drop the conversation.

"Are you heading back soon?" she asked after a beat. Her voice was softer, but the disappointment still laced its edges.

“Twelve minutes, give or take as we speak,” I confirmed.

“I think he is still there, waiting for you,” her voice trailed off, slightly distracted.

I knew by the tone she was restraining herself. She was trying to respect my space, but the worry in her voice was almost palpable. It felt the same as how badly I wanted to vent about everything, but couldn’t as it would only worry her more. If guilt could occupy a physical space, there would have been no room left for me in this car.

“I have no doubt,” I answered, forcing a little sarcasm to replace the sense of dread I was actually feeling.

My mother hesitated before replying. I sent her curiosity and concern playing tug-o-war with her restraint, “Please let me know when you get there.”

I silently relaxed at the hope she would disconnect the call, before I filled her in on everything anyway. Keeping it from her killed me almost as much as knowing if I told her, she’d beg me to move back to Wisconsin.

“And thank Kendric for me. With Adam gone, it’s good to know you still have someone there looking out for you,” she added before she finally let me off the phone.

I stared at the road while an eerie silence filled my vehicle. I could turn on the radio, but music wouldn’t change the stark outlook for my evening. Until my mother hung up, the reality of the situation hadn't set in. The rest of the drive was filled with nothing, but anxiety and guilt.

As expected, Kendric's truck hadn't moved by the time I pulled into my driveway. The only thing that was out of place was a blue bouquet of flowers that sat perfectly on my front porch. It wasn't until I approached them that I saw what the flowers had been placed in.

Instead of the traditional pottery, the flowers had been put inside of a battle-worn combat boot. I bent down and picked up the boot to admire the forget-me-nots. They were my favorite flower, although not many people in my life knew about it.

When I readjusted my hold on the awkward "vase," a deformity on the left side of the sole caught my eye. Trying not to panic, I balanced the boot as the evening light reflected off a sliver of metal tucked behind the latter threaded strings.

Gingerly, I loosened the bootlaces. I didn't have to pull it out to know the piece of silver metal was a dog tag. I pulled out the stamped identification tag, but the imperfection on the rubberized tread was almost like a fingerprint. I dropped the flowers at the startling realization of who sent them.

My front door opened as Kendric's eyes bore a hole into me. I stared at the scattered flowers, unable to look away. They confirmed I hadn't gotten everything Adam had left behind. I had personally helped him pack the winterized pair of boots for his deployment.

How did the stalker know those flowers had meaning for me? It wasn't something he would have learned from Adam. Mainly, because Adam had been jealous of how I had first discovered them. I often thought he brought me sunflowers, and called me Sunshine, to replace the memory.

An uneasiness suffocated me as I caught that detail the stalker probably hadn't intended to expose. Them using Adam had never been anything, but a way to break me down. Aside from my mother, Kendric had been the only person to give forget-me-nots to me.

June 7, 2018

Kendric

Adam and I didn't talk about the night he confessed his concerns about his ability to be a father. In fact, I wasn't completely sure he had remembered it after our olive branch ritual. I had no problem pretending it never happened, but I wondered if he hadn't brought it up because he didn't want to relive it either.

What kind of friend was I, that the mention of marrying my ex didn't feel nearly as devastating as the idea of her being pregnant with his child? It was questions and self-hate like that kept my lips sealed tight. I was stuck in a never ending loop of guilt and resentment toward him because as hard as I tried, I couldn't get her off my mind.

It had been weeks since that night. The longer I waited to say anything to him, the more it felt like I was overreacting. I needed to accept that my pipe dream of having a life with her was over. Anytime I thought I had a handle on it, I'd see Adam and the loop would be back in full swing.

Every time I saw his face, all I could picture was Del and how she'd look big and pregnant. The jealousy of those thoughts started to reflect in my interactions with anyone unfortunate enough to cross my path. The whole idea of her being pregnant by him rubbed me the wrong way.

Knowing I needed to get my personal feelings in check, I walked out of the bunk and braced myself. To my surprise, Adam wasn't standing with the others like he usually was. No one in our group seemed to think it was abnormal, but not everyone noticed patterns like that.

I kept an eye out for him, on high alert, waiting for any signs that something else was off, but the rest of the morning went as expected. Two hours later, we had our orders. Still, Adam was still nowhere to be found.

I barely registered the mission objective as the gut feeling that something was wrong ate at my focus. Logically, I knew it wasn't uncommon for a member of our squad to be reallocated to another when the numbers were low. If he had been at the usual spot this morning, it wouldn't have bothered me.

With no more answers than I started with, my squad headed out for the mission without Adam. I needed my head in the game. We were escorting Staff Sergeant Henry Lake to negotiate a deal with a local merchant in an area that was known for frequent and violent attacks from the Taliban.

I was to escort Lake and the interpreter, Mohammed, into the building. The moment Lake mentioned my name, I watched our interpreter smile at me nervously. I returned it with a reassuring smile of my own. Anytime I had worked with the man, he seemed genuinely spooked by just existing. I didn't want to give him one more reason to be afraid.

We entered the small rundown shack as Friedman stayed outside. His least favorite shadow, Murphy, in toe. I was thankful that I hadn't been stuck with the man. Where

Friedman put on a good show with his frat boyish behavior, the entitlement that oozed from Murphy was entirely genuine.

Something about the calmness when we arrived had my senses heightened. Once the building was cleared, Lake began to pitch the first offer. I couldn't help, but notice the older gentleman couldn't have cared less.

Before the pitch was finished, a cry came over the coms from the part of our squad securing the back of the home. A group of three hostiles were approaching and they were taking fire. Lake and I raised our weapons.

Seeing our actions, Mohammed's eyes grew wide. I was worried he would be a liability, but the merchant took our reactions as the sign he had apparently been waiting for. The older gentleman rattled off something so fast I couldn't catch it before he darted into a room.

Gunfire sounded off just outside of the building behind us as I approached the side of the door the merchant had ran off to. Lake and Mohammed flipped two of the tables in the room we had been standing in before he had him crouch down between them for cover. I waited for Lake's signal before I pivoted, to gain a line of view into the room.

Standing toward the back of a windowless room stood the merchant that had set up the ambush. His back was slightly to me, as I heard the sound of the lighter before he turned toward us and I saw the flame. In his hand was what appeared to be a makeshift molotov. I lined up my shot, the flame caught the strip of fabric threaded into the glass.

Without hesitation, I fired my rifle twice in his chest as he brought a molotov cocktail over his head. My third shot sent his head backwards, dropping him while holding the explosive. As he fell to the ground, the bottle shattered on impact, sending the tiny room up in flames.

Friedman radioed in as two more men were incoming toward the direction we drove in. He was so close to the building, I could hear his voice from the other side of the wall. Cutting off his call over the coms, bullets tore through the front door.

Smoke quickly began to fill the room we were pinned down in. Crouching down on either side of Mohammed, Lake and I lined up our rifles. There was only a door into the shack and no windows were big enough for us to fit through.

Gun fire and yelling echoed outside for the longest few seconds of my life before the door was kicked open. The first insurgent and I locked eyes just as I pulled the trigger. The way his eyes widened in surprise as his body dropped to the floor burned into my brain.

A second man entered with hate and anger radiating his entire being. As he tried stepping over his fallen comrade to walk through the entryway, I watched a bullet from Officer

Lake tear through his forehead. Trying to keep my breath as level as I could, I waited for anyone else to enter.

Mohammed's shaking vibrated the side of my leg as he stayed curled over his knees, clutching the back of his head. As the fire spread out of the room it had started in, I heard him repeat the same phrase over and over before I realized what he was saying; he was reciting a prayer.

The all clear was announced over the coms a few moments later. As the three of us inside made our way out of the building, the room we had been in completely caught fire. My breath caught as I saw one of Friedman's boots the minute we had made it outside. I held that breath as I waited for any sign of life from my fallen comrade.

I waited for Murphy's confirmation as he checked Friedman's pulse. I rushed to help administer life saving measures as Lake radioed for a medic when ours didn't respond. Murphy applied a tourniquet to Friedman's left biceps as I held pressure over a bullet wound just under Friedman's right clavicle.

I saw the moment Friedman stopped breathing just before the shack behind me exploded. My body propelled forward from the impact as if someone had shoved me. A white hot burning sensation ripped through my side seconds later, thanks to my adrenaline delaying the pain. I can remember trying to push myself off of Friedman before everything went black.

I woke up in the hospital sometime later. The dimly lit space only added to my disorientation. A small sniffle came from my side as my eyes adjusted to the light.

“Didn’t anyone in training explain that fire and explosive materials shouldn’t be mixed?” Adam weakly teased as I found him sitting in a chair at my bedside.

“Didn’t help we were a man down,” I defensively replied unfiltered as my body screamed for caffeine.

Adam’s forced smile dropped as something heavier took its place. He swallowed hard and averted his eyes as if worried I would see the tears in them.

“I’m sorry,” he said barely above a whisper, but I heard the break in his voice.

The emotion behind his words had been so strong it felt like more than grief for our fallen comrade. The worry I had felt about Adam’s sudden absence resurfaced as I watched him practically break apart in the chair.

“No, don’t be. I was being a dick,” I tried to apologize, but I noticed the packed bag on the floor beside him.

Before I could ask him what was going on, the crinkle of paper in his hands diverted my attention off the bag. I didn't have to see the whole thing to realize what he was holding:

He had the envelope with Del's letter.

"Why do you have that?" I asked nervously as I scrambled to take in everything I was seeing.

Adam looked down at the object in his hand as if seeing it for the first time before he sat it down on the table beside him. For a second, he seemed to struggle to let it go. As I watched him and waited for the answer, the packed bag and strong grief in his body language came crashing down.

"Why was it addressed to my wife?" He volleied back.

I stared at the faced down envelope and silently thanked the gods it still appeared to be sealed. Looking back at him, I debated on lying.

"I was writing goodbye letters, in case…I just hadn't written yours yet," I halfway fibbed as he took it in.

He nodded as if understanding. I waited for more questions about it, but none came. When he began to stare into nothing silently, I couldn't hold back my questions.

"What happened to Del, Adam?" I asked, not sugar coating my question.

I knew his emotional state could have been from the loss of a friend, but it felt uncharacteristically strong to be over Friedman. In response to my question, he bent forward to cradle his head in his hands. Any strength he was trying to fake crumbled as soft sobs erupted from his chest.

“Tell me she is okay,” I begged, waiting for him to calm down enough to speak.

Panic filled me as I tried to sit up to get to him, but a sharp pain ripped through my side like before. I winced and stopped moving. Adam tried to straighten himself and suck in a couple of fragile breaths.

“I got the message this morning. She was in an accident last night and she's in the hospital...but God! Kendric, it's bad. It's really bad,” He rushed out in a heartbreaking confession between hyperventilating breaths.

The world seemed to stop around us as I waited for more information. Whatever else he had been holding back seemed to be physically painful to say out loud and the thought of that was ruining me.

“My flight is in a few hours,” he followed up and I resisted the urge to demand more information.

I needed to know she was going to be alright. The word “hurt” didn’t tell me nearly enough. He knew more than he was saying and in the middle of my worst case scenarios, the one topic we didn't talk about popped into my head

"And the baby?" My mouth spat out before I could stop myself.

The moment I said it, he shattered, breaking back down into uncontrollable sobs as he shook his head, unable to say anything. I wished I knew what I could have said to comfort him, but we sat in the unspoken confession for a long time.

By the time he left to catch his plane, I was reeling with everything. Aside from what I had learned from Adam, I was being sent home for recovery a week later when the hospital could release me for travel. I found out later that between the ambush and the explosion, Friedman was the only casualty, but I was one of three with serious injuries.

Chapter Fourteen

February 19, 2024

Delaney

Kendric didn't say a word as I silently processed the flowers; I didn't want him to. I had enough I needed to fill him in on and didn't want to voice the newest detail yet. If he realized the significance, the last thing I wanted to do was add more awkwardness between us.

When I was finally able to function, he just simply held the door open for me. Even though I knew I should have cleaned them up and threw them out, I couldn't stomach the idea of touching them again. The only thing I hadn't dropped was the dog tag and as Kendric turned to walk further into the house, I stuffed the piece of metal in my pocket.

His silence didn't stop after he shut and locked the door behind us as I thought it would. On a mission, he marched toward my bedroom. Confused, I followed closely behind.

He glanced back at me for a second as we entered my bedroom before he threw my closet open and rummaged in the bottom of it. The sheer audacity of this man had me flipping total 180s as I began to feel my sense of privacy being invaded.

“What the hell are you doing?” I scolded as the question slipped from my unfiltered mouth.

Kendric didn’t pause or hesitate as he pulled an old suitcase out and laid it on my bed.

“That psycho knows where you live, Laney. I’m taking you home with me,” he said nonchalantly as he pulled open a dresser drawer and grabbed a handful of my clothes, tossing them into the luggage.

I stared at him like he had lost his freaking mind. I was fully capable of making my own decisions.

“You can’t be serious. This isn’t something you get to decide for me,” I challenged as I grabbed the clothes from the suitcase, preparing to put them back where they belonged.

“Don’t start with me, Del, I will take you with me, with or without clothing,” he warned and I felt the heat creep into my cheeks at his unfortunate choice of words.

I clutched the clothing in my hands, nervously fiddling with the fabric to calm my nerves. Pesky and pornographic thoughts in his favor only made staying defiant harder. I had nothing keeping me in the house. Kendric being there made it feel less depressing, but I didn’t know if I could handle being in his playing field.

“Should I recap the last couple of days for you? Or how about we take a trip down memory lane?” I asked as a last ditch effort to hold onto my control.

Finally, my words made him pause, but I didn’t miss the low growl he instinctively gave in response. I had hit a nerve and I hated the part of me that liked it.

“Do I need to remind *you* what role your admirer played in the last few days?” he snapped back and I swore my pulse shot up in the hundreds.

“Of course not! It wasn’t exactly sunshine and rainbows for me either, but we don’t work, Kendric. And we don't know how he found me here in the first place,” I attempted to sound calmer.

Kendric looked up at me then. All of his rage and concern was so heavy in his eyes it stole my breath straight from my lungs. Without warning, he stalked toward me, never breaking eye contact.

Before I could think about moving away from him, his strong hands were on either side of my face as I let the clothing in my hands drop to the carpet. I staggered backward from him in shock, but his hold on my face caught me from losing my balance.

"I don't care...If you think I'll let you stay here alone, ANYWHERE alone for that matter, you have another thing coming," Kendric's voice became a bit softer, but I felt all the primal instincts he was trying to hide.

I focused on my breath instead of the heat that radiated off my cheeks at his touch. I couldn't be this close to him and he couldn't keep saying things like that. My willpower started to crack as his thumbs absentmindedly caressed the sides of my face.

"W-we can't..." I pushed out, trying to counter my desire to give in.

As if reading my mind, his eyes drifted to my lips. I reached up to his hands, trying to remove them from my face so that I could think clearly. His breath caught the moment we made contact.

"Why won't you let me protect you?" he asked this time, his voice so tender it was almost a whisper.

What was I supposed to tell him? It wasn't like I could be honest and tell him how I thought I had developed real feelings for him...again. Hell, until he looked at me a moment ago, I had convinced myself it was a stress response mixed with grief.

“I can’t,” I choked out the best I could before hesitantly pulling his hands off my face.

Frustration and confusion clouded his face for a moment as I stood there, reeling silently in my revelation. He turned away and went back to my dresser, collecting clothes for my kidnapping.

“You don’t have a choice. That fucker knew your favorite flower…” he growled out as he zipped up the luggage and stared at me, waiting for me to argue it.

I stilled at what he said. Part of me hoped he hadn’t remembered… It would have been easier.

“Were. They *were* my favorite,” I lied and I caught the small smirk across his face.

“Not according to Adam,” he teased as I paled.

When I didn’t answer him, Kendric glanced over at me. His brows pulled together. It felt like I was exposed in front of him, the rawness of it both terrifying and intoxicating.

“I’m sorry. I shouldn’t have…” he started, but I shook my head as I fought the guilt threatening to escape, one deeply rooted.

Kendric had always been a sore point in my marriage. At first, I was the jealous one. The break up had been so unexpected and harmful and Adam got to keep Kendric in his life. When Adam came home from their first deployment together, we switched sides.

My husband took the green-eyed monster over after an argument we had on the day he came home. I had told him how the wreck happened and we grieved the baby together. When it was his turn to fill me in on the things that he could, he told me Kendric had been wounded on a mission. All my hurt and the anger dissipated the moment he explained the extent of Kendric's injury.

To Adam, Kendric wasn't anything to me anymore, so Adam didn't understand why I felt the need to see him. When I heard they had been deployed to the same place, I had felt some peace knowing Adam was there and they would keep each other safe, but something had snapped in me from the news.

Adam's argument had brought me to my senses and until a few days ago, I hadn't thought about that fight in years. From that point on, anything that reminded Adam of my past relationship set him off. Those flowers had been the ignition point of the biggest fight Adam and I had ever had.

"It's okay. I just didn't realize he told you about that fight," Back in the present, I tried to put Kendric's mind at ease.

Kendric's spine straightened as confusion filled his expression.

"He didn't mention a fight."

I closed my eyes and cursed at myself for saying too much, "It wasn't a big deal," I dismissed, but it was obvious Kendric didn't believe me.

"Who else knew about the argument?" he inquired and I realized where he was going with that.

"Just Adam and my mother," I sounded perplexed.

In classic Kendric fashion, he decided he was done talking and grabbed the suitcase by its handle. Making a beeline to my bathroom, I followed behind him as he grabbed my toothbrush. Thinking of everything, he crouched down to grab the feminine hygiene supplies from under my bathroom cabinet.

The longer he ignored me, the angrier I got. I wasn't a child and I could pack for and protect myself just fine if I needed to. Not that Kendric would have ever believed me.

"Kendric Tate, you are literally packing to kidnap me from my home. Why does it matter?"

Kendric packed the toiletries away in the bag and raised an eyebrow at me.

"Think of it more as…protective detail," he teasingly shot out, avoiding answering.

I blocked the doorway where he stood. I wasn't going anywhere until he stopped being so evasive. Not that I really had room to talk.

He looked down at me as amusement soaked his poorly restrained smirk.

"Who's keeping who against their will now?" he teased. I narrowed my eyes on him.

His smile dropped slightly as he finally gave into my demands.

"Whoever this is knows the flowers are important. If they are using Adam to hurt you, then it means they knew of the fight most likely," he explained, but as logical as his reasoning was, it didn't explain the way Kendric's name kept being a key factor.

In my gut, I knew he had been the connection. Although it had been entirely possible Adam had told someone else about it. It wasn't like my mother had been a secret-vault either.

"How do you know the forget-me-nots weren't picked specifically because of you?" I pushed back, trying to show him a little bit of trust.

Kendric swallowed, his earlier amusement completely erased from his face.

“Because the last time I bought these for you was for prom. Seems like a stretch that someone would hold onto that, but use Adam’s phone as the medium,” he reasoned.

I could hear the uncertainty in his voice, but I wasn’t sure what exactly he was doubting. Did he not think he was part of the ruse my stalker was using? Or did he not want to accept that he had been a factor in my marriage not being perfect?

“Fair enough,” I replied even though I didn’t feel it.

Kendric clenched his jaw as sensing my lie. “Unless that fight hadn’t been over flowers,” he pressed and I diverted my eyes, tired of this game.

“I need my charger,” I evaded as I walked away from Kendric’s prying look, taking a page from his book.

April 7, 2020

Kendric

It had been two years since Adam and I had the heart-to-heart in the hospital. I kept telling myself that eventually the idea of him and Del wouldn't destroy me. Between that deployment and seeing how much he loved her, the damage done to our friendship seemed to heal part of that resentment.

Maybe it had been selfish of me in the beginning. At first, keeping that friendship close had been the only way I could remain close to her. Not that she and I had really ever talked, but in his letters, I got to know about her life and who she was.

Those letters became my safe haven, my lifeline to the woman I would forever love, but never have. It wasn't until months after the letters began I realized I had become invested in both of them. Until that moment, I hadn't realized how much I missed them.

I folded the most recent letter from Adam and placed it in a drawer beside my couch. I had cleared out the end table specifically for them since often I rarely made it to my bed. I was heading to redeploy and knowing these written treasures were here waiting for me gave me a little peace.

I wouldn't receive another one for a while and Adam had just redeployed. I had hoped he and I would cross paths over there at some point. I spent the whole flight wondering if Del would be okay after the trauma she sustained the last time.

Adam had been trying to convince me that the three of us needed to meet up if we were both ever on leave at the same time again. I kept praying the Army would make that impossible. It wasn't that I didn't want to see Del. I just hadn't been keen on the idea of seeing how they interacted with one another.

In the time before our reconnection, I had grown used to not seeing Adam. The brief time we had on the last deployment had been something I never knew I needed. I would have been content if all I ever got after that was ships that passed in the night, but the Army had a funny way of surprising me. Not long after I arrived at base, I ran into him again.

"Someone told me the new Sergeant was a piece of work, but no one told me it was this asshole," Adam's voice rang out behind me as he was joking with a couple of other soldiers.

I turned around at the sound of his voice to see him smiling from ear to ear. I returned a wide grin.

"And here I thought I'd be fighting beside some stand-up guys," I teased back as he pulled me into a quick hug.

"There's no one else I'd trust as much to have my back," he looked me over.

I nodded, thankful. The feeling had been mutual, but the voice in the back of my head wondered if he would have felt the same if he knew I still harbored feelings for Del.

The two soldiers he had been talking to stared between the two of us awkwardly, waiting for our reunion. I eyed their names and ranks as they waited patiently for the introduction.

"Gary Donaldson, Caroline Greene, this is Sergeant Tate, the guy I was telling you about," Adam introduced me to the pair.

The two soldiers looked me over as if scanning my worth. Donaldson stood up straighter, looking nervous I was doing the same. His expression was tense as if I was about to call him into inspection at any moment.

The smaller blonde woman, PFC Greene, greeted me warmly with a smile, reaching her hand out to shake mine.

"You can call me Caroline. Adam has told us a lot about you," She said as if amused.

I shook her hand and raised my eyebrow at Adam. It wasn't uncommon for us to refer to each other by our first names, but something in the way she said this made me wonder how well they knew each other.

"Kendric," I added to match her effort.

Using their last names was something I had done to keep my distance from my fellow squad members. It was the easiest way not to let my emotions get the best of me and keep my head in the game. Friedman wasn't the first person I had lost over here and the rigid rule kept that from destroying me.

"Jeez Gary, he isn't as scary as Adam made him sound. You can relax," Greene jested and Gary's cheeks flamed a bright red.

I let out a chuckle and glanced back up at my friend, who was smiling mischievously at me.

"You told them I was scary?" I matched Adam's wolfish grin.

"I believe the term I said was…'impressively intimidating,'" Adam chuckled.

The rest of that week consisted of hearing things like that. Adam had been my biggest hype-man, but the more I heard, the more insecure I felt about my abilities as their superior. Their expectations had been planted by a man who was completely biased.

I tried to swallow the imposter syndrome like I had been doing with my guilt over Del, but it felt like there was no room left for it. My growing insecurities created a monster in the pit of my stomach. The creature taunted me with threats of exposure at just the mention of Adam's name.

I masked my emotions behind an indifferent expression as I joined the group of soldiers waiting for me. Adam gave me an excited smirk as soon as he saw me approach. Donaldson immediately tensed as if he still believed my only purpose in life was to make lower ranks miserable.

"Just wait guys. I am telling you he is a legend," Adam boasted as I came to a stop near the group.

My stomach rebelled against my growing self-doubt.

"We should focus more on getting our heads in the game than campfire stories," I urged past the ease that took root.

Adam leaned in closer to whisper, "Come on, man. Half these guys act like I made it all up."

I clenched my jaw as if needing the physical reminder to stay outwardly calm. I should have told him then that there was a difference between fairytale reminiscing and the real thing, but I nodded. My insecurities kept the words hostage on my tongue.

One by one, we loaded into the convoy. We were delivering supplies and given it was a common assignment, I figured everyone there had done it before. It quickly became clear however, one of them hadn't.

The longer we drove, the more uneasy Donaldson appeared beside me. He had shifted in his seat so many times, we could have made a drinking game out of it. I knew that nervousness all too well.

“First mission?” I asked quietly, trying not to draw the attention of the others beside us.

Donaldson’s eyes widened as they shot up to mine. Hesitantly, he nodded. I patted his shoulder as the vehicle slowed to a stop just outside our target.

“Alright guys. Change of plans. Donaldson will be with me. Anderson, you will be with Sullivan,” I barked just before we exited the vehicle.

Adam looked at me with confusion, but didn’t argue. We separated into our designated groups and parted ways. I was to lead eleven of us as we provided threat evaluations and established a perimeter. Adam and his team were to deliver the supplies.

Donaldson and I had barely reached our position when I spotted one of my men appearing to be scoping out a local merchant twenty yards from where he should have been with his assigned battle buddy. I glanced at Donaldson, who looked around the area as he was paranoid of the wind.

“Adonis-two, have you reached the arena? Over,” I radioed through my teeth as I watched the squad’s designated slimeball ignore my page.

“Adonis-two, come in. Over,” I radioed louder and more aggressively.

Murphy’s head shot up and looked for me as he handed over something to the merchant. He and I made eye contact before he took a pack of cigarettes from the merchant's hand. He shoved the pack in his pocket before he reported in and headed back toward his partner.

Donaldson looked at me to gauge my anger, but didn’t say a word. His expression told me he had questions, but wisely chose not to ask. I watched as Murphy scurried back to his post.

“Adonis-two in position,” Murphy radioed back a few moments later, showing little remorse that he had been caught.

The supply run finished without incident as we headed back to our vehicles. The tension in Donaldson’s shoulders relaxed as our armored vehicle came into view. I slowed slightly, using the privacy to check in with him.

“It gets easier,” I lied as I watched Adam walk over to Greene.

The closer we got to our ride, the more I noticed how comfortable Adam and Greene seemed to be. I tried to remind myself that Adam wasn’t *that* guy, but the way he took her medic bag to carry for her set off a ton of red flags. It wasn't unusual for men and women to be friends, but it felt like his whole demeanor changed.

I hadn't realized Donaldson had replied to my earlier statement, nor was I aware he had been watching me and waiting for a response. His voice caught me off-guard as it pulled me from my ridiculous thoughts.

"They live near each other on base. Neighbors or something," Donaldson answered although I hadn't asked.

"What?" I replied a little short as my brain struggled to absorb his statement.

"Anderson and Greene. Them and their spouses are friends," he elaborated, sparing me from having to ask the difficult question out loud.

I looked down at the PFC and debated on denying the thought process he clearly had read from my face. Thinking better of it, I didn't respond.

"You know his wife, right? Anderson said you guys were all friends in school or whatever."

I gritted my teeth at Donaldson's use of the word *friends.* Logically, I knew that had been the better way to describe us. It was less awkward than telling everyone the overly inflated beast had also been his wife's ex-boyfriend, but the omission had left me feeling territorial.

"Yea, we were something like that," I said curtly when Murphy came into view, straggling behind the rest of the squad.

I stepped aside to let Donaldson into the vehicle as my jealousy turned into anger. It had been the wrong time for Murphy to gain his second strike for the day. I knew from experience how insubordinate Murphy could be, but abandoning his battle buddy twice in a short period had been more fuel to my growing aggression.

"PFC Murphy," I commanded as he came within earshot.

Murphy's careless grin dropped at the sound of my voice. I knew I probably should have waited until we got back to base, but I needed an outlet before I took it out on someone less deserving.

"Yes, Sergeant?" Murphy answered as he came to stop a little more than an arm's length from me.

Someone from inside the convoy cleared their throat, sensing my hostility. I forced the impulse to glance at the other members of my squad as I became aware I was being watched.

“When we return to base, you and Tucker will report to me for a lesson in personal safety,” I barked out, trying not to cave in front of my team.

Murphy’s eyes furrowed in irritation as he accepted the order. The punishment had been meant for both him and his partner, but his partner hadn’t earned a second strike.

“You will also discard whatever you bought from that merchant before you step foot in the vehicle,” I ordered as I watched the frustrated look on Murphy’s face turn into heated rage.

Murphy’s upper lip twitched as he pulled out the pack from his pocket. As he went to put it in my hand, he hesitated before tossing the pack on the ground at my feet. I kept eye contact as I bent down and picked it up before turning my attention to the opened door and prying eyes.

Glancing at Donaldson, I tossed him the cigarettes, and dismissed Murphy to the other vehicle. Ignoring the way Murphy fumed with every step, I climbed in next and took a seat beside Donaldson.

“A lesson in personal safety?” Adam asked as we departed from the village.

“Being tied to their battle buddy may remind them to stick with each other in the field,” I huffed under my breath as the discontent toward Murphy's actions and Adam's stories simmered quietly beneath my skin.

Adam looked toward Greene as Donaldson averted his eyes to the floor. The rest of the ride was silent aside from the hum of the engine. I was grateful for the quiet. The last thing I wanted to do was talk to Adam.

Chapter Fifteen

February 19, 2024

Delaney

It never crossed my mind that Kendric would live off base. I had to force myself not to think about his life outside of our interactions for so long, the idea he had a home that wasn't part of military housing felt foreign. Much to my surprise, he had chosen a place right between the base and our hometown.

He sat my suitcase down on the old wooden porch as he unlocked his front door. The warmth on the other side seemed to beckon us inside as if the house had missed his presence. It was odd that this place felt more like a home than my own.

"It's not much, but the surrounding woods keep this place pretty secluded and I have a whole security system. You'll be safe here," he reassured as we stepped inside.

"Says my captor," I commented mischievously as I took in the first room in sight.

A small couch that appeared to be from the seventies sat against the wall across from the front door. Two floor to ceiling windows on either side showcased the forest he had mentioned in his reassurance. I smiled softly as I recognised the end tables from when we went to school together.

“Are those your mom’s?” I walked over to one, ignoring the way he tensed as I lightly touched the familiar piece of furniture.

“They had been my grandmother’s first,” He answered as he shut the front door behind him and snapped the lock back into place.

I smiled softly at the way the memories seemed to be absorbed into the wood under my fingertips.

“Do you want something to eat or drink? I need to hit the store, but I should have enough for tonight,” he offered stiffly as if he had never brought anyone else here.

“Not unless you also keep moonshine in your freezer,” I joked.

Instead of a sarcastic comment like I had been expecting, Kendric’s departing footsteps served as his response. I spun around to see him disappear into a doorway just to the right of the front door.

Quietly, I followed him into what appeared to be a kitchen that matched the theme of his couch. He opened a mustard yellow cabinet and pulled out two glasses. He glanced in my direction as he turned to open his freezer.

"You don't seriously have some stashed away after all the trouble you gave me for mine?" I said suspiciously as I remembered the surprise on his face the night we exchanged shots and raw confessions.

He grinned as he shut the freezer door with a frosted bottle in his hand.

"Sorry, but you will have to settle for whiskey," he chuckled as he started to peel off the wax seal.

I scrunch my nose up at the reminder of whiskey powered regrets in the early years of mine and Adam's marriage. I forced those memories down where they belonged, but the confessions Kendric and I had the other night quickly replaced them. I cleared my throat to get his attention.

"It's probably better that I leave that alone," I laughed as a contagious grin spread across his face.

Without saying a word, he reached for something obstructed by the appliance, soon revealing a pulled out warm can of off brand cola. I beamed up at him gratefully as he poured half of the can in my cup and the other in his. Replacing the unopened bottle, he grabbed a try of ice for our drinks.

"You can drink something not far off from gasoline, but whiskey is out of the question?" he laughed jokingly at me.

Once again, I made a face at the unspoken reason for my response. He watched me closely as I sipped the carbonated beverage. I closed my eyes, ignoring his stare as I sank into the feeling the house had.

“I never said I couldn’t handle it,” I volleyed back when I opened my eyes to find him still staring.

“Fair enough, but one of these days you’ll have to tell me the story behind that,” He halfway ordered.

I glared at him, even though we both knew it was only for show. The thought of escaping to the bottom of the bottle was too tempting to be a good idea. Especially after I had kissed him earlier that morning.

I nodded and leaned into the feel of the cool glass against my fingers. The physical touch of it seemed to ground me back to reality. Unable to handle his unwavering attention, I glanced around the kitchen.

It was eerie the way the interior looked like it had been frozen in time. It was as if Kendric had been afraid to change anything he didn’t need to in order to preserve it. Even stranger, it seemed to fit him perfectly.

“This place was my grandma’s too,” he explained as my eyes landed on a palm sized porcelain pig in the window.

“Where you used to spend your summers?” A distant memory of an old phone conversation filtered in.

Kendric nodded as a pained expression crossed his face.

“Then I need to see more of it,” I demanded, mocking his normal tone before I turned and wandered out of the kitchen.

Being in the same room as him felt heated, as if all the things we couldn’t say bounced between us. I tried to conceal my reaction as my phone vibrated in my pocket, but I was not wanting to disturb the closest thing I had felt to peace in days. Whoever it was would need to wait. Yet, in the back of my mind, I worried what I would find later when I checked the notification.

I took a right outside of his kitchen and started up the stairs. I could hear his footsteps landing softly behind me, making my skin buzz, but I tried desperately to ignore it.

“You know, usually the host offers a tour before their guest noses through the home,” He said quietly, seeming to try to bait me into another playful debate.

“I never expect proper manners from you, Kendric Tate,” I challenged back, turning my head so he could see the smirk he had caused before returning to my mission.

The more we playfully bickered, the further into taboo territory we headed. It had always been his favorite form of flirting and if I was being honest, it had become mine as well. I walked a little quicker to put some distance between us.

As I got to the top of the stairs, the space opened to what appeared to be a small hallway containing four doors. I paused, halting Kendric's steps behind me as I contemplated which I should open first.

"The first door on your right is my bedroom, the second your guest room," he rattled off as he impatiently waited for me to move forward.

I knew he had given the information in hopes I would choose one of the rooms he had listed, but the unknown of the others left me feeling rebellious. I headed to the first door on the left without a word. He let out an annoyed breath as he followed.

Behind the door I chose I found a bathroom complete with a clawfoot tub and a breathtaking view that looked out over the forest. I downed the rest of my glass to keep from looking at Kendric in awe. It might have been my favorite place in the house.

Gently, I shut the door to the bathroom and took a step toward the last door Kendric hadn't mentioned.

"It's just storage," he snorted quickly as I reached for the handle.

There was an edge to his voice I couldn't decipher. I turned the knob anyway. This time, it didn't open. I looked over my shoulder at him in question, but he only averted his eyes.

"I'm sorry. That is one room I like to keep private," He sheepishly apologized before I could ask why he would lock it if kidnapping me had been a spontaneous decision.

I didn't press the issue even though questions about his secrecy flooded my mind. It wasn't abnormal for him to be closed off and that room didn't feel any different from the things he kept locked inside of his head. I nodded in acknowledgement and crossed the hall to the room that was meant to temporarily be mine.

As I opened it, sunlight flooded into the doorway. Specs of dust settled as I took in the little room painted in a soft gray. It had been the only spot in the house I had seen that had been updated from the dated decor.

I walked over to the bed and admired the hand embroidered quilt that he had chosen. The soft blue thread stitched blue forget-me-nots on every block. I couldn't control the gasp that left my lips as I turned to find Kendric's eye; he had been waiting to see if I would notice them.

"I can change it out," he said hesitantly, gauging my response as he continued, "if it makes you uncomfortable after —-"

Feeling guilty for my reaction, I cut him off, "No, no. It's perfect."

I knew I should have reacted differently. He had been right to try and mention the flowers that had led to me staying here, but that hadn't been my first thought. In fact, the stalker had been the furthest thing from mind.

All I could think of was the fact the cover had been as dated as the rest of the house. The realization filled in a piece of our history I had never known. It must have been his grandmother's and the only thing in the room he hadn't felt like changing.

"Why did you keep it in here when you redid the rest of this room?" I asked without thinking, needing to confirm my theory.

Kendric took a deep breath as if debating on lying to my face. His eyes drifted from me to the quilt that seemed to hold significance.

"It had been in this room for as long as I could remember. It didn't feel right to change that," he vaguely answered, but I couldn't let it go.

"And this was where you would stay when you visited her?" I dared even though I knew I was dangerously approaching a sensitive subject.

Kendric downed his cola and nodded, unable to look me in the eye. Long before he had ever given me those flowers, they had been a symbol of his safe space. I softly smile in realization that he had offered me the chance to create one of my own, with a piece from his.

June 8,2020

Kendric

The dynamic between Adam and I this deployment had been different from the last. Something about him had changed and it wasn't the same kind of change you saw in someone after they joined the military.

At first, I thought my feelings for his wife had colored my perspective.

Two months into this deployment, I found myself watching Adam more and more closely. It was like my subconscious couldn't trust who Adam had become because I couldn't pinpoint what had felt off about him. One night, as he was coming back to base, I received the answer I had been waiting for.

I had been reallocated to a different squad that day to fill in for someone they had lost. My temporary assignment allowed me to return a couple of hours before Adam. I'll never forget the exhaustion that seemed to consume him before he caught sight of me and forced his mask back into place.

I stapled an equally fake smile as he patted my shoulder in greeting. It had been a striking reminder that we weren't as close as we once were. We all had our ways of coping, but at some point, I became someone he couldn't be completely open with.

I told myself I kept my distance because of the feelings I still had for Del. If I had been a real friend, I would have intervened when I noticed the smell of alcohol on his breath had become a frequent occurrence. My experience with my father should have tipped me off that the unwinding ritual had become less of a last resort and more a means of self medicating.

Adam and I had gotten into the habit of meeting up at the end of the day when we could, so I headed to the usual haunt to find him. Our main space had been this area just past our housing where someone had placed handmade wooden benches.

I shouldn't have been surprised to find Caroline Greene there with him. Their friendship had gotten closer over the passing months, but I paused as they came into view. Him and

Greene had been sitting on the same bench. Both of them were straddling the wood to face each other, caught up in what appeared to be a humorous conversation.

Something in the way Adam's cheeks flushed a bright red gave off the impression I would have been interrupting a conversation they preferred to have in private. I should have turned around then, found something else to do to occupy my limited spare time, but the protectiveness I felt toward Del, wouldn't let me.

"No, I'm serious. Laney will be livid," Adam chuckled nervously toward Greene.

My ears perked up at the sound of Del's name. I swallowed the jealousy and scanned the rest of the area for anything else to pay attention to. Unable to move away, I leaned against the metal support beam for a housing unit.

"Well, she will have to get over it. This is exactly what she signed up for," Greene laughed too before stealing a drink of Adam's bottle of water.

Neither of them seemed to notice I was standing there and maybe I shouldn't have used that to my advantage. Until I had seen Greene's reaction as she swallowed the drink, I had full intentions to leave. Whatever had been in that bottle definitely wasn't water.

"It's not that. Today was the anniversary of her wreck. I missed our call," Adam's voice became a lower and more serious tone.

I knew what he had meant and the story hidden between his words. Instantly, their conversation rubbed me the wrong way. It would have been close to ten in Missouri. There was no reason he still couldn't have called to check in on her.

"Besides, she knows you would have been there if you could. I'm not sure D would be so...understanding," Greene retorted with a distance glint in her eyes that told me there had been a story hidden in that statement too.

Instead of answering, Adam took a long drink from his bottle. I was sure he had done so either from his own guilt or to keep from commenting on her marriage. Either way, it looked like the wrong kind of trauma bonding waiting to happen.

Oblivious to my presence or lacking the will to care, Greene scooted closer to my bunkmate. If he had been the man I thought he was, he would have moved away, but then again, he also would have been on the phone instead of drinking with his neighbor. When he didn't budge, I made the decision to leave.

It took everything in me to keep to the direction of my bed. I couldn't tell if I wanted to turn around and confront him because of my feelings for Del or to protect my friend from making a mistake. Either way, I knew it wasn't my place.

Nothing I could have said or done would have changed the fact that Adam's relationships were none of my business. It wasn't like we were as close as we once were, even though I didn't realize that until he flashed the fake smile at me earlier. I wasn't even sure I wanted to be that close to him, given the man he was becoming.

When I got to my makeshift housing, I found myself at a loss. Pacing the floor, my mind went in all the directions it shouldn't have.

My brain kept telling me I was reaching for patterns every time I saw Green and him together, but I couldn't deny what I had just witnessed. I couldn't understand how he would choose that conversation over Del or how I seemed to be the one who couldn't let her go. It was like I couldn't decide who to be mad at; him for crossing the boundaries with Greene or me for caring.

When the thoughts wouldn't stop, I finally sat down on the edge of my bed and I pulled out my contraband bottle from the newly built end table. I knew without a doubt what had been in his bottle when I noticed mine was empty. Remembering how both of us had restocked our stash a week ago, the weight of his addiction hit me.

I drifted off, remembering all the times I had smelt it on his breath, knowing if I had been trying less to reserve the new found friendship, I would have put a stop to it. Closing my eyes and forcing myself to sleep was the only way I could cope with the war inside of my head between my selfishness and my anger.

I woke up sometime later to the sound of something heavy crashing to the ground. Growls and mumbles echoed through the space as my eyes adjusted to the dimly lit room. Immediately, my fight-or-flight response was triggered.

Evaluating my surroundings, I quietly crawled off the side of my bed to my knees. A shadowed figure stood hunched over the foot of Adam's bed. Keeping my eye on the intruder, I reached for my duty weapon tucked safely under my headboard.

The retrieval of my weapon wasn't as silent as I had hoped. Noise of the metal scraping the floor alerted the other person I was there. The darkened figure snapped around on unsteady legs, revealing Adam's empty space.

When the figure took a step closer toward, the early morning light shining through a window illuminated my best friend's face. The ease I should have felt evaporated as I saw the familiar brainless stare behind his eyes. The eerie similarity to my father's painted everything in a different kind of terror.

Adam wasn't awake like I was, not completely. I knew it like I knew how to breathe. The memories of those long nights in my past kept me momentarily frozen in place.

"You're lying," Adam snarled at me as I caught sight of the knife in his hand and the sweat gathered on his forehead.

I pulled my rifle up with me as I stood and prepared for the worst. Even if I woke him, there was a possibility I was going to need something to keep us both from getting seriously injured. I stood and readied myself.

"Adam!" I shouted as he walked closer, stomping his feet, but just like my father, it didn't seem to phase him.

For every step he took toward me, I took one away from him, glancing around for anything else I could use for our protection. The moment a wall prevented me from going further, I raised my rifle.

"Adam...wake up," I tried desperately once more, but it was no use.

He had been trapped inside of his nightmare and I was going to need to fight for my survival. I winced as his shin bounced off the frame of my bed when he stalked toward me. He growled out more words I couldn't quite understand.

"Let her go!" He let out in a heartbreaking roar as he found his way around the obstacle.

His eyes widened with wild terror as if his brain was struggling to keep hold of his hallucination. He lunged forward and his free hand pinned my shoulder to the wall as he brought the knife back, preparing to strike.

"I'm sorry, brother," I apologized as I swung the stock of my weapon directly into his face.

Letting out a sigh of relief, I watched Adam crumple to the floor. What the hell had just happened.

Chapter Sixteen

February 19, 2024

Delaney

The quiet stayed between Kendric and me throughout the rest of that evening. I wasn't sure if my prying questions left him feeling awkward or if it was my presence. Either way, we didn't fill the evening with small talk.

We couldn't talk to each other like strangers, but there was an unspoken rule in place, like a wall, that kept us from conversing like close friends. Still, there were these moments where it felt like nothing changed between us.

The sun set hours before he walked into the living room holding something in his hand. I was focused on a book I stole from a built-in bookshelf under the stairs and to be perfectly honest, I hadn't realized he even left the room. Holding my spot on the page with my thumb, I raised a brow at him when he stood quietly in front of me.

That was when I saw my phone in his hand. When it had buzzed in my pocket a second time after the tour, I told Kendric I needed to grab a glass of water. I had found a peace at his house that I hadn't felt in days, so when I saw Adam's name on my phone, I put it on the windowsill next to that porcelain pig. All I had wanted was a little bit longer to live in that serenity.

Leaving him in the dark was never the intention and I kicked myself as I awaited the lecture on hiding it from him. I just wanted a few hours where those messages didn't hang over me and occupy every thought. I wanted to feel safe.

"When were you going to mention you received another message?" he asked without looking up at me.

Unable to answer, I watched in horror as he held the device out for me to see the screen. In almost slow motion, he unlocked the device and clicked into the message notification. The text thread opened, but I couldn't watch him anymore.

I stood and headed toward the stairs, not staying around long enough to read the newest threat from the unknown party. Kendric's focus was on the device, so he didn't have time to stop me from leaving the room before I made it to the base of the staircase.

"Where the fuck are you, Del?!" a male's voice roared from the speakers of my phone and I paused.

I felt the ice crystalize in my veins as my blood ran cold. Hearing the voice only solidified my reasoning for avoiding it.

When Kendric turned to look at me, I was already heading up the stairs.

My mind raced as my feet continued on autopilot. I didn't want to discuss it with Kendric after he pointlessly ruined the only peace I had felt in months. The closer I got to that guest room, the angrier I felt toward him, even though deep down, I knew he didn't deserve it.

"Laney, we need to talk about this," he called after me as I made it to the landing.

We didn't *need* to do anything until I could process the voice message. He wouldn't understand that and I saw no point in arguing. I ignored him.

His footsteps echoed up the stairs as I entered my room, but I shut the door behind me. I was too focused on figuring out why that voice had sounded so familiar to tell him to back off. The closed door should have been enough of a hint.

In the safety of the empty room, I closed my eyes and ran my fingers through my hair. The nagging feeling that I knew that voice saturated every one of my thoughts. It sounded so familiar, but off at the same time.

The sound of the door opening pulled me from my spiral. My panic quickly turned into aggravation as I turned and saw

Kendric in my doorway. Seeing the irritation in his eyes only made me more upset..

“Is it so hard for you to give me a moment to process?” I snarled at him.

He traced his tongue along the tip of his incisor as he descended into the room. His eyes trained on me like a sniper at a target. He raised the phone to point at me in disdain.

“Probably as hard as it is for you to let me in,” He cursed as he tried to walk in my direction.

I held my palm up, causing him to stop just out of arm’s reach.

“That’s the problem, Kendric. Maybe I would if you showed an ounce of patience. All I wanted was a few hours to not think about that psycho,” I scolded.

I wasn’t sure if it was the irritation or the fear that made me shake, but I prayed he didn’t notice. Trying to hide it, I crossed my arms tight against my body.

“Hiding from it won’t solve anything,” he caught me.

I let out a humorless chuckle and glanced around the room before glaring back at him. He had been the one who practically pulled me from my house to keep me here. What did he think this sleepover was? Instead of solving anything, Kendric made this whole thing a scavenger hunt.

“Funny, because I thought you brought me here to literally hide from that problem,” I choked out, hating the way my voice trembled.

He lowered his eyes and shook his head before he turned to leave, tossing my phone on the bed. That had been exactly what I wanted from the time he barged into this room, but something about the look on his face changed my mind. He was holding something back, but had the balls to lecture me on being too closed off.

“And there you go, demanding me to let you in with one breath and shutting me out with another,” I spat at his back, causing him to stop in his tracks.

He turned to give another glare at my accusation. The flames of his anger reflected in his eyes as he stalked back toward me. I didn’t stop him this time. His steps faulted in front of me so close I could feel the warmth of his breath on my cheeks.

“Fine. You want openness? I didn’t bring you here to hide you. You are so determined to handle everything yourself that I couldn’t trust you wouldn’t get yourself killed,” He hissed.

I gritted my teeth as the first tear spilled down my face. I hated the way I reacted to any form of heightened emotion, but angry crying had been my least favorite. Even though I knew I needed to get my emotions in check, I held his glare.

"I am not one of your soldiers. You don't get to dictate how I fight back on this and I'm not even sure why you keep trying, " I shot out before my filter could prevent it.

His eyes widened before his brows pinched together in frustration. Just saying the words out loud made me feel like I had crossed another invisible line.

"You are my best friend's wife," He answered, even though we both knew that wasn't filled with conviction.

"Okay. Openness. You got it," I let out in a calmer voice before squaring my shoulders to make myself feel bigger, "I *was* his wife, but he died and loyalty isn't inherited. So please, help me understand why any of this is now *your* obligation just because once upon a time, the two of you were besties."

With restrained desperation, he grabbed the sides of my face in response, but I couldn't look at him any longer. The rawness of my truth left me feeling exposed. I closed my eyes and wished I could take the confession back.

His heavy breath filled the awkward silence before he gently rested his forehead against mine. I could feel his anger wane as his hands shook from how hard he was holding himself back. I tried to steady my breathing as we stood there, unable to pull away from him.

“That’s the problem, Laney. Any loyalty I felt for him weakened the moment I knew you took his last name,” even though he whispered it, I still heard his voice crack..

This time, he let me pull back enough to face him. All the stone in his features was quickly melting by the guilt that spread across his face. Staring at him, I attempted to understand his confession, but none of what he was saying made any sense given our history.

“My loyalty to you was never inherited and I can’t let you do this alone. So, use me as your punching bag or your distraction, but know I’m not going anywhere,” His words rushed out of his mouth when I didn’t respond.

The way my brain caught his use of my nickname, calling me Laney, stuck out like a sore thumb as I slowly absorbed his meaning through my shock. The nagging feeling of the voice memo in my chest pulled at the term of endearment, dulling my ability to think clearly.

The stalker called me Del. There was only one person who called me that still. The flowers, the nickname, the jealous messages about Kendric; they all connected to the man standing in front of me.

Unable to process the information ricocheting off my skull, I did the only thing I knew to do, to drown out the thoughts. My eyes drifted to his lips as I focused on the only words that stuck from his openness.

“Then be my distraction,” I challenged breathlessly.

Without a fight or judgment, he obliged. His lips crashed against mine, hesitant at first as fingers threaded through my hair, pulling me into him. All thoughts of the psycho at the other end of the phone faded as I fell into my safe place.

June 9, 2020

Kendric

I sank to the floor as I stared at Adam’s body. He was out cold and thankfully no longer a threat. I’m not sure how long I sat there, watching his breathing as I tried to figure out what I was going to say to him.

I leaned my head against the wall as the adrenaline settled. Flashbacks from my father’s night terrors played like a messed up sideshow through my mind. I was six years old at the time of his first episode…

My father had been home for a year after his last deployment. He had been a part of Desert Storm and it was clear from the moment we first saw him that he wasn't the same person who deployed. My mother and I had been picking up the pieces while my father had failed to fully acclimate to the civilian world.

His drinking had started the first fourth of July after he came home. The neighborhood was known for constant fireworks for weeks leading up to and after the holiday. I began to fear the change in him after I found him one night in our bathtub curled into a fetal position.

I remember waking up in the middle of the night to fear fueled screaming as firecrackers sounded off overhead like gunshots. Being the proud son of a soldier, I leapt into action, grabbing a plastic bat and prepared to help my father defend the house. The last thing I imagined fighting was my father's personal demons.

When I found him, I didn't see any monsters. Instead, I saw the empty bottle of bourbon he had been cradling as if it was his duty weapon. Sighing in relief, I had turned to go back to bed, but my mother was watching us in the doorway.

I'll never forget the worried look on her face as she glanced between me and my sleeping father. In my memories, that moment lasted longer than the seconds it did in reality. It was like the morbid calm before the storm.

I jumped when I saw her, dropping my weapon and almost peeing my pants. The echo of the hollowed out plastic reverberated through the tiny bathroom as another firecracker popped and fizzled out. My mother's worry turned to pure horror as she pulled me into her in the same breath his empty bottle shattered against the wall where I had been standing.

My mother spent years using that night as a reason he needed counseling. Instead of seeing the damage he caused, he saw it as a sign he should have volunteered for a longer deployment. The alcohol eventually took his ability to serve and six months after I left for basic, it took both of their lives.

Adam shifted restlessly, bringing me back to reality. Memories of my father's similar ailment melted into the moments I had overlooked Adam's drinking habit. I kicked myself for missing the obvious cries for help, even though I knew why I turned a blind eye to them.

I stood up from the floor as Adam struggled to wake up. Regardless of missing the precursors, I saw them now. I knew what I needed to do and that he would probably hate me for it, but I couldn't live with myself if I let him become that monster.

"Why does my face hurt?" he groaned out as he rose to a seated position and adjusted his eyes to the morning light.

I ignored his question as I scanned the room. I could recap his PTSD adventure after I fixed the last threat to his safety. Without a word, I walked over to his half of the space.

Adam watched me with confusion as I took his rifle that was propped up on a wall near his bed.

"What are you doing?" He asked as I removed the clip and checked the chamber, making sure it was emptied before I began.

"I'm taking out your firing pin," I informed him calmly as I removed the hand guard.

Adam scrambled to his feet, but swayed, delaying his ability to come after me again. He watched me as I pushed in the pin and pulled back the charging handle to remove the bolt and carrier. The guilt swallowed me whole as I focused all of it on my task at hand.

"What the fuck, Kendric," He cursed.

I shot him a glare before returning to my mission and pushed out the pin before locking the bolt into position. By the time he took another step toward me, I had dumped the pin into my hand, pocketing it. Returning his glare, I tossed the pieces of his weapon to his mattress.

"How long have you been having those nightmares?" I interrogated instead of justifying my actions.

Adam's eyes widened. He stuttered out a couple of syllables before he sat down on my bed in shame.

I watched him silently, waiting for a real answer. It was hard to see him as the kid I grew up with, when all he reminded me of was the man I escaped from. Crossing my arms, I leaned against the wall as he gathered his bearings.

"How. Long?" I repeated through my teeth as he looked up at me with tear-filled eyes.

"Everyone has nightmares, man, I'm not suicidal," he argued as he adverted my stare.

The way his desperation hung on the last word left me feeling unsure in my aggressive approach. I couldn't tell if he was avoiding the question out of embarrassment or if he really didn't understand how bad it was.

I watched as his eyes located his knife that rested near my feet. His attention snapped back up to face before he gingerly touched his nose. Scanning me from head to toe, he let out a small sigh of relief.

“Not all of us act them out,” I said a little softer.

He fell apart at that as tears soaked his cheeks, taking in the seemingly new information. All doubt that he had been evading my question for self-preservation faded. The absolute self-hate that crossed his face told me this was the first time.

“You need to get help and I have to ensure our safety until you do,” I informed and gave my explanation for disassembling his weapon.

He stared at the knife in response. Chewing on what I just told him, he sat there quietly for a moment.

“It isn’t this place,” he started gesturing at the tiny living quarter, but meaning the deployment. “It was the alcohol and that freaking anniversary.”

My father’s excuses echoed in my mind as Adam’s ‘reasons’ were spoken in the same tones he used to use. *I shouldn’t be here. The dreams are just a sign I need to go back. Alcohol is the only thing that keeps me sane.*

“With everything you have seen here, you don’t think this place has any influence? I had to physically harm you to get you to stop trying to kill me,” I snapped, hating the way he blamed his episode fully on the loss of his child when it had been his decision to drink away his grief.

Adam stared at me, his guilt edged with defensiveness.

"You can't tell anyone! They will kick me out," he pleaded in a hushed voice.

If I hadn't felt such blame for missing his patterns, I would have ignored his statement. Neither of us had mentioned Del, but she hung there between us in unspoken implications. The moment he was sent back, the nightmares would fall on her and there was no promise he'd seek out the help he needed.

I rubbed my face with my hand as I struggled with how to respond. The soldier in me knew it needed to be reported. The realities of what could happen if it didn't get addressed ate at me, but my past replayed on a loop in my head. It wasn't like I could trust the VA's mental health system.

The longer I looked at him, the more I worried Del would have to face this like my mother did. She was smaller and kind and I knew when someone was trapped in that state; it didn't matter how much you loved someone. I felt the low growl build in my chest before I finally replied.

"Then we will handle this discreetly, but so help me God, Adam. If you don't play this by my rules, I'll report it without a second thought," I halfway threatened as I watched his shoulders sink in relief.

"Whatever you say, I'll do it," he let out as he cradled his head in his hands. Once again, the desperation practically dripped from his words.

I uncrossed my arms and put my hand in my pocket. The firing pin almost burned in my fingers as I debated my decision.

"As of this moment, you are on the road to sobriety. No more excuses, no crutches. You do your job and you keep your nose clean," I laid out as he pulled himself together.

"Anything else?" he asked with spite in his tone as he straightened his spine and rubbed the wetness from his cheeks.

"You find a therapist off base the moment you land in the states and Del isn't kept in the dark about this," I listed my last requirements, naming the only reason I had agreed to his request.

I knew I shouldn't have said her name. From the moment I found out about their relationship, it was a boundary I had respected, but I couldn't get her out of my head. I knew she wouldn't have the heart to hurt him and this risk was the only way I could prevent it.

Adam's eyes shot up to mine the moment she was referenced and something more than anger flashed across his expression before he hesitantly nodded.

"Do we pinkie swear now or do you want my blood to seal the deal?" he spoke through his teeth as he waited for another lecture.

Deep down, I knew it was probably an empty promise for the sake of his career. I didn't really care. If he thought I wouldn't ensure he would follow through, then he was risking more than I was.

"Consider it done, but understand I will sink us both if you give me a reason to doubt you again," I threatened once more before tossing him the firing pin against my better judgment.

He caught the missing piece of the weapon and nodded. He knew I wasn't doing this for him and I didn't care. As far as I was concerned, if he hadn't been so cozy with Greene, he could have worked through that grief with his wife and maybe prevented this whole conversation. All I was doing was trying to protect her.

I couldn't look at him without feeling rage at the way he was blowing this off. He had no right to the jealousy he was presenting at the mention of keeping his secret to keep her safe. Not when she appeared to be more of an afterthought.

He had been the one who convinced me not to propose before graduation. Every reason he gave that talked me out of my decision, he had no problem with doing in my stead. The longer I watched him fiddle with the pin in his hand as if I provided another excuse to neglect her, the weaker my filter became.

“Call your wife and handle your shit. Regardless of what your buddy out there said, you and I both know Del had no idea *this* is what she signed up for,” I dismissed in a deadly calm before I opened the door to leave.

I knew by his returned glare that I had gotten my point across. My loyalty wasn’t to him or my career. I just prayed I made the right choice, keeping him there where I could monitor him.

Chapter Seventeen

February 19, 2024

Delaney

I closed my eyes as Kendric provided the distraction he promised. In the darkness, the world fell away as he pulled me closer to him by my waist. His hesitant and gentle kiss turned hungry as he walked us back toward the bed.

“This wasn’t what I meant by distraction,” he whispered against my lips in a moment of morals while we gasped for air.

I barely heard him over the earth shattering around us. We both knew as he said it, he was offering me an out, but no matter how wrong this was, I couldn’t take it. Being with him didn’t feel wrong when his lips met mine and I didn’t care if the guilt ate me alive later as long as he was touching me.

I opened my eyes to scan his face for the same signs of assurance, but in my search, my eyes fell to his swollen lips. Any thought of doing the right thing left the room as a small groan erupted from his chest at my lusty stare.

"You can't look at me like that," he gasped, only further melting my resolve.

I looked up at him innocently to hide the temporary bitter taste his torn expression gave me. He wasn't concealing his emotions this time. I could see them all. His need, the war he was having with himself, and the guilt he was trying to push off until later.

If he asked me if I wanted this, I knew I would come to my senses. We both would, if only for the other's sake. I selfishly ignored every impulse to stop, praying he wouldn't come to that same realization.

"Look at you like what?" I teased, giving him an out in the form of flirtation.

Stepping me backwards until my calves hit the frame of my bed, he gave me his answer. I controlled my growing nervousness as he studied my face one last time for any hint of regret. Breathing heavily, he gathered the hem of my t-shirt in his fingers, waiting for me to call his bluff.

"Like you need me to fuck you, Laney," he challenged.

I reached down and unbuttoned his jeans, making it clear I had no desire to change my mind. The feeling of his skin against mine felt too much like the peace I had been missing for months. In terms of self destruction, I couldn't think of a better reason to hate myself for later when my actions came down on me.

Firm in my decision, I undid the top of my jeans and slipped them down slowly as he watched with bated breath. The moment they hit the floor, he pulled my t-shirt over my head, and it became less like a game of poker and more like a race. I clumsily slipped his jeans down his well-defined thighs, leaving them on the floor next to mine.

We were playing a dangerous game, but all that seemed to matter was how desperately we both wanted to play it. Everything we couldn't say hung between us, intensifying everything. The conflicting nervousness and intimacy of the moment made the air thick with anticipation.

I unhooked my bra with shaking fingers as Kendric hooked the straps and slipped them down my arms in a way that felt more like a caress. I inhaled sharply as the material stretched tight against my sensitive nipples in the painfully slow descent. Once more, he seemed to silently ask for my consent as his eyes found mine.

It felt as if I was slowly losing my control, bracing my palm against his chest. Everything felt too real and too raw, but it also seemed like a delicious escape from our reality. Trying to memorize the moment, I took in the scars that made him who he was now.

It was hard to believe he was the same guy I fell in love with all those years ago. For the first time, I saw his military service marks like a road map on his skin and it took everything in me not to trace it with my fingers.

Instead, I slipped my hands just under the scar above his hip. The second I did, he sucked in a nervous breath. I wasn't sure if my touch had been what shook his confidence or the fact my hand now rested below a big piece of his history, but his lips were now dangerously close to my collarbone. His heated exhale pricked my skin with goosebumps and I forgot all about my fantasized trailing. Even though he was the first to discover my weakness, I wasn't sure if he would remember it.

One gentle kiss to my neck turned into the soft pricks of his teeth as he worked his way down to my kryptonite. An uncontrollable moan escaped my lips as my body melted in his hands. I unraveled as he answered my unspoken question and bit down on the soft spot between my neck and my shoulders.

That one spot had always felt like he could use it to claim my body for his. As his teeth sunk into my skin, an uncontrollable moan escaped my lips and my nails dug into his flesh to keep hold of the feeling. I all but panted as heat shot straight to my core.

My reaction brought on a similar response as his own as it broke any restraint he seemed to have. He picked me up and sat me on the edge of the bed as his thighs spread my legs apart to press himself against me and my now ruined panties. I felt our equal desire and need.

At first, all I could acknowledge was how good he felt. Until his body tensed under my hand and just as quickly as it began, I was snapped out of the euphoria. He had completely stilled as the intimacy faded between us. When I looked up at his face only to find that damn granite mask, I heard it.

Vibrations echoed through the silent room and I traced Kendric's furrowed stare. Sitting on the bed behind me, Adam's name and number lit up my screen. My stalker had now escalated to calling me.

My distraction was shattered as I scrambled off the bed, and immediately it felt like I was being watched. As I tried to cover myself with Kendric's t-shirt, he shot me an apologetic look and reached across the bed for my device. All consent went out the window as he answered the call and placed it on speakerphone.

“I see you didn’t like my flowers,” the voice on the other end answered.

If Kendric remembered I was still standing there, it didn’t show. He gripped the phone tighter as the only emotion that broke through his well crafted shield came out in flames of anger.

“Who the fuck is this?” Kendric growled with hate and venom practically dripping off his words.

“So Del *is* with you,” The stalker snarled as if I had personally betrayed him.

Once again, the creep had used my nickname, but this time, I watched as Kendric caught it. Frantically, he replayed the voice memo, listening for the hint embedded inside of it. His eyes shot to mine with nothing, but that fire behind them, our moment of peace forgotten.

“Who else calls you that?” he asked, looking at me as if I already knew who that voice had belonged to.

There was a territorial undertone to his words as if that nickname was supposed to be his and his alone. In all honesty, to me, it had been. He was the only one I had ever let me call me that. At first, that had been because everyone else respected my wishes not to. I couldn't pinpoint when it had stopped feeling like an act of disrespect when he said it and turned into a term of endearment for me.

"Just you," I answered barely above a whisper as my eyes caught the full size of his scar above his hip.

There was no doubt in my mind it was caused by the wound that led to one of the biggest fights Adam and I ever had. The sudden realization triggered the guilt of our distraction to crash down on top of the panic I was already feeling from the call. My legs trembled beneath me as I tried to remain calm and focus on the interrogation I was under.

Kenderic's anger morphed into concern as he saw my reaction to everything and tossed my phone back onto the bed, realizing his mistake in answering it to begin with. He had just noticed me a little too late. As I felt myself slipping into fight or flight mode, I looked away from him and held his shirt tighter to my body for comfort.

My eyes fell to his scar again, hoping the guilt would swallow me whole before the panic could fully set in. Hating myself was easier than the feeling that I couldn't escape the stalker or the concern I had that Kendric was somehow connected to him. Desperate to hold onto my sanity, I replayed all the ways I had just disrespected my late husband's memory.

“Laney, I…” Kendric started in protest as tears gathered in the corners of my eyes.

I thought if I could lose myself into the destruction, I could prevent myself from having to run away from him yet again, but the feeling of his guilt on top of my own felt suffocating. I knew watching me break down would only hurt him as much as I was willingly hurting myself. I needed to get out of the room.

I shook my head as I hurriedly gathered a fresh set of clothing. The room felt too small and the longer I stayed there next to him, the less air seemed to fill it. Nothing he could have said in that moment would have prevented my inevitable breakdown.

“I need to…Can I take a bath, please? I just- I need some time alone right now…” I choked out as I turned to the only excuse I could use to prevent him from following me.

He stared at me for a moment, as if debating on protesting my escape. Everything in me urged him to provide an explanation, but I physically couldn’t bring myself to do it. He would only break his own heart in an attempt to save mine, but I couldn’t let him do that.

“There are fresh towels in the cabinet by the sink.”He finally spoke and I knew by his voice, I was too late.

Relieved he hadn't fought my decision to flee, I let out a trembling breath and thanked him before quickly shutting myself behind the bathroom door. Finally in the safety of my seclusion, I broke down, masking my sobs with the running water. Maybe my stalker was nothing more than karma.

August 12, 2020

Kendric

Two months had passed since Adam and I came to an understanding. It took me telling him what it took for me to stop him during his night terror for his anger to finally fade. If it wasn't for his continued relationship with Greene, my resentment might have faded as well.

I woke up that morning planning to talk to him about it so that maybe I could heal that jealousy. My plan hadn't been to accuse him of anything, but I needed to know why he had gotten so close with her. At least, that was the plan until we got our assignments.

"Ready for snake training?" Greene perkily asked as she approached the group of us by the benches.

I focused on my poor excuse for coffee to hide my biases against her. When none of us answered in anything other than frustrated groans, she shrugged her shoulders. Everyone knew it was meant to be a joke, but the truth behind her statement wasn't something anyone was ready to laugh about.

The assignment had been part of a program to help the Afghan Army against their fight with the Taliban. The military had figured if they could fight like us, they wouldn't be so overwhelmed. The problem was that this country was dangerous to even their soldiers. More often than not, the men we trained used those newly learned skills against us as a means for survival. It became hard for them to differentiate the people who had trained them and the threat they were fighting.

"At least we aren't kicking up moon sand waiting to get shot," Murphy blurted out as he stood from his seat.

I zoned out of the conversation as Greene pulled Adam to the side. It was impossible not to watch them as Adam bent down for Greene to whisper something in her ear. Whatever she had said, immediately angered her.

He glanced back to where our command was stationed before turning to take a step in that direction. I had hopped up with the full intention to investigate, but Greene grabbed his arm discreetly and shot him a pleading look. Hesitantly, he stopped, but I could tell by the torn look in his eyes he didn't want to.

Donaldson let out a small chuckle to my left, pulling me back to the conversation. Adam soon rejoined us as he shook off his irritation, but Greene kept her distance as she hung her head in regret. What the hell was I missing between them?

"Did you see how many were fucked up the other day? I get there is a language barrier, but 'grab your gear' seems to take some of them on a completely different kind of trip," Donaldson criticized as the group of us stared at him.

He wasn't wrong, but it wasn't something we talked about.

"Do you think it makes the blood splatter more entertaining?" Donaldson added in a comic tone to lighten our moods.

I didn't miss the way Murphy shifted uncomfortably from the statement or how he averted his eyes to anywhere other than his friends in the conversation. No one laughed at Donaldson's poorly timed morbidity as the four of us stood there distracted by our own demons. As horrible as the assignment was, at least we weren't going out there completely in our own heads.

"Let's just get this over with," I snapped as I poured the rest of my cup on the ground, displeased.

When the training day was over, we silently went about our day. Those assignments never felt like we were saving anyone. They were guaranteed guilt as I forced down the question of how many of my comrades would die because of what we taught that army.

Desperate to erase my mandated betrayal, I grabbed the water bottles I had set out that morning and headed to take a shower. The heat from the sun guaranteed warm water and it became a healthier ritual as I pretended it washed away my day. It might not have been as effective as the vodka, but it wasn't one more thing I'd hate myself for later.

Before I could reach my destination, I saw Adam. I had the full intention to say hi and pass him, but as he came closer, the tension in his jaw caught my attention. Even though I told myself I had stopped him because we were still friends, I wanted to know if it had anything to do with that hushed conversation he had with Greene that morning.

"What's up with you today?" I inquired when he gave a half-hearted greeting.

He looked down at the ground for a moment as if debating on answering me. Glancing behind him, he shook his head, unsure if he could trust me.

“Don’t worry about it,” he tried to dismiss me.

The defensiveness in his voice wavered as he said it. I crossed my arms and raised an eyebrow at him. He took one look at my face and knew I wasn’t going to drop it that easily.

“Look, I don’t know what's up with you and Greene, but when it puts you in a piss poor mood all day, it’s my job to worry about it,” I countered.

His eyes widened at my audacity to pull my rank at his refusal. It had been a shady move on my part, but he had made it pretty clear he wasn’t going to tell me unless he had to. Using my authority seemed to be smarter than accusing him of having an affair.

“What makes you think she has anything to do with this?” he shot back defensively and I forced myself to relax my posture.

There was no proof anything was happening with them, but my gut was convinced what had been between them wasn’t strictly friendship. Everything in his face told me he didn't need me to be a superior. He needed me to be his friend.

"I saw her pull you aside earlier. I'm not accusing you of anything, but I have eyes and both of you seemed a little agitated. I just want to make sure you both are alright," I said quieter than I intended. I wanted them both to be solid for different reasons.

He relaxed softly and rubbed the back of his neck before glancing around us for prying ears. Satisfied no one was eavesdropping, he closed his eyes for a moment and debated on if he should explain it to me.

"Look, you aren't hearing this as our Sergeant, okay? Whatever I tell goes straight into that vault," he started waiting for me to agree before he went any further.

Hesitantly, I nodded. I wasn't crazy about the way he needed to clarify that I wouldn't act on whatever secret he was about to divulge, but he wouldn't tell me unless I did. Even then, he seemed to be overly guarded.

"Caroline's husband is a grade A asshole and I can't exactly give you any details about why I say that, but when she called him last night, he got mad because she was ten minutes late to their phone date. He even tried to use Laney to make her more upset," he admitted vaguely.

He paused in his explanation as he gauged my reaction to his wife's name. I didn't know Greene's husband personally, but the anger behind Adam's voice as he said it sent chills through me. I forced down any concern I had for Laney so he couldn't use it as an excuse not to finish.

"Apparently, my wife was a tactic he had used before to make Caroline jealous, but she knows Laney now and it didn't work like he had been hoping. Things…escalated. I told her before if he made any more threats, I'd make her report it or I'd report it myself," he finished, unknowingly letting the detail of the ultimatum slip in his rush to get it out, the look on his face immediately showing it.

My protective nature rebelled against my better nature. Narrowing my eyes at him, I opened my mouth to ask what exactly he meant, but he stopped me.

"I know you want details and if I gave them to you, you would have no choice, but to report it. I need you to trust me enough to handle this. I promise if she doesn't report it, I will do so myself. I'm just trying to convince Caroline to come to you first. I don't want either of us being the reason Laney or Caroline becomes collateral damage," The shame of his request reflected in his eyes.

I stared at him shell-shocked as he asked me to protect another one of his secrets. Even though I wanted to refuse it,

Adam had a point. If we forced Greene to confront this, her distraction could put the whole squad at risk.

Going against my better nature, I agreed to keep his secret. Affair or not, I couldn't imagine he would put Laney at risk. Still, I couldn't help the uneasy feeling I had that she was back home alone with this man who Adam felt was a big enough threat to go to command over.

"Is Del safe living next door to him?" I asked for my own reassurance.

He nodded before glancing toward someone coming our direction. I made him promise to keep me in the loop as I rethought every interaction I had witnessed between him and Greene. Maybe I had been wrong about their relationship.

Chapter Eighteen

February 20, 2024

Delaney

I didn't see or talk to Kendric the rest of that night after he had answered that phone call. By the time I had gotten out of the bath, he must have gone to bed. When I woke up that following morning, he was in his kitchen, making coffee.

I came down the stairs, ready for work and I braced myself for his reaction to the fact I would be leaving the safety of his farmhouse. He would not be happy that I was going, but I didn't have a choice. The job was now my only source of income and I had already been off for a few extra days as a reward for the overtime I had pulled the two weeks before.

He looked me up and down in question before he quietly handed me my daily caffeine fix. Exchanging an awkward good morning, he waited for an explanation of my formal breakfast attire, but I had no intention of arguing with him before I had finished the cup in my hand. I could tell as he watched me sip the hot liquid that he was waiting to interrogate me.

“I need to leave for work soon,” I answered his questioning stare as I returned the coffee mug to the sink.

Kenderic’s face immediately contorted to one of concern as he choked on the sip he had just taken. I forced down a laugh at his clumsy reaction, I patiently waited for the argument I had been ready for.

“I don’t think it's safe right now,” he did at least try to dampen the protectiveness in his voice.

In six months, I would be evicted from the home I had on base and I needed this income to secure another place to live or I would have to move back in with my mother. Somehow bringing it up felt like the wrong thing to say because he was the only reason I wanted to stay.

“I need this job, Kendric. I can’t just stay here and wait for the stalker to lose interest,” I protested gently as I left out the reason why I needed the income.

Sighing heavily, he rubbed his face in frustration. He knew I was right and it wasn’t like he didn’t have a job of his own to worry about. I knew from Adam that even when home, as long as he was in contract, he had assignments from the base. Either way, I would have to spend the day on my own.

“How long is your shift?” he wondered, unable to hold up his side of the argument in the face of my logic.

I let out a breath of relief, happy it didn’t take as long to make him see reason as I had been expecting. It was getting harder to fight with him. After the last couple of months, I found myself taking his opinions to heart. It made it clear that our past disagreements had only been one more way to drive a wedge between us on purpose.

“Should be twelve hours, but they have been pretty short staffed lately.”

Kendric’s brows furrowed as if he hadn’t been thrilled that I would be away from the house for that length of time. It wasn’t until that moment I realized he had no idea what I did for a living

“If it makes you feel better it's not open to the public,” I tried to put his mind at ease.

Since he drove us both here, I didn’t have my car. It definitely made me feel better knowing I wouldn’t have to walk to my vehicle all the way to the end of the lot reserved for the staff. At the same time, it meant I’d have to tell him where I worked.

“Just tell me when and where to be and I’ll be there,” he offered, slightly distracted by his own thoughts.

I hesitated in telling him where exactly it was that I worked. When I had first told Adam, he flipped out for justifiable reasons. In terms of overprotectiveness, Kendric had my husband beat in spades.

“Alderman’s Rehab in Oakview. We should leave here in about thirty minutes to beat the morning traffic. I should get off at nine tonight,” I hesitantly admitted, bracing myself for Kendric’s response.

Alderman’s had a bad reputation for a good reason. It wasn’t the same kind of rehabilitation where someone detoxes from drugs or alcohol. It was an extension of the local prison, where they had sent sex offenders for a specific form of therapy.

Kendric stared at me as if he was waiting for the part for me to tell him it had been a joke. For a moment, I wished it had been, but it was a good paying job and the relocations thanks to Adam’s career left my resume less than desirable.

Kendric’s face went beet red when he realized I was serious, “You work around violent perverts all day and didn’t think once you should have mentioned it? What the hell Laney?

What makes you think the stalker isn't linked to that place?" he rushed out as he stared at me in disbelief.

I blinked back at his reaction. The person on the other side of that number had been using Adam's phone number. It would have been pretty damn hard to get it or even spoof it from a locked down facility. Whoever it was also seemed to have a link to Kendric, so it was ruled out as a potential connection the moment he was mentioned in the texts.

"I didn't mention it because my job has nothing to do with this. The patients there are locked behind maximum security. Not to mention no one there knows anything about my personal life outside of my job. It's not like they took a day pass to send those pictures of us in my bedroom," I snapped back.

Even though he seemed to understand why I saw no connection, my work still seemed to eat at him. He was quiet during the drive there until we made it into Oakview. The whole ride, I could see the wheels turning behind his distracted expression.

"Please tell me this place isn't as dangerous as I've been told," He spoke out of nowhere, breaking the silence in the truck.

I swallowed hard, not wanting to lie to him. The whole reason the place didn't bat an eye at my spotty work history wasn't because they understood the military moved people around like pieces of a board game. The turnover rate was high thanks to the long hours and injuries caused mainly from understaffing.

"I can't. It is a dangerous job, but I have a good rapport with most of the guys. Right now, I am as safe as I can be. I can promise that," I answered honestly and his fingers tensed around the steering wheel until his knuckles turned white, but he didn't say any more.

The goodbye before I exited his truck had been as awkward as our good morning. I carried it with me, hating myself and knowing he would worry about it for the rest of the day. Making a mental note to check back in with him on my lunch break, I headed to my supervisor's office for my meeting with her to catch up on what I had missed in my absence.

When I walked into Lacey's office, she greeted me with a huge smile, unaware of my sour mood. Not everyone could say they liked their boss, but my supervisor had become a friend. Forcing myself to put my morning and Kendric aside, I returned her warm welcome.

"Hey there girly! Welcome back to the shit show," she offered me the chair across from her desk.

I took the seat gratefully and prepared for her to fill me in on the patients. She started with a new patient that had been admitted to my assigned hall while I was off. From the start of her debriefing, I knew this guy was going to be a handful.

As she dove further into his background, it was easy to tell she found him unsettling. Then again, most of the guys here had similar histories that could make someone recoil in disgust. It wasn't until she looked up at me to make sure I heard what she was about to tell me that I started to feel uneasy.

"Just be on your guard with him. He doesn't look like he would be a huge threat, but from my understanding he's very manipulative. He has already convinced Johnny B. to act out again these last couple of days," She warned, holding my eye contact.

Johnny was the biggest client we had in the facility. Even on days where the facility had been fully staffed, it was a struggle to break up the fights he had caused in the past. Before I had started, he sent almost a whole shift to the hospital because of one fight, but since then, he had been working the program religiously.

"I thought Johnny was close to going back because of good behavior?" I was hoping she had gotten the name mixed up with a different patient.

She shook her head beside herself. He had been so close to being a success story for the facility, but the fact he was manipulated by someone new couldn't have made someone in her position look good. Our building hadn't been big enough for her to separate them and I knew they couldn't afford to send anyone back.

"That's what I am saying. We have no proof yet, but some of the staff think our new guy is starting it," She answered and I paled.

I swallowed hard in understanding as I kicked myself for trying to convince Kendric I was safe at work. If the new guy set Johnny off during my shift, there was no telling what kind of danger I would be in. More often than not, I was the only staff in a room and it automatically would make me a target.

"Noted," I answered numbly as I took the new patient's file from Lacey's outstretched hand.

It wasn't until I opened the file that I realized she had never mentioned his name. I looked back up at her before flipping frantically to the intake form to find the copy of the photo taken for his ID. Sucking in a shaky breath, I came to terms with the threat he posed to my safety.

"Do you know him?" she immediately noticed my reaction.

I nodded, not ready to tell her just yet how I knew him. Unable to stop myself, I scanned over the reason he had been brought to our facility and felt the bile rise in the back of my throat. It had been almost ten years since I had seen his face, but the moment I did, Kendric's words repeated loudly in my thoughts.

"He was that teacher in high school I told you about," I finally answered.

Kendric might have been right. David Gilliam's transfer hadn't been mandatory like the rest of the offenders there. His case manager had specifically requested it. Given the paperwork in my lap that detailed his ability to manipulate others into doing his bidding, it was entirely possible he had someone on the outside taunting me from Adam's number.

February 20, 2024

Kendric

I sat in the truck outside of Laney's work, watching for any sign of the creep who had been harassing her. It felt like the harder I fought to keep her safe, the more threats came out of the woodwork. The only thing that kept my mind off of what she could have been facing on her shift was my search to track down the identity behind her stalker.

The only thing I had definitively found out was that Donaldson had packed up the things Adam left behind after the attack. I was waiting for a call back from him when his squad returned to base, but that wasn't expected for another couple of days. When Laney finally crawled into the passenger seat, I had been mentally making a list of the questions I needed to ask him.

Laney gave me a tired greeting as she fastened the seatbelt and I knew by the sound of her voice, it had been a long shift. I didn't blame her for not venting about it as we drove most of the way home in silence after the way I had reacted that morning. I shouldn't have snapped the way I did, but I had grown up hearing stories about that place. It had become somewhat of an urban legend.

Most towns had some creepy monster children feared like women in white or a man with a hook for a hand. Ours had a story of an escaped patient that stole children from their beds. It wasn't until I left high school that I heard more realistic stories of the despicable creatures that lived behind the fence.

"Mom worked there after I left for basic," I revealed when the silence became suffocating.

Out of the corner of my eye, I saw Laney look at me in surprise at my confession. I knew it was something she would have never expected. Everyone had just assumed she had been a stay at home mom until the day she had died.

"I didn't know that," Laney replied, but I could tell my comment had brought up questions she wasn't sure she could ask.

The last thing I wanted to do was dampen the mood by saying too much. I wasn't sure how much about my parents Adam had filled her in on.

"She was trying to save up to leave my father."

I had hoped if I opened up to her a little more about my life, she would return the favor. She had been the one who voiced that this was a two-way street and I was trying to make an effort. I didn't think talking about my mother would be this hard.

"Is she still in Morley?" Laney asked.

I clenched my jaw, struggling to answer her question. As I had predicted, neither of my parents had survived my father's alcoholism. He had been so worried that she would use her job as an excuse to cheat on him, he picked her up from work and they wrecked on their way back home.

"No, she- she's not. Both of them died shortly before my first deployment," I told around a lump in my throat, ignoring the way her eyes took in my face.

Without saying a word, Laney reached out and took my hand that rested on the gearshift. I squeezed her fingers gently, grateful she didn't give apologies for my loss. I think we both knew by now that sentiments like that, no matter how genuine, had lost their meaning.

"I'll have to ask around to see if anyone remembers her. I might even be able to find photos from their staff parties if she attended," she offered.

I smiled at the gesture. Laney had no idea what it would mean if she could find one. My mother didn't like having her photo taken. The last photo I had of her had been from my twelfth birthday.

As I put the truck in park in the driveway, she hesitated before unbuckling the seat belt. Before I could even ask her what was up, she looked at me with a conflicted expression. I got the impression with my attempt at being more open, she felt safe to do the same. It had worked in my favor.

“We got a new patient while I was out. Legally I can’t tell you anything about him, but you need to know it could be a lead behind the messages. Think you might have been right this morning,” she confessed and I took my hand off the driver-side door handle.

“I thought you said they couldn’t be connected to the facility,” I asked, trying not to be so demanding.

She unbuckled herself and looked away from me. I could tell she was nervous by the way she bit her bottom lip as if worried she would choose the wrong words to say. Immediately, my stomach filled with dread from her reaction.

“I don’t know for sure that he is a solid suspect, but based on everything I read, it's possible he could have used outside help. It's someone we knew in highschool, so he’d know things about me, about us, that I don’t share.”

I stilled. It was one thing for this just to be one deluded creep, but the idea of it possibly being more than one made the situation seem more unpredictable. I couldn’t imagine how overwhelming it had to be for her.

“Do you have to see him on your shift?” I asked as the realization hit me.

She nodded and opened her door to exit the truck. Reaching behind her seat, I pulled out a gift I had bought her while I waited for her shift to end before I followed. When we got inside, I handed it to her, unsure of how to explain it.

"I got this for you. Since we don't know how tech savvy your admirer is, I wanted to make sure he couldn't track your movements while I was pulled away," I explained.

Her eyes widened as she found the new cell phone inside of the bag.

"You didn't have to do this," she protested, staring between the device and me.

Her expression fell as if I had bought the device out of pity. I needed her to understand that I was not doing any of this because I felt like she was helpless. Even though I thought I might have made it clear the night before, I hadn't done it for Adam either.

"I just want to keep you safe. He may still track the old one and if you are okay with it, I'd like to take it with me when I leave the house. The new phone is under my name and it will be harder to track. I didn't want you to feel you were trapped here because of him," I replied, but I barely got the statement out before she launched at me and wrapped her arms around my neck.

I reveled in the feel of her against me as I folded my arms around her to prolong the hug. After I had messed up and answered that call last night, I wasn't sure she'd let herself close to me like this again. I hadn't brought it up because I was terrified that she would tell me she thought it had been a mistake, but to me, it had been everything.

As she pulled away, I caught a glimpse of the guilt she kept trying to hide from me whenever we got too close. I couldn't shake the feeling that she regretted it every time and I desperately needed clarification. Driven by that gnawing concern, I felt compelled to tell her I didn't think we had made a mistake.

"About last night..." I started. I couldn't look at her face as I let her past the walls I had spent so many years building. If she had regretted everything, I didn't think I could fully get the confession out.

"I'm sorry. I shouldn't have— " she began before I had a chance to continue, but I cleared my throat nervously, cutting off her apology.

She was always the one taking the blame for other people's actions and feelings and I couldn't let her apologize for my inability to control myself around her.

"I'm not sorry, Laney. Not for kissing you or feeling the way I did when it happened, but I am the one who needs to apologize here. I should have never answered that call last night. I'm sorry for stopping and answering it without thinking of how it affected you," I rushed out, barely taking a breath.

She didn't say anything to my confession. Instead, she leaned up on her toes and kissed my cheek softly. Interrupting the moment, my phone rang in my pocket and I made no attempt to reach for it. Smiling, Laney nodded toward the noise and walked away to head up the stairs.

These phones would be the death of me. Inwardly cursing at the fact we seemed constantly tied to these devices, I fished mine out of my pocket.

"Tate," I answered, waiting for the other person to speak.

Donaldson greeted me as static filled the empty air on the other line. Someone had sent him word that I had called for him and he knew it had to be serious.

"Do you have a bit to talk? I need to ask you about Adam Anderson," I responded before glancing up the stairs where Laney had disappeared.

Eventually I would need to tell her everything I had learned about this part of Adam's life, but for now, we had to focus on the person using Adam's cell phone. Maybe by the time we stopped the harassment, I could find a way to tell her I was home for good.

Chapter Nineteen

March 25, 2024

Delaney

The month had been a blur after finding out about Mr. Gilliam's admission into Alderman's and Kendric's raw confession. Work had become my personal hell and the stalker continued to message my old phone every day, growing increasingly irritated at his lack of access to me. Even though Kendric and I had grown closer, we still kept each other an arm's distance away emotionally.

Even work had grown into something resembling my own personal Hell, as I feared at any moment my old teacher would recognize me. At least Lacey had been trying to ease me back into the hall as slowly as she possibly could given the facility's inadequate staffing numbers. The only comfort had been the fact my stalker hadn't mentioned Alderman's once in his many messages and voicemails.

Still, I needed to ensure Mr. Gilliam was in no way involved. After a while, it was like Kendric had forgotten the new patient all together. It felt as if he was wrapped up in an investigation of his own and I often heard him behind that locked storage room door. Even though I wanted to ask him about it, I couldn't bring myself to pry.

At first, I didn't understand his secrecy, but when I started to hear bits of the phone calls before he disappeared behind the locked door, I started to understand. They seemed to pertain to experiences he and my husband shared on deployment and understandably, it didn't feel like he wanted me to hear them. We both had things we couldn't share and I thought it had been best to respect that boundary as he was respecting mine.

I didn't want to add to his plate more than I already was, especially if he knew that starting today, I would be back in my hall full time. When David showed zero signs of remembering me, Lacey was convinced nothing would be triggered by putting me back into my full duties. As much as the idea of being around that man for twelve hours straight made my skin crawl, it was the perfect opportunity to get the information I needed to eliminate him as a suspect.

What no one at the facility seemed to realize was just how good of an actor David really was. They didn't see what I had seconds before he forced himself to look right through me. I saw the recognition and the hate in the brief moment before he did.

Today I was sure it would be no different. He knew if he was to give away that he knew me, his chances of getting out of there were slim. I didn't second guess that as I listened to the daily breakdown of each patient's progress in the program.

Unluckily for me, my first opportunity for getting those answers waited for me on my first assigned task for the shift. For the first four hours, the aids had been divided up to supervise a specialized therapy session. The one I would be watching over had been the worst one of all and no surprise he had to be in it.

It was a targeted class for lower level patients who were either new to the facility or not working the program. Every time I had to sit through one, it felt as if a piece of my soul died by the time it was over. I learned rather quickly to disassociate as the patients recounted in graphic detail the worst offenses they had taken part in.

If I had any hope of gathering clues that could link him to the person using Adam's phone, I couldn't zone out this time. As much as I hated this group, I needed it. Putting on the mask I had perfected from watching Kendric, I headed straight to the room where I had been assigned.

I mentally prepared myself for the stories I would hear. Some would detail abuse they received from their parental figures that taught them the wrong meaning for love while others would relish in moments where their violence made them feel powerful. I didn't know which version David would tell, but I needed to get my head on straight so I could bear it.

I knew the moment I sat down that I was in for a long four hours. Already sitting close to my designated chair sat David and Johnny. I hadn't been sitting there for more than a couple of minutes when Johnny leaned in to whisper something in David's ear before David looked at me and nodded. A vicious smirk spread across his villainous face.

For over three hours, I listened to heartbreaking and gut-wrenching stories, waiting for David to speak. As soon as he was done, I could shut everything off, but the longer I waited, the more he seemed to savor my discomfort. I wished I could have convinced my peace of mind that I could tune it all out without missing his testimony.

If the counselor hadn't hand picked the order himself, I would have thought my nemesis had waited so long to give his retelling on purpose. Finally, second to last, it was David's turn.

"Many of you have heard this story before, but not all of you know the ending. As you know, about a decade ago, I worked as a teacher in a small high school not far from here," He started.

Any worry I had that his recognition was all in my head was immediately erased as I felt the anxiety grow in my chest. Judging by the restraint he showed not to look at me as he talked with a wolfish smile, he had been waiting for this moment since he found out I worked here.

“I spent five years before that, being cautious, switching schools before I could get caught, forcing students into acting out my fantasies. Freshmen were my favorite,” he oozed out as the class sat silently like children hearing a fairytale.

I glanced at the counselor who wouldn’t look up from his notepad. Out of the seventeen of us present, only seven of us seemed utterly disgusted by the pride in David’s voice. I held the statue-like demeanor out of pure desperation, refusing to give David the satisfaction he was hoping for.

“Anyway, at this last school, I had gotten reckless. When the rumors had died down to campfire ghost stories, I chose my next victim too prematurely. She was a helpless thing, with fiery hair and a smart aleck mouth. Before I could teach her a lesson, that little bitch had set a trap. She recorded the whole thing, but waited months to catch me off guard by playing it for the whole school and landing me here,” he hissed but with venom.

At David’s tale, the counselor looked directly at me. Lacey must have mentioned my encounter to him. I didn’t blame her for doing it. It was her job, but she hadn’t warned me anyone else knew about that shared history between me and the patient.

I dropped my eyes to my hands as I ignored the feeling of watchful eyes on me. It had been a sign of weakness I was hoping to avoid, but the last thing I wanted to do was be evaluated like I was one of them.

"Then, I got my revenge. I waited, just like she did, for the right opportunity to exploit her vulnerability," he began and my ears perked up.

I had skipped my last class with him to broadcast that video. He was escorted out of the building and until a month ago, I hadn't seen him since. At first I thought he had been talking about the stalker, but this hadn't been the admission I was looking for.

"I am not anything if not patient and I have realized that with the right friends, I wouldn't have to lift a finger. We waited until she was all by herself. They made sure I got what I deserved after all the trouble she caused me," he continued his veiled threat.

I could still feel the counselor's eyes on me, but I was no longer looking at him. Even though nothing David had said proved otherwise, I no longer believed he was talking about the harassing messages.

"Mr. Gilliam, in this class, we don't tell stories with vague meanings. You either have to go into detail or we will move on to the next person and you will not receive credit for participating in your therapy, " the counselor warned.

David smiled at me while he pretended to debate his answer. When he didn't add in details of my stalking, we both knew there were no details to give, because none of it had happened yet. He couldn't have cared less about his participation.

"Forgive me; I'm new at this. Jonathan, would you mind?" David spoke in a deadly calm, giving the order to Johnny B in the form of a question.

In slow motion, I watched as the counselor turned his attention to Johnny just in time for a fist to crash into the side of his face. Two patients darted from their chairs out the door, leaving me with the fourteen other patients. Judging by the way they looked at each other and then to David, it was clear none of the others were in on it.

I hit the alarm built in beside my assigned seat before I stood, but I couldn't leave the counselor in here defenseless. I wasn't even sure if running would have been the smartest move, considering there were several patients between me and the door. I looked at the other patients that didn't seem sure of David's plan in the hopes that they could buy me some time for the staff's show of force.

Preparing to put up a fight, I grabbed the chair I had been sitting in and held it in front of me to swing at anyone who dared to come close. David stayed put, patiently waiting for his plan to unfold, all the while modeling a soulless smile. I didn't see the patient head toward the door until I heard it slam shut.

"Hold it closed, Abner," Johnny instructed, looking toward David for acknowledgement.

When David didn't break my eye contact, Johnny upped his game. I wondered if he knew he was playing the role of Mr. Gilliam's new puppet as he handed out instructions like a frazzled personal assistant.

"Rider, get that freaking chair. We have to make this quick," Johnny demanded.

I turned my attention to Rider, who was expected to follow the command. He took a hesitant step toward me before Jerry stepped out in front of him.

"Why does he have to be the one to grab the chair? If you want her so bad, you do it," Jerry challenged.

Making a mental note to advocate for him at his next review, I silently thanked the behemoth that came to my defense, even if he had only done so for his own sake. Jerry was, in no way, the salt of the earth, but he had been one I had the best rapport with in the room. He was also a few months away from being transferred to the next level of the program and obviously didn't want to be stuck there.

Johnny snarled at Jerry as David's smile dropped in the face of his defiance. It was almost satisfying to realize David believed he had everyone left in the room under his thumb. Heaven forbid the group of heathens cared about hurting one more stupid girl.

"Hurting me only keeps you here longer guys. Why risk that when he won't lift a finger to damage his own chances?" I added to Jerry's argument and watched as the others seemed to turn on Johnny.

I had found the weakness in David's not so perfectly concocted revenge plan and he rose from his chair. Nodding his head to another of the patients, he silently ordered them to take Rider's place. The moment Harlow came at me, I swung my weapon, knocking him to the ground. A leg of my chair caught his jaw hard enough that I heard his teeth connect.

It had been the wrong move and David had been counting on it. Two other guys came at me, but I only managed to hit one before the other yanked the chair from my hands. Johnny rushed at me as Harlow used the distraction to regain his foothold, grabbing ahold of my arm. Both men pinned me to the wall as my rescue party arrived.

The alarm continued to sound at ear drum bursting pitches, yelling and banging echoed from the door Abner was barricading. Jerry seemed to be the only one not afraid of gathering riot. David must have been grooming most of them for the moment he was admitted and his grudge made me the perfect target.

He started toward me as I forced myself to look at the only ally I had. With his eyes, Jerry pointed toward the door and I knew what he was planning. It was easier to take out the one guy preventing my rescue than it would be to fight the group of men circling me, waiting for blood.

By the time I looked back at David Gilliam, I came face-to-face with his fist. He sneered at me as he licked my blood off of his knuckles, completely unaware his party was about to end. I sneered back at him with bloody teeth.

At the sound of bodies colliding at the door, I spit a mouth full of blood at David's feet. By the time any of them noticed the rescue attempt, it was already too late. Even as security filled the room, the men holding me down refused to let go. In a moment of angry desperation, David retaliated one last time by grabbing my chin and forcing my face in place.

"You win this time," David snarled, furiously pressing his lips against mine before he was finally pulled out of the room.

I forced down the urge to vomit as Harlow was the next one to be ripped away from me. The only patient left holding me in place had been Johnny. His death grip around my arm was so tight, I thought he'd crush my bones from the struggle.

No matter how hard they pulled back on him or how many staff members were added to the rescue attempt, all they managed to do was yank me along for the ride. As I dug my heels into the laminate floor with no avail, I heard someone in the crowd call for a sedative. It would have taken the same amount to subdue the giant as it would to take down a rhino and I knew it was pointless.

Even if they got the medication here at the speed of light, there was no telling what he would do when he realized he was going to let David down. I was unwilling to find out how deeply Johnny's brainwashing had gone. I did the only thing I could think of and turned toward the giant. In an act of pure survival instinct, I kicked David's lackey square in the balls.

As the mountain of a man collapsed to the floor, I realized David had won, even if it hadn't been the way he had intended. Regardless of the fact I did what I had to in order to survive the attack, getting physically aggressive with a patient would cost me my job. I headed straight for Lacey's office to fill out the incident report and hand in my badge, with zero remorse for my actions.

March 25, 2024

Kendric

I broke every speed limit between the base and Alderman's after receiving the call from Laney's supervisor. Every horror story I had ever heard from that place played through my mind as I raced to get to Oakview. All she would tell me was that Laney had gotten injured in an attack.

It didn't help anything that when I answered the phone, her supervisor called me to her emergency contact. She didn't want Laney to drive herself home and urged me to talk her into getting checked. Apparently, Laney was adamantly refusing to let them send her over to the local emergency room.

The only comfort that gave me was that Laney had been alert enough to still be stubborn. I knew in my gut the newest addition to that facility had been the root cause. I wasn't sure how I would talk her out of returning to work for her next scheduled shift, but I knew I couldn't live with myself if I let her.

By the time I made it to the parking lot, she was waiting for me outside. I had barely placed the truck into park when she opened the door and crawled into my passenger seat. Willing her to look at me, I didn't move as she buckled her seat belt and stared out the window.

"Are you okay?" I asked quietly when she didn't talk, relieved that Laney didn't look as horribly disfigured as I kept imagining.

She didn't turn to face me as she sat there almost numb to everything around her. The quiet that radiated off of her chilled me to the core as I recognized that kind of stillness. It had been the same thing I had seen over there with my squad when the trauma from a mission managed to shatter a piece of us in the process.

"I'm fine. Can we just go, please?" she was barely audible over the engine.

Unable to handle it anymore, I shut off the truck and reached out for her hand. I needed to see her face, but the moment I touched her, she flinched so hard I jerked back. It wasn't the same kind of reaction someone had when they were startled. It was more intense and only scared me more.

Sensing my fear, she finally gave in. When she hesitantly faced me, I realized why she was trying so hard not to. Dried blood was caked underneath her chin. A pretty rough busted lip glared at me and immediately I saw red.

Acting on impulse, I reached for my door handle, but her hand caught my arm and stopped me. I glanced back at her, trying to wait for whatever argument she had, but I caught the fresh bruising speckled across the side of her jaw line. Flinging the door open, I got one foot out of the cab before she called after me.

“You won’t get past that gate,” she reasoned and the guard that came out to stand at the entrance proved that she was right.

I sank against my seat and closed my eyes, trying not to break my teeth from the pressure. All I could think of was how many ways I could kill whoever had hurt her, but I wouldn’t have even known where to begin or how many patients I’d murder before I got the right one. Laney grabbed my hand and I held onto it as I tried to calm down.

“Please, just take me home,” she begged and the defeat in her voice broke something inside of me.

Unhappily obliging, I shut the door, too angry to talk. She didn’t seem to mind my silence as we drove back home, still holding on tightly to my hand. I pretended not to notice how she seemed to sink further into her hoodie the further we got from the building.

As we walked into the house, I tried to make myself drop it. I knew she would talk about it when she was ready, but the scenarios in my head were driving me insane. Unable to stop myself, I snapped knowing we were finally in a place she felt safe in.

"What the hell happened?" I begged to know as I locked the front door behind us.

I knew I shouldn't push her, but seeing the evidence of the attack was torture as my mind went wild trying to figure out how she got the marks on her face. She just shook her head in response. I should have listened, but something inside of me couldn't let it go. We had gotten too far for her to push me away.

"You don't get to shut me out of this one. I don't need the graphic details, but fuck, Laney. I can't stop thinking of what might have happened. So, please, talk to me..." I started out in a frustrated tone, but it melted into more of a plea than a demand.

I hated the way my words only seemed to make her breakdown more, tears flowing down her cheeks and dripping to the floor. For once, she stopped fighting me and listened, even if it had only been for my sake.

“I had to supervise a therapy session, but it turned into an ambush and they pinned me to the freakin wall. I thought he was going to kill me, but I got lucky and a patient helped me by letting the staff into the room. I had to fight back and I got fired,” she rattled off so fast I barely caught it.

My brain was torn between the fact that it had been more than one patient that attacked her and the fact that one in particular had made her fear for her life. I couldn’t help, but wonder if he had been the one who left the marks on her face as if grabbing it so hard he intended to crush her jaw.

“You thought he was going to kill you?” My brain lagged on her explanation.

“Mr – the new patient. The one I thought was behind the messages,” I didn’t miss how she almost said his name.

My eyes widened as hers did. Laney had mentioned we knew him. There was no way she had been talking about... When she paled, I knew I was right.

“What do you mean they pinned you to a wall?” I asked instead of seeking confirmation.

I didn't want to stay on the topic of Mr. Gilliam and let her realize I had picked up on the one piece of information she never intended to let slip. It wasn't something I was ever going to push for and she had enough on her mind without the guilt of confessing something she could legally get in trouble over.

"I can't talk about that right now," she turned to walk up the stairs.

Logically I knew she was safe here, but the moment she started toward the second floor, I panicked. The last thing I wanted to do was let her out of my sight. I ignored the voice in my head that told me she needed the space.

I took the stairs two at a time as I followed her to the bathroom. She left the door open to start the faucet over the tub, but when I walked into the room, I had no idea what I would say. I slowly approached her as she watched me through the reflection of the bathroom window, figuring she would tell me to leave.

When she didn't, I did the only thing I knew to do; wrap her in my arms gently. I held her there like she was glass until the tub had filled with steaming hot water. As she broke out of the hold to shut it off, I went and grabbed a clean rag from under the sink.

"Let me clean that up. I'll get out of your hair too," I offered. She nodded, sitting down on the edge of the tub.

She averted her eyes as I dipped the washcloth into the warm water. Her eyes stayed trained on the floor as I delicately wiped away the blood on her chin. The whole time, I tempered my rage and convinced myself to walk out of that room when I finished, even though every nerve in my body told me I shouldn't leave her alone.

"Good as new," I whispered as I caressed her chin with the pad of my thumb softly, prolonging my exit a few seconds longer.

She caught my wrist with her fingers as her emerald eyes finally met mine, answering my unspoken prayer/

"You are welcome to stay."

Chapter Twenty

March 25, 2024

Delaney

From the moment Lacey told me she was calling him, I knew it would either bring me closer to Kendric or force new walls up between us. We had this awful habit of pushing each other away when our feelings got too real for us to handle. But the moment he got a good look at my battle wounds, it had broken him. Until he cleaned away the blood from my face, I worried that seeing me like that would shut him down completely.

His act of kindness had seemed to heal something in both of us. It felt like he was washing away the trauma behind the attack itself. The tenderness behind his actions quickly turned into something far more intimate and I think he felt it too.

We stood there as he studied my face in response to my invitation for him to stay. I could see what he was wondering, worried that I had only offered it because of my current state of mind. As hard as he tried to fight it, I could also tell he wanted to stay as badly as I needed him to.

"I shouldn't," he answered softly with a furrowed brow and conflicted expression.

He didn't want to take advantage of my mindset, but he had no idea how much his presence was helping it. We had been playing this game of chicken for so long, we both convinced ourselves it was wrong when we collided. I needed that peace I felt in those moments now more than ever.

"If you say that because you honestly believe it, I understand, but if you are only declining it for my sake, stay here anyway," I began to undo the top button of my jeans.

He swallowed hard as his eyes fell down to my hands slowly as I slipped my pants down toward the bathroom tile. His thoughts were so readable, a rarity. Kendric closed his eyes, fighting his better nature, torn between what he wanted and what he thought was right. When he opened them again, he undid his belt buckle, trusting me enough to give into my request.

The moment of relief I felt was fleeting as my fingers bunched up the hem of my hoodie and my arms ached from the bruises he hadn't yet seen. A busted lip had been one thing, but the banding on my arms due to being held in place during the struggle, a struggle painted on my flesh. He now saw I hadn't been exaggerating when I said I had to fight for my life today.

He must have taken my hesitation for nervousness or pain as he stepped in closer to replace my hands with his to help me undress. My heart rate increased to break-necking speeds when the warmth of his fingers enveloped mine. I froze from the fear of how he would react. If the smell of him and the fire between us hadn't been so damn intoxicating, I probably would have tried to warn him, but I couldn't think straight enough to speak.

Instead, I kept quiet as he slipped the hoodie gently over my head. When it fell to the floor, I watched as his breathing turned ragged at the deep purple hand prints left by my attackers. We stood there in silence for a moment as he took it all in.

"I'm glad you aren't going back there," he whispered, breaking the tension as pulled his shirt off in return.

I nodded, grateful he was willing to pretend it wasn't killing him inside at the picture I knew the marks exposed. I think part of him knew I wasn't ready to go into more detail on how I got them. Part of me knew he wasn't ready for them, either.

His breathing didn't return to normal until after we were undressed and he sank down into the tub. When I finally lowered myself down in front of him, I closed my eyes to sink into the feeling of his skin against mine. The world fell away as I focused on every rise and fall of his chest.

Being this close to him had a way of making everything feel lighter, even though I knew he had no idea he was doing it. I felt his fingers gently trace the temporary handprint left by Johnny's iron grip. When I opened them again, I met his in our reflection.

"I'm okay, really. It looks worse than it is," I tried to reassure, but the heartbroken look on Kendric's face didn't change.

His fingers stilled only seconds before he slipped his hands in the water to wrap them around me,and pulled me in closer to him. He knew I had been lying about being alright, but he didn't realize how much he was doing to heal the wounds that he couldn't see. Kenderic wasn't a distraction this time, like he probably thought I needed.

"I just can't stop thinking how worse it could have been," he whispered in my ear like an apology.

His words only reminded me of the worst part of David's assault. I wanted Kendric to erase it like he had when he nursed my busted lip. Without thinking, I turned slightly and kissed him at the awkward angle, but it had done exactly what I had needed it to. That one kiss turned into a hungrier need and I felt it in both of us.

I winced slightly at the sting and he pulled back out of guilt as if he had been the one to initiate it. Making sure he knew what I wanted, I laced my fingers through his and I brought one of his hands from my ribcage up to the bottom of my breast. Turning to meet his eyes again in the window, I watched as he hesitantly followed my silent command.

I pulled my hair over one shoulder, tilting my head to offer my neck to him and watched his gaze darken. But he indulged. The further down he kissed my neck, the more he teased me with his fingers. I hadn't planned for this, but I couldn't seem to stop myself from wanting more.

When he finally took the tightened bud in between his fingers, I gasped. My back arched against him and my knees parted slightly in response to the electric feeling of him pulling at my nipple so softly. It was driving me to the point of begging for more. His teeth sank into the soft spot between my neck and shoulder and from that, I thought I would come undone just from the throbbing between my legs alone.

That was when I felt the hand he used to hold me in place start to slip down lower. Once again, he held eye contact with me as he worked his way down to between my thighs. Drunk on the power he felt watching me through the window, he spread me apart with his fingers.

I needed him to touch me, to touch that bundle of nerves the sides of his fingers were resting against. The tease had worked me up enough that I lost all train of thought and his tongue dipped down and traced the swollen indentations left behind by his teeth. A whimper escaped my lips and his fingers closed in around me and pulled slightly, pulsing like he was doing to my nipple at the exact same time.

His merciless movements pulled and released in rhythmic fashion, pushing me closer and closer to the edge. I had never come so close to imploding so quickly and him watching us only intensified everything. He didn't break the stare, as I came unraveled from his fingers alone.

March 25, 2024

Kendric

No sooner than she came, her hands stopped mine before she turned her head to kiss me again. For a moment, I thought we had gone too far, but I knew she wasn't done the second her lips met mine. When I felt her shiver slightly, I realized we couldn't finish it in the water.

"Come with me," I ordered the moment our lips parted.

She raised her eyebrow in question, but she didn't protest. I helped her out of the tub, leading her to my bedroom. Neither of us said a word as I took her hand and forced down everything inside of my head telling me this was wrong.

I knew we shouldn't have been doing this. The attack earlier in the day had left her too vulnerable, but every time she looked at me, her green eyes told me this was what she needed. Every reaction she had to my touch and the way she looked at me in that reflection made it impossible to refuse her no matter how wrong it might have been to give in.

The gasp that left her lips was no different as she sat down on the edge of my bed and I forced her legs far enough apart to situation myself in between them. Bending down, I kissed her once more, trying to be mindful of their tenderness, reaching for a condom in the drawer of my bedside table. I didn't find one in time before she wrapped her dainty fingers around the base of hardened arousal and all train of rational thought poofed from existence.

Slowly at first as if gauging my size, she stroked me and I groaned at the feeling of how small her hand felt around me. Looking up at me with a devious smirk, she pushed me back slightly with the palm of her hand pressed firmly on my chest. As if recreating an unspoken fantasy, she leaned over her hand, and let her saliva drip onto my shaft, working it in as she stroked me a little faster from base to tip. I watched in pure ecstasy as she wrapped her pout perfect lips around my swollen head.

"Fuck!" I moaned as the tip of her tongue licked away the bead of my excitement.

She was perfect. Trying to deserve it, I wrapped her hair around my hand to keep it out of her way, but she moaned around me as I accidentally pulled it tight in the process. The tighter I held it, the faster she went. Before I could stop it, I was losing my control.

I wasn't someone who liked to take it slow and gentle, but I hadn't had an emotional connection to my past partners like I had with her. Judging by the way she cupped my balls and taunting me, she didn't exactly want vanilla either. I pulled her hair tighter before I tested the waters and thrust into her mouth until she gagged around me.

I wasn't ready to come yet and the more of her esophagus I felt around me, the bigger of a threat of climaxing was becoming. It wasn't her throat that I wanted to spill inside as the primal need tightened in the palm of her hand. I pulled myself out of her mouth and ordered her to lay back on the bed as I focused on my breathing instead of the intense urge to see if she'd swallow.

Her head barely hit the mattress before I spread her legs wider and slid my hands down between her thighs. She was so wet I could feel it before I got to her silky center. Repaying her tease from earlier, I ran my thumb down her soaked slit with a groan.

She was already so swollen and ready for me, but I wasn't done teasing her. I needed to calm down and I wanted her almost begging for it. I admired the mess I created between her legs as I slipped two of my fingers inside of her, stretching around them so perfectly the thought of trying to wreck her made me throb.

Once I found that sweet spot, I curled my fingers, stroking her ribbed edges until she squirmed from my prodding. Her legs pressed against me as she moaned, tightening around my fingers, preparing to come around them. I applied pressure to her sensitive bundle of nerves with my thumb.

"That's my girl..." I purred in approval as I felt her legs shake against mine and she soaked the palm of my hand.

Unable to wait any longer, I pulled out to grab ahold of her thighs with both hands and pull her ass off the edge of the bed. Lining myself up at her entrance, I eased her down on top of me as I slid in like a warm knife through cold butter.

I let her adjust to my size, slowly sliding her up and down me at first, but by the time I had reached the edge of my undoing, it had gotten primal. I could feel her drip down my manhood with every slam of my hips against hers. The way she bucked against me almost made it hard to hold on. She came close to her fourth as I tried to slow in order to prevent mine.

“Please…don’t stop,” she begged as I felt her walls tighten around me.

It was taking everything I had not to fill her, but the need in her voice pushed me over the edge. I quickly grabbed my base to pull out of her, but she placed her palm on my chest to stop me.

“Kendric! Oh God…I’m so close,” she cried out.

All it took was her name to fall from her lips and doing the smart thing was instantly forgotten. I pounded into her until she had milked every drop out of me and I didn’t stop until she shattered that fourth and final time.

We fell asleep with her head on my chest not long after, but I awoke some time later to the sound of my phone ringing from the bathroom. Careful not to wake her, I crept to my jeans, closing my bedroom door behind me gently. I had missed the call before I was finally able to pull my device from the back pocket.

Cursing under my breath, I redialed Donaldson's number as I went toward my storage room. He was supposed to call back when he found out who had packed away Greene's things like he had done for Adam. The man couldn't have had worse timing.

"Hey! I thought I missed you." His voice appeared on the other line.

I unlocked the door as I balanced the phone between my shoulder and my ear. "No, no. I just had my phone in the other room. What did you find out?"

I listened to the static fade in and out of the line as I flipped on the light and waited for him to answer. Shutting the door, I locked it as quietly as I could, hoping I hadn't woken Del.

"PFC Gunner packed away her things. Said it was two boxes in total. It was shipped to somewhere in Morley, Missouri," He reported and instantly, I tensed.

"Can you get the exact address for me?" I asked as I opened one of the boxes I had pulled out earlier that day.

As I sat on the phone, I flipped through the contents of the box, not wanting to wait until morning to find what I was looking for. If I was awake, I figured I should make myself useful.

“Sure, but I have more,” he went on as I pulled my grandmother’s ring from the bottom of the box and paused.

I thought I knew what he had for me. On our last phone conversation, I asked him to reach out to a buddy of his to find out if their tech skills could figure out if Adam’s phone had gotten or received calls from Alderman's. Something in his tone had told me it wasn’t exactly good news.

“I got to see a copy of Adam’s inventory when we boxed everything up. Like I said, his winter boots were included along with his personal cell phone. It got me thinking, and you mentioned only seeing two stacks of letters and that letter from his mom, right?” he pressed for clarification.

I tried to remember everything I had found in that box the night Laney let me open it and confirmed his information. He sighed heavily as if dreading to tell me what he had to do.

“There should have also been another letter addressed to his wife in that box. One of those goodbye letters you had us write just in case. I remember putting it in there myself. clipped it to a picture of him and his wife,” he rattled and I stilled.

There was nothing clipped to that photo when I found it. I knew by her reaction when I looked through that box Laney hadn't touched it yet. The news of that missing letter made my skin crawl.

"Did you hear back from that friend of yours yet?" I inquired as the worry settled in.

He cleared his throat, it popping through the static.

"Yeah, he said the only calls made to and from that phone in the last few months had been to the number you gave me," he answered hesitantly.

For a moment, I was relieved that the stalker hadn't been connected to the guys who had just attacked Laney. That was until Donaldson continued.

"But are you sure you gave me the right number, Sergeant?" He sounded nervous.

"Yea, if that's the only number that phone has called or relieved calls from, it's definitely Adam's," I answered slightly confused.

Once again, Donaldson anxiously cleared his throat before he explained himself. He hadn't been asking what I thought he had.

"I don't mean to overstep here Sergeant, but in the search, the last call made from that phone showed it had been made from Caroline's house on base. I recognized it from a letter she had sent out a week before the accident. I thought you gave me her husband's number by mistake," he answered.

His statement made more sense than he realized, even if his assumption was wrong. I knew there was a reason I disliked Daniel Greene and it took Donaldson's findings to remind me why. I had completely forgotten the conversation Adam and I had about him on our last deployment together.

Chapter Twenty-One

May 10, 2024

Delaney

Sleeping with Kendric had been a mistake. Maybe the collision was bound to happen, but I didn't think I would wake up to an empty bed after. I had stupidly convinced myself I meant more to him than a one-night stand, but he grew distant afterwards and proved me wrong.

When I got up this morning, I figured he had already left for work. That was his favorite excuse these last few weeks when he left before I woke up and spent his evenings behind that locked storage room door. I had given up on trying to break through the concrete walls he secured between us after that night. To my surprise, when I made it down the stairs to grab my routine cup of caffeine, he was at the kitchen table waiting for me.

The moment the smell of his coffee hit my nostrils, my stomach rolled. I don't know if it was the way he seemed to look at me for the first time since that night or if it was the pent-up feelings I had over his behavior that made me so queasy and anxious. Yet, the instant reaction to *him* made me want to run out of the room. I swallowed the bile in the back of my throat as I turned to leave to do exactly that.

It never crossed my mind that he would find this behavior out of character for me. In fact, I found it hard to believe he thought about me at all now that he had gotten what he wanted; my body. I was surprised when I made it halfway up the stairs before he stopped me.

“Laney!” he called out and I froze at his unexpected attention.

I closed my eyes and willed myself to turn around to face him even though the acknowledgement I would have begged for weeks ago made me angry now. When I did, I met his questioning stare, trying not to glare at him for having the audacity to expect me to want to stay in the same breathing room as him.

“I thought we could have coffee together this morning. I know I’ve been…absent these last few weeks…” he tried, but he was too late to suck me back into whatever it was he wanted.

Maybe if I had fully woken up before he attempted to mend the bridge he willingly burned, I wouldn’t have been so short with him, but he didn’t seem to have the patience to wait for that. The stench from his mug at the bottom of the stairs only seemed to fuel that irritation more. How dare he try to warm up to me now after it felt as if he had abandoned me the day after sleeping with me.

“Work is work, right? I need to get ready for mine and I’ll be out of your hair,” I replied a little bitter.

The forced smile on his face dropped at my tone and he nodded without a fight. I don’t know which was worse; that he didn’t argue with me like he would have before or that I wasn’t surprised when he didn’t. I just wished I didn’t want him to.

When I turned to walk back up to my room, the wave of nausea hit at full force. Running up the stairs as quickly as my legs would carry me, I darted into the bathroom. Dry heaving to no avail was the clearest sign that it was better for me to go back home. The heartbreak from being here with him had started to wear on me physically.

As soon as I was sure Kendric had pulled out of the driveway, I called out of work and packed my bags. Instead of feeling guilty for doing it behind his back, I reminded myself of how little he seemed to care until this morning. He should feel victorious that he had finally pushed me away like he had been trying to do since Adam brought him back into my life.

It wasn’t as if we had planned for me to live there forever. We both knew I would have to move eventually. Widowers were only given a year after the death of their soldier before they were forced off the base. Kendric made it alarmingly clear I had no reason to stay.

After the attack at Alderman's, my stalker's texts and phone calls seemed a lot less terrifying. If I had survived three grown men, I could survive one man who hid behind my husband's phone. I might have been piling on the reasons to run, but not even the psycho held more power over me than the self-hate I felt for staying with Kendric Tate.

Sitting my bags outside of my room, I went to leave a note on my freshly made bed, but I couldn't find any stationary in the room. I knew I couldn't text him my goodbye. He might not have cared enough about me to fight it, but I wasn't sure I could say the same about his sense of honor. Remembering the stack of papers in his bedside table from our disastrous sleepover, I made my way back to his nightstand.

It wasn't until I saw the familiar morning sunshine light up the room where I made my last mistake with him that everything came crashing down. It felt like I was finally closing a chapter in my life that I should have locked away after graduation. I didn't know who I was anymore and it felt like I had spent the last eight years trying to figure that out while I let the men in my life dictate my life.

Forcing down my self-loathing, I made my way over to his nightstand. Nestled between random envelopes and miscellaneous letters was the notepad I had been looking for. As I went to close the drawer, I caught Adam's name written on a stack of letters held together with a thick rubber band.

Unable to fight my curiosity, I grabbed them and sat down on the edge of Kendric's bed. The longer I stared at my husband's name, the more the cursive seemed written by a woman. Curiosity got the best of me before I could decide if what I was doing was wrong.

All it took was to read the first one to wish I had never found them. One by one, they laid out my husband's affair like a timeline, dating back to the last deployment he shared with my soon to be ex-roommate. Judging by where I had found them, there was no doubt in my mind that Kendric knew about it and never told me.

I didn't bother to write that goodbye note to him. Instead, I left the love letters scattered across his bedding along with the phone he had gotten me for my safety. By the time he found them, I would report my old device as lost and a chunk of my savings would have gone to replacing it.

Officially on my way home to pack, I adjusted to the overwhelming feeling I had that I was starting over. I wondered if Daniel had been feeling the same way or if he had known about the relationship my husband had with his wife. Trying to distract myself from all of the betrayal, I called up my old friend, for comfort.

May 10, 2024

Kendric

Donaldson's lead had gotten me nowhere. As far as I could tell, there was zero connection to Daniel and the addresses the boxes had been sent to. Either way, I had found enough information to know I didn't want him anywhere near Laney. Based on the hospital records, I realized the connection between Adam's last words to me. It was less likely that he had been sleeping with Greene, and more likely he had been trying to save her from her husband.

I let the investigation for the identity of the psycho consume me after that. After this morning, I realized I had let that obsession take me too far away from the girl I loved. By the time I had figured it out, she was too upset with me to let me explain.

I didn't blame her. At first I had been too worried she would tell me that night had been a mistake. I used Donaldson's call as an excuse to avoid the conversation. I should have realized how it appeared when I wasn't there for her when she woke up.

I didn't know how to tell her that I had spent the time in-between phone calls trying to figure out where I had stashed Adam's letter. When he had died, it felt cruel to add to her grief over feelings that at the time, I thought were fake. If I wanted to ask her to marry me, she needed to read them and know that he died an honorable man who wanted her to be his last goodbye.

As I got into the truck to leave that morning, I placed my grandmother's ring in the glove box. I would not give up on having a life with her this time. I had been so caught up in my plans to make up for my mistakes, I didn't notice that her old phone had been eerily quiet until I finally made it home.

It was when I noticed the only light in the house came from the kitchen. Immediately, I dialed her number, but it rang until the voicemail picked up. I would have assumed she was still at work, but the daycare she started at weeks ago had already closed over an hour ago.

Cursing, I made my way to the front door only to find it unlocked. Something wasn't right about any of this. As quietly as I could, I made my way into the house with my gun drawn, but I seemed to be the only one in the house.

"Laney?" I called out, hoping to hear some sign of life, but there was nothing.

The hope that she was still somewhere in the farmhouse dwindled as each room I entered was empty. For every scrap of optimism I held for finding her here vanished as I entered my bedroom. The moment I flipped on the light, I knew why she was nowhere to be found and instantly my heart sank.

I didn't have to read what was on the letters to know they were Greene's. They had been littered on my bedspread as if she laid them out in chronological order. It wasn't until I heard the ringing underneath one that told me she had left her new cellphone for me to find as well.

Picking up the device, I saw her mother's contact light up the screen. The last thing I wanted her mom to do was worry, so I picked it up, not sure how I would explain her daughter's abrupt absence.

"Ms. Martin," I answered, trying to control the emotion behind my voice, but my carefully curated stone wasn't working.

She didn't try to hide her surprise at my voice before a small knowing chuckle came through the line. I winced at how wrong her thought process was.

“I was making sure Laney was doing okay. She didn’t call on her way home this afternoon like she normally does but I guess I know why,” I could hear the smile in her voice.

I paused. Regardless of how upset Laney had been, it wasn’t like her to dodge her mother’s calls. When I didn’t immediately respond, Ms. Martin’s cheerfulness quickly dropped a couple of octaves.

“She is okay, right?” I wished I could honestly answer her.

I didn’t know. I wasn’t even sure where Laney was right now and the fact she left her phone behind only worried me more.

“She’s not feeling well today. I’ll have her call you back as soon as I can pass along the message,” I said weakly as I tried to cover for her daughter.

There was a moment of silence from the other end of the call and I worried she could tell I wasn’t exactly being truthful. Wherever Laney was, I was certain she didn’t feel the best after reading the notes from Greene, so I hadn’t outright lied.

“Well, tell her I love her and make sure if she doesn’t shake that stomach bug, she needs to go to a doctor. You know how stubborn she can be. I trust that you will make her,”Ms. Martin rattled.

What stomach bug was she referring to? I hadn't noticed Laney feeling off, but I hadn't exactly been around. I would have asked, but I knew it would have blown my cover.

We said our goodbyes, hanging up. It seemed her mysterious illness wasn't the only thing I had been out of the loop on. Unable to shake the uneasy feeling, I pulled her old device out of my pocket, realizing there was only one reason she would leave the new phone behind.

The moment I unlocked it, I knew I was right. The whole reason her old phone had been quiet that day was because it now no longer had service. I glanced down at the letters and realized what I should have the moment I saw them.

She knew I was aware of the cheating and hadn't told her. It wouldn't have mattered that I had taken them to protect her or that I no longer believed it was an affair. I betrayed her trust after avoiding her for the last several weeks. How was I supposed to make up for that?

Without thinking, I fished my keys from my pocket and headed toward the door. There was no longer a doubt in my mind where she had gone. I had been the one reading how increasingly obsessed with locating her the stalker had been since I took her phone with me everyday to work. She could hate me all she wanted, but I would not let her sacrifice herself for my mistake.

The whole way there, I tried to call her old number from my phone, but every time, it went straight to voicemail. I must have imagined a hundred scenarios in my head for how it would all go down, but I hadn't been expecting to find Daniel's car in her driveway when I got there.

Every suspicion I had of that man filtered through my head as I parked the truck across the street from her house. I might not have found concrete evidence to support the fact he was behind those messages, but I didn't have enough to say he wasn't. When I got to her front door, it swung open before I could knock.

Daniel's surprised expression morphed into one of unrestrained frustration as he straightened.

"Daniel?" I heard Laney call out behind him in concern at his sudden stop in her doorway.

I stilled. There were several things I wanted to do to the man in front of me, but talking to Laney had been more important at that moment. I didn't want him to take any tension between her and I as an open invitation.

"Kendric's here," he snitched as he turned to the side so she could see for herself it hadn't been a joke.

She shot me a glare as she nodded to Daniel as if letting him know it was okay to leave. Who the hell did he think he was to play the role of protective friend?

"I'd like to speak to you alone, please," I said directly to Laney, ignoring Daniel's presence.

He looked toward her again to judge her response, but this time, all Laney did was cross her arms in front of her chest. For a moment, I thought she'd refuse, but she took a deep breath before dismissing her friend once more and casually walked toward us.

"It's alright. I'll talk to you tomorrow," she told him.

Hesitantly, he obliged and pushed past me with a glare, a poor attempt at intimidation. If he was the person behind Adam's phone, he definitely seemed more confident behind that screen than he did facing off with me in person. I was pretty sure he didn't have the balls to leave the bouquet on her doorstep.

"I appreciate you giving me the chance to explain things…" I started as I turned my attention back to her, only to be welcomed with the door beginning to shut in my face. By some grace of God, I managed to stop her before she could completely close it.

"I don't need you to explain anything to me. I read the letters, so I'll say it again; your loyalty to my husband isn't needed anymore. Consider yourself dismissed, Sergeant," she ground out through her teeth before slamming the door in my face.

I stood there for a moment, absorbing what had just happened. In all the scenarios I had imagined, I would knock again or use my key, but the moment I reached up to rap on the solid wooden surface, I heard her. She had slid down against the door and started to cry.

Just like I hadn't been prepared for her old neighbor to be there, I had been expecting her to be angry with me. Hearing her breakdown made me realize that the secret I kept and my actions had also broken her heart. Unable to bring myself to hurt her more, I sat down on the porch and waited for her sobs to stop.

I didn't have to be in the house to protect her from the stalker. When I couldn't hear her anymore, I climbed into my truck. If I had to sit out there to keep her safe, I'd do it, including keeping Laney safe from me and the damage I seemed to create.

Chapter Twenty-Two

June 14, 2024

Delaney

Kendric had become my stalker. He didn't send me daily messages professing his love in cryptic threats or call me like my other did. Instead, I often woke up and went to bed with him parked across the street from my house.

It had been over a month since I heard his voice, and for the first time in a while, I woke up wishing I could hear it. The moment it crossed my mind, I immediately shut it down. Missing him didn't change the fact I didn't know if anything he and I had was real or if he had only done what he needed to in order to get me into his bed.

I thought he had been a version of the same guy I loved in high school. And I saw firsthand the changes the military can have on a person's character, but I had been so wrong about my husband. I couldn't help, but wonder what I missed with Kendric. The only thing I knew I could count on was his dedication to his soldiers and hiding Adam's affair seemed to fit into that category. How could I believe that Kendric never stopped loving me when he didn't love me enough to be completely honest or to fight for me before I was already gone?

Watching him in the mornings while I drank my cup of coffee had become a habit while that question played through my mind like a broken record. It felt like I was doing so to prevent complete withdrawal syndrome, but I was terrified that if I stopped, it'd destroy me like it did when he broke my heart the first time. For the first morning in weeks, watching him sitting out there hadn't been the only reason I got out of bed.

As if hearing my silent plea for help, my phone rang inside of my pocket. I turned my back from the window and cut myself off from my new found addiction as I answered the call without looking at the screen.

"Hi, mama," I answered, forcing a cheerful tone to my voice.

This had been another new routine of mine. Ever since I had called to see if her spare room was still available, she felt the need to check up on me daily. I don't think she realized I was serious about the request until she found out I had put in my two weeks at the daycare.

"Are you still flying out tomorrow evening?" she asked right on que.

I think she hoped I had given in and talked to Kendric, but my answer was the same one I gave her for the last seven days in a row. I know she thought if I just heard him out, he'd change my mind, but I hadn't told her about my husband's affair or how Kendric covered it up. I think she had hoped he and I were finding our way back to one another.

“Yes ma’am,” I said in a mocking sing-song tone.

Even though she hadn’t tried to convince me to tell Kendric goodbye in the last few days, I prayed she didn’t try to on this call. The guilt for taking off without saying another word to him already felt like it would eat me alive.

“And the doctor thinks it's okay to fly?” she questioned.

I rolled my eyes, knowing she couldn’t see it. My stomach had been in knots since the day I left the farmhouse and she was convinced I might have some rare disease that needed immediate attention. I didn’t have the heart to tell her I never went to see anyone.

“I told you, I’m fine. It's calmed down the last couple of days, so I think it’s just the stress from the move,” I lied.

She sighed heavily at my evasive answer. We both knew as many times as I had moved the last few years, I had this down to a science. If I could have invented a way to keep everything in convenient collapsable boxes that matched the decor, I would have.

“You still have a month before you have to leave. You could give yourself some time to get everything done…and tie up loose ends,” she tried again without saying his name.

At her second not-so-veiled reminder, I turned to glance at Kendric’s truck. She did not know how hard it had been to come to terms with the fact he wasn’t a loose end anymore. I couldn’t risk being pulled back in by him, even if it meant never having closure.

“Everything I need to do is already done, aside from the walkthrough today and maybe a couple of boxes. I need to leave here, mom. Everything is just a reminder of my old life and I can’t heal until I do,” I recited like a scripted answer.

Once again, I heard her sigh as I watched Kendric pull away. Maybe it had been her constant attempts to help me make peace with him, but for once, I wished it had been a day that he was off duty. As irrational as it was, I found a bit of comfort when he was out there all day.

“Well, call me this evening and let me know how it goes, please,” she said her goodbye with nothing, but displeasure.

I willingly agreed and said mine before disconnecting the line. Eventually, she would understand my decision. At least, that was what I hoped, but I would need to tell her about Adam. She wasn’t his biggest fan and where I knew she thought Kendric could do no wrong, she'd get why I didn't want to be surrounded by the shame and the lie that was my marriage.

With Adam in mind, I sat my phone on the counter and grabbed the bottle of his moonshine from the freezer. Heading toward my bedroom, there was one more box I was finally ready to take care of. When I first got home, I couldn't look at the package his squad had sent me after his death. It took three nights on the couch before I gathered enough courage to move the damn thing out of sight. Opening the closet door, I stared down at the box of Adam's things.

Swallowing my mixed emotions from seeing it, I opened the top of it and placed the bottle inside the cardboard tomb. I didn't bother to look at the contents because it felt like Caroline Greene had tainted everything. That box had represented everything I lost when the IED went off almost a year ago, but throwing it away felt like I was getting rid of all the lies.

I didn't look back as I left it in the dumpster and headed back into the house. There might have been the possibility that I would regret my actions later, but I knew if I kept it, the time capsule would be a glaring reminder of all the reasons I hated who I had become. I had sacrificed enough of my life to him and Kendric. I would not keep it and risk my ability to move on from them.

The only thing left to do was wait for the guy who was supposed to inspect the apartment, but I had already packed away the remote to the TV. With my appointment being less than two hours away, it felt like the perfect time to binge social media. I should have expected to see the text waiting for me the moment I unlocked my screen.

Hubs:

I knew he couldn't sit outside your house forever.

I knew the stalker was still watching me. It had been the only reason I didn't call someone to escort Kendric from the area the first time I noticed he was parked outside. It felt like his presence had been one of the reasons my stalker kept his distance.

Dismissing the notification, I began my pre-planned scroll fest, trying not to let the message bother me. If I hadn't packed the living room first, it might have taken me longer to get caught up on my social media platforms. I blamed my honed in moving skills for the internet spiral I found myself in an hour later.

One thing led to another and I found myself reading random stories about everything from fashion fails to accidental medical discoveries. That was when I stumbled upon a story where a woman detailed how she had similar symptoms to mine. The reason for her mysterious illness had been from the mold she found growing under her bathroom sink.

As focused as I had been on packing everything, I realized as I read the story, that I had forgotten one more area of the house that I had left to pack. I had saved it for last because I had been due to start my period at any moment and I didn't want to rummage through boxes to find a tampon. When I didn't actually start, I had forgotten to pack it entirely.

Grabbing an empty tote bag, I headed to the bathroom, praying to find the same mold as the lady in that story. I had thrown everything into that bag except for the last item shoved all the way in the back of the cabinet. I had bought the pregnancy test for when Adam finally came home.

He had promised me this was the last year he would be on active duty and his deployment took up the last few months of his contract. After we had lost our child and Adam had the problem involving his night terrors, we agreed to wait until he was home for good before we tried again. As I held the box in my hand, I reminded myself that there wasn't a point in keeping it.

The longer I held the box, the more I panicked about how late I really was. I figured there was no harm in taking the test if all I was going to do with it was throw it away anyway. With every second I spent waiting for those results, I counted how many weeks I had been late and tried to convince myself everything had been caused by my extreme stress.

The closer it got to my three-minute alarm, the more my brain circled back to the night I spent in Kendric's bed. I didn't care for the way my night with him and the correlation to the days I was late seemed to line up perfectly. When my alarm sounded, I held my breath and picked up the test.

"You have to be kidding me," I cursed as I barely registered the positive result in my hands.

Before I had a chance to properly process the karmic joke from the universe, a loud knock came from my front door. Falling in line with the rest of my messed up life, the inspector was early. I raced to my door and tried to shake off the earth shattering discovery.

I realized I was still holding the box and test in my hands as I reached for the door handle. Stuffing the test into the box and then the box into my purse by the door, I took a steadying breath. I had until tomorrow to figure out how to handle the situation, but for that moment, I needed to let the inspector inside with as little awkwardness as possible.

Mentally preparing for the last Army regulated hoop I would have to jump through, I opened the door to greet the inspector. To my surprise, it wasn't who I had been expecting to see. Standing on my front porch with a polite smile on his face stood Kevin freaking Gear.

The blast from my past and the test that haunted me from my handbag left me too stunned to greet him immediately. He didn't seem to notice as he stepped inside without a word and I had been too stunned to register that us being alone was a red flag.

"I'm sorry, Hi, Kevin! What on Earth are you doing here?" I finally greeted.

The smile reached his almost black eyes at his name and he grabbed the door as if to shut it behind us.

"I hope you don't mind me stopping by. I was visiting Daniel, and he told me about Adam. I thought I would stop by and check in on you," He answered, but he still hadn't shut the front door.

"No, not at all. How do you know Daniel?" I wondered, registering the weird charge to the surrounding air.

His smile dropped slightly as his eyes narrowed on me. "He married my cousin Caroline," he informed me as he watched my reaction to her name.

I stilled. For a reason I couldn't explain, my heart raced and it felt as if he was trying to block my only exit.

"I don't know if you would remember him, but you actually just missed Kendric Tate," I tested, as I registered a horrifying familiarity to Kevin's voice.

The moment I mentioned Kendric's name, all the kindness in Kevin's face vanished. As I took a step back to put some space between us, he reached for something behind him.

"I told you he couldn't wait out there forever," my stalker replied, a wolfish grin distorting his face.

Pulling a gun out from behind his back, he pointed it directly at my chest. He finally had me exactly where he wanted me and I only had myself to blame.

June 14, 2024

Kendric

Everyday since Laney shut me out seemed impossibly longer than the last. I raced back to stand guard at her house that evening at a speed I probably should have been arrested for.

Something about the day felt off, as if I wasn't where I needed to be.

When I put my truck into park, my phone rang loudly over my engine. I wondered if she was finally telling me I needed to go home, but the thought completely vanished when I noticed no lights were on inside her home. Distracted by the completely dark windows, I answered the call without looking at the screen.

"Tate," I greeted.

The man on the other side cleared his throat as if he expected me not to answer.

"Just thought I'd let you know, the inspection didn't happen today as promised," Henderson answered and I let out a small sigh of relief.

He had owed me a favor for the last five years and until I had learned that Laney was planning to move, I had never pictured myself using it.

"Thanks, man," I answered, observing my surroundings through my mirrors.

As uncomfortable as it had been to practically live in my truck, it seemed my presence had kept the stalker away. Where Henderson had bought me some time, it didn't appear I would have any luck trying to talk to her tonight. Judging by her car in the driveway, I figured she was already asleep.

"Of course, but I still technically owe you one. I left her a message to call me back, but she hasn't yet. I'll let you know when she reschedules," he said with a chuckle and I clenched my jaw.

I forced down the uneasy feeling I had at his admission. From my understanding, she was scheduled to fly out tomorrow and it would have taken her at least a week to get a new date for him to come by. As him and I gave our goodbyes, my phone beeped in with a call from her mother, only adding to a growing sense of dread in my stomach.

"Mrs. Martin?" I answered, trying not to let my worry reflect in my voice.

Faint shuffling filtered over the line before her voice came through.

"I know you guys aren't really talking right now, but she told me you have been showing up before and after your shifts. Can you tell me if she's at home?" Mrs. Martin rushed out, skipping the hellos in her panic.

I glanced toward her parked car in the front of her house again. Even though she could have been out with friends, I knew she wasn't crazy about letting anyone else drive after her accident. It took a lot for her to trust me enough to do it.

"Her car is here, but the house is completely dark. I think she went to bed early for her flight," I answered, although I didn't feel like that was the case anymore.

I heard her mother let out a sigh, but it hadn't been a breath of relief. She didn't know what to think either.

"Her flight isn't until tomorrow evening. She promised me this morning that she'd call back after the inspector left," she replied absentmindedly, but I was already getting out of my truck.

If she had been expecting Henderson, it didn't explain why she would ghost him. Something kept trying to pull me back here all day long and I was wondering if this had anything to do with that strange feeling.

"I'll check it out," I reported as I got to the front steps of Laney's porch.

Her mother made me promise I would keep her updated before we said our goodbyes and I disconnected the line.

The last thing I wanted to do was worry the woman anymore than she was, but I knew something definitely wasn't right.

When I reached for the doorknob, I found the source of that gut feeling. Even though the door looked to be shut, it wasn't closed enough for the door to actually latch. Maybe she had left in a hurry and somehow, that only terrified me more. Going back to my truck, I called her mom and let her know her daughter wasn't home. I was planning to sit out there tonight regardless, but I didn't sleep a wink as I waited for Laney to come home.

Chapter Twenty-Three

June 15, 2024

Delaney

I hadn't seen Kevin Gear since our graduation from Morley. The more messages that were sent from Adam's phone, the more I thought it would be connected to his life or Kendric's from their deployments. I never thought I'd recognize the face behind it or that it'd be someone who had always been so kind to me.

I had also always assumed the bet and games Kendric warned me about had all been Quinton's idea. Kevin had seemed to just be playing along. He wasn't a spineless kid trying to fit in. He was an absolute psychopath.

"Good morning, Del," Kevin greeted as he entered the small room he had locked me away in overnight.

He had driven me to a house in Morley not far from the home Adam grew up in. I could tell by the shrine of his highschool football days it was probably his childhood bedroom. He missed my glare as he admired the photos he displayed on the walls.

"Why are you doing this?" I demanded to know, skipping the pleasantries.

His smile dropped slightly at my question as he stalked toward me holding a paper bag soaked with grease. The smell of the fast food rotted my stomach lining. More at the disgust toward him, not the morning sickness I was now aware I had been having.

"Careful now. Your brainwash sessions are showing," he warned.

The whole way here, he had ranted about how Kendric and Adam had filled my head with lies. He was convinced the only reason I hadn't been with him sooner was because they had blinded me to anyone else. It quickly became clear I had yet to become the target of his rage and if I wanted to escape from him, I needed to remember that.

"I'm just trying to understand," I tried again.

I couldn't get past his reasoning for keeping me there. He knew even back then I never thought of him that way. I hadn't seen this man in almost a decade.

He just pinned me with a calculating look as he came to sit down on the edge of the bed he had tied me to. Trying not to touch him, I brought my knees to my chest, but he didn't seem to notice my aversion. The moment I pulled away from him in the only way I could, he gently placed his hand reassuringly on my knee.

"It's time to eat. I can't have you wasting away on me. We can talk about it later when you are ready," he avoided the question as he removed his hand from my skin.

Even if I wasn't being held against my will, I hadn't exactly been able to keep down much of anything lately. I wasn't even sure you could consider what he had in that bag as actual food, but I didn't know how he'd react if I refused it. Forcing myself to at least try to appease him, I nodded and plastered on a small smile.

My only hope of survival was to play along as much as I could until Kendric realized I was missing. I tried not to think about the fact he would find out I had planned to leave today. If he knew about it, there was a chance he would assume I just left early to avoid his final attempt to apologize.

Kevin opened the bag and immediately, I felt the panic. I turned my head while he rummaged through it, praying I wasn't about to vomit from the smell of the burgers alone. I closed my eyes and gathered my strength as I swallowed the bile already rising up the back of my throat.

When I turned back to face him, he patiently held out a fry for me with a hopeful stare. This seemed to be a test and I didn't want to find out what he would do if I failed it. I made my mouth open for him while I forced back the tears that were threatening to show from my fear that wouldn't keep down.

Almost lovingly, he fed it to me and watched as I chewed it slowly. I tried to swallow it, but it tasted like it had been fried in old oil. Immediately, my body rebelled. Unable to control it, I choked before spitting it back up on the bed beside me.

Terrified of his reaction, my eyes shot up to his before I began to profusely apologize. I watched his kindness morph to absolute rage as if I had done that out of nothing but spite. Trying to think quickly on my feet, I shot out the only excuse I could think of.

"I'm sorry, Kevin. Really, it's not you. I caught a stomach bug from the daycare. You can call my mother. She will tell you how she had begged me to see the doctor for days now," I explained and something I said seemed to trigger his paranoia.

"You don't have children. Don't lie to me," he challenged with a humorless laugh.

The way he said it seemed to imply he already knew everything about me. He had no idea how wrong he was. I shook my head adamantly to hide the fear that he would figure out exactly what caused the biological reaction.

“I don’t…I’m not…I promise. I had to get a job after Adam…” I trailed off as his nostrils flared at the mention of my late husband’s name.

“I work at a daycare here in town,” I answered and it seemed to be enough to satiate his jealousy for the time being.

He nodded in acceptance at my excuse before he reached back into the bag, as if he planned to ignore the fact I couldn’t seem to hold down the breakfast he had bought for me. I tensed as he brought his hand back out, expecting him to force feed me another bite, but he had brought out a napkin instead. I froze as he reached over me to clean up the mess I had made on the bed.

“We will try again later,” he threatened.

As he stood to leave the room, I reminded myself that I needed to play into his delusion. The longer he thought I was trying, the more time I was giving Kendric to figure out where. I forced the most sincere smile to my face that I could manage and cleared my throat to grab his attention.

“T-thank you…for taking care of me,” I stuttered out, hoping he believed I had meant it.

He returned my smile and tilted his head to the side as if my appreciation had seemed almost random.

“Of course, Laney. All I want is the chance to show you I could have been doing this all along,” he promised with nothing, but honesty in his voice.

I knew if I had left it at that, he would have walked out of the room leaving me alone for a little while longer. As much as I needed that time to myself to figure out a way to escape, I needed him to think I was understanding his insane train of thought.

“I know and I-I trust you. You have always been so sweet to me.”

I swore I saw a blush creep across his cheeks before he quickly turned to leave. As he shut the door behind him, I pulled at my restraints in the hopes I would feel some kind of give. They didn’t budge and I wished he had tied my hands together instead at opposite sides of the bed.

Leaning back against the headboard, I focused on the photos along his walls instead. In most of them, he was wearing his uniform. He had been in almost all of them and in over half of them, he had been standing beside Quinton.

In every photo, I could clearly see that his smile didn't meet his eyes. In fact, the only ones he wasn't forcing a smile for were the ones where he stood beside a man in a crisp suit and tie. The way Kevin seemed like a younger carbon copy of the man in the blazer made me believe it had been his father.

I switched my focus on the photos that didn't seem to match the others. That was when I saw the photo he had pinned to the wall. It was the only photo he displayed that covered the other person's face with a thumb tack. I recognised the background before I recognized the man.

Mangled metal reflected behind both of them and the camera had cut off someone holding a red solo cup on the side of the photo. It had been taken at the Spring Fling. I knew the person standing beside Kevin hadn't been Quinton.

Quinton hadn't worn his letterman's jacket to the event. Squinting, I tried to make out the number on the jacket. I did a double take as I realized the embroidered patch read the number seventeen, Adam's number.

The sound of the doorknob stopped my search for clues in its tracks. I waited for Kevin to enter in hopes I could use what I found in my favor, but I hadn't really learned a ton of information I didn't already know. As obvious as his rage was for the pin placement over my late husband's face, I had already learned he was a topic to avoid if I wanted to get closer to my captor.

"I'll give you one chance to prove to me I can trust you," Kevin said through his teeth.

This time, he hadn't said it as if he was full of just anger. There was something else behind his words. I carefully scanned him, using the same observation skills I had used for years to find my way through Kendric's armor.

"I'll do anything," I offered as I noted the cell phone clutched in his hand.

The whites of his knuckles and the way he avoided my eyes told me everything I needed to know. Something happened that scared him between when he had left the room and now. In my gut, I knew it had something to do with Kendric Tate.

"Call off your dogs," his tone was deadly serious, confirming my assumption.

Swallowing hard, I nodded and watched as he unlocked my cell phone. Hesitantly, he headed over to my side of the bed and placed the device on speaker phone close enough for me to speak.

"Laney! Where are you? Are you okay?!" Kendric rushed out in pure panic as he answered the call.

I forced down the guilt as I looked up to keep eye contact with Kevin. His expression told me he was waiting to see if I had just lied to him.

"I've said it once and I'll say it again; I'm not seventeen anymore. You need to move on and accept I am going to my mother's and for the love of God, stop freaking calling me," I declared, hoping he would catch my hidden clues.

Satisfied at my response, Kevin disconnected the line before Kendric could respond. I waited to see if my stalker bought my carefully curated lie.

June 15, 2024

Kendric

The line disconnected as I stood in Laney's living room. She had sounded so convincing, but there was something in how she said it that didn't feel right. As I stared at the boxes that only confirmed her response, I told myself I was reading too much into it.

I headed toward her front door as I tried to convince myself she wouldn't have answered if she had been in any real trouble, even though I must have called her ten times that morning only to reach her voicemail. It wasn't like the stalker would have let her keep her cell phone. All I knew for sure was how badly I had messed everything up with her.

Her statement replayed in my head and for a moment, I repeated part of her statement as I placed my hand on the door knob. In all our conversations since we reconnected, that comment she made over the phone had been the only time I could remember her referring to herself when she was seventeen. Maybe she had said it as a way of telling me she wasn't a child, but it didn't feel like that had been her meaning.

It felt strange that she would refer to the same age she had been when she and I had broken up, but part of me felt I was grasping at straws. I needed to accept that I had lost the only chance I had left with her. Shaking my head, I went to open the door to leave when a knock on the door startled me back to reality.

Without debating on if I should answer, I opened it. I wasn't about to wait for whoever it was to get back into their car before I could take her advice. The longer I stayed there, the more I would psychoanalyze her cowardly goodbye, only forced by my persistence to get a hold of her. I shouldn't have been surprised to find Daniel on her doorstep.

"Daniel," I greeted, unamused.

His eyes widened as he saw me before irritation replaced his momentary shock.

"Kendric? I need to speak to Laney," He quickly dismissed as he tried to look for her over my shoulder.

I straightened my spine, mimicking the way he tried to keep her out of my sight the night I came to explain why I had kept his wife's letters a secret. I didn't hide the smile on my face as I dismantled his hope of seeing her.

"She's not here right now," I started to close the door behind me to leave, forcing him to take a few steps backward.

Daniel returned a cocky grin as if I had been lying to him in an attempt to block his access, "Nice try, Kendric. Her car is in the driveway," he reminded me.

He was right. It was and at his reminder, I leaned back into her entryway to glance at the shelf that usually held her keys. If he hadn't said anything, I probably would have missed the most concerning clue of them all.

I found her keys still laying on the shelf untouched. Her door had been left slightly ajar. Would Laney forget her keys like she did locking the door? And if she had run out of the house to visit friends, why did she leave her purse on the hook just below them? Concealing my concern for her safety, I stoned my features before turning back to the jerk who stood there impatiently waiting for my answer.

“And you are convinced everyone else she knows is incapable of driving?” I retorted, hoping he didn’t know about her need to be the one to drive.

I knew before I said it that my tone would make him angry. Even though I knew I shouldn’t have been trying to push his buttons, it helped to calm my nerves. His immediate response to it made this game almost too easy.

“No, but I find it pretty hard to believe she’d willingly let you into her house after you kept her husband’s affair from her,” he hissed and I stilled.

I knew Laney well enough that when he said it, she would have told him who she thought Adam was sleeping with. He didn't seem too heartbroken about the fact it had been with his wife.

"I was trying to protect her, but you don't seem surprised that your wife played such a key role in all this," I volleyed back and he curled up his lip at my response.

I had struck a nerve. I couldn't lie and say it wasn't therapeutic, but I wondered if Laney had known I wasn't the only one keeping it a secret.

"My marriage is none of your concern and neither was Laney's for that matter," he warned in a low voice, reminding me he thought she was still somewhere in the house behind me.

"That's funny because her husband made it my concern when you spouted off threats while your wife was serving our country," I snarled back, done with his attempts to make himself seem like he respected his wife.

I had found records from four different hospitals that detailed how little he cared for Greene's well-being. Daniel wasn't going to sit there and play the affair card when I was well aware of the truth behind those letters he was trying to use to his advantage.

Daniel's eyes narrowed on me in pure anger as he leaned in closer to me as if making sure his voice didn't carry to Laney's ears. Still unaware she wouldn't hear them no matter his volume.

"I heard about you, you know. The great Sergeant Tate, who shamelessly pined for his best friend's girl. Do you think Laney would believe a word you told her if she knew you were only using her husband's death as a way to stay close to her?

Instead of the reaction he had hoped for, all I could do was smile at his failed attempt to scare me out of her doorway. Calling his bluff, I offered a question of my own. It was clear that she didn't tell him I had already confessed the fact that my rekindled friendship with Adam had been solely to keep her in my life.

"Maybe not, but I am not the one who texted her from her husband's phone from your house for months now. Before you try to say you didn't, you should know that's not what it says when you trace his phone," I volleyed back to gauge his reaction.

Daniel stilled before confusion tainted his furrowed brow. It was one more confirmation I had needed. He wasn't the stalker and he was wasting my time trying to argue over her like property.

“What the hell are you talking about? I haven’t even texted her from my phone,” he shot back.

Realizing he was about done with this conversation, I knew I had one last chance to make sure he was not an accomplice before he gave up and walked away.

“So last month, you did not know someone was texting her from your place with his phone? Someone has been stalking her for months and all the evidence points to you,” I bluffed.

For a moment, he looked just as lost as he had been when I mentioned the phone the first time, but a hint of realization crossed his face before he went quiet. He might not have had any idea about the messages, but it became alarmingly clear he might have known who had Adam’s phone.

“Forget this. I’ll try her again later,” he spoke distractedly before he tried to turn and leave.

Wrapping my fingers in the back of his shirt, I stopped him. If he had any information that could help me find her, he wasn’t going anywhere. I’d do whatever I had to in order to force whatever he was hiding out of him.

Chapter Twenty-Four

June 15, 2024

Delaney

I watched nervously as Kevin placed my phone in his pocket as he paced the room. I tried to read his emotions in fear he had noticed that I had tried to tip Kendric off, but I didn't know my stalker well enough. He threaded his hands in his hair before he let out a frustrated growl. When he stopped and looked at me, I was sure I had sealed my fate.

"You aren't ready," he forced out as he looked toward the door, debating on what he should do.

I was too afraid to say anything. It wasn't as if I was trying to reason with someone who was stable enough to see the logic. Afraid anything I said would only make it worse, I watched Kevin as I focused on my breathing, trying to remain calm. If he didn't know I had left any clues, I didn't want to give it away by my reaction.

He crossed back to the side of the bed and pulled out a folded picture out of his pocket. Keeping the back of it toward me, he sat down on the mattress and stared at it for a moment without saying a word. It took everything I had not to scoot away from him this time like I had the last, but I needed him to think I was warming up to him.

“This was supposed to be us, before *he* ruined it,” Kevin said barely above a whisper.

It sounded like he was talking about an arch nemesis like he wasn’t the villain who had kidnapped me and stalked me for months. When he sat the picture down on the bed, I recognised it immediately. It had been taken on the same day as the photo tucked into the case with Adam’s flag.

Kevin followed my bewilder stare to the photograph of me in Adam’s arms. Using his index finger, he forced the picture down onto the bed so hard, the photo curled around it. I tried not to glance at the picture where a thumb tack was stabbed in my husband’s face.

“You were supposed to smile like that at me and I know you felt it the night of the Spring Fling. *He* ruined everything,” he spat out like he was exhaling fire.

I tried to mask my confusion as I processed his words. Kevin and I had been friendly at best. Outside of that night when he offered to walk me home, he had barely said more than a couple of words to me. The venom in his voice made it sound like he didn’t remember he was talking about a dead man.

"Adam's not here anymore. He hasn't ruined anything. I promise," I tried, hoping he still believed he could win me over.

I needed Kevin to believe he still had a chance if I was going to survive this. It had been the one thing I had retained from all the crime shows I had binged. He needed to think he had gotten everything he wanted in order for me to buy myself more time.

"Adam's betrayal was paid for by karma. I'm not talking about him," he growled in response.

As he said it, the remaining pieces fell quickly into place. The flowers and the nickname. Kevin had been mimicking Kendric. He was the one who interrupted us that night. Kendric had also been the reason my stalker had been expelled because he called the police on the party when he was trying to find me.

"Kendric isn't standing in our way either. He covered up Adam's affair. There's nothing between us anymore," I reassured.

Kevin only confirmed that Adam hadn't been the only one to see what I had been in denial over for years. Even my own mother thought I had married the wrong man. I needed Kevin now to believe that there was nothing between Kendric and I if I had any hope at escaping.

As unbelievable as it felt to think it, I felt lucky that he kidnapped me when he did. I knew the moment I saw that positive test I wasn't going to go anywhere. If Kevin didn't get the chance to grab me when he did, my pregnancy would have been harder to hide. There would have been no convincing him that Kendric wasn't a threat at that point.

"He has spent a decade in love with you. If he used his best friend to find you before, he will find a way to do it again. He thinks you belong to him, but he's wrong. You are *mine*," he cursed and I tried to follow along.

He hadn't used Adam. They had been friends long before I had been in the picture, but I knew there was no point in arguing it. Instead, I tried to add on to the doubt I could see behind his eyes.

"He never loved me, not like you do.You saw how he used me to get to you. Men like that never change and you are right. I was nothing more than property to him," I lied.

Kevin looked at me as if I was the one who lost my mind. I matched his bewildered stare with questioning eyes so he couldn't see past my deception. Reaching over to a desk across from the bed, he pulled out an envelope from the top drawer.

As he opened it, I saw my name in Kendric's handwriting. He began to read it out loud.

"This was dated for May, 2018. 'Laney, I must have written this a hundred times. We have been nothing to each other for longer than we were dating, but there isn't a day that goes by that you do not cross my mind…'"

I listened to him recite the letter as my brain spiraled. That had been the same year Adam and Kendric reconnected. Kendric hadn't lied to me when he said I always had his loyalty. He just hadn't told me he never lost the love he had for me all this time either.

Unable to control my reaction to his letter, I felt the tears trail down my face. I knew Kevin noticed them the moment he finished reading. The loud rip of the paper refocused my mission as I made deliberate eye contact.

"Regardless of how he felt or feels, that relationship ended when he chose the Army over me. Just like Adam did," I tried again, but Kevin didn't seem to buy it.

He shook his head and threw the pieces of paper to the floor in disgust.

“After tonight, it won’t matter,” he hissed out as he stood.

Panic filled my lungs as I caught the deadly meaning behind his words. I wasn’t sure what exactly he had meant by his statement, but the way Kevin said it sounded like a threat. It was clear I wasn’t the only one in danger.

“What happens tonight?” I asked before I could stop myself.

He looked at me with dead eyes as he weighed his ability to trust me enough to give me an honest answer.

“Once we make sure he can’t follow you to the ends of the Earth, we can start our new life. You will never love me like you love him until we are away from the constant reminders of Kendric Tate,” he promised before heading toward the door.

“Let me help you. If he still has feelings for me, he won’t pass up the chance at trying to talk me out of leaving,” I offered out of pure desperation.

Even though I had no guarantee that Kendric had caught my clues, I knew this was possibly the last chance I had to warn him. It was also another way for me to convince Kevin to trust me. I needed him to believe I was falling for his plan and for him like he wanted me to do.

He studied my face before turning toward me to hear me out.

“But I have one request, please. I want to be there to see his face as he realizes you finally won,” I added.

A sickening smile spread across Kevin’s face at my offer to help him gloat. I had successfully baited the hook. I just prayed Kendric and I both survived the trap I was setting as my last Hail Mary.

June 15, 2024

Kendric

Daniel turned to look at me in disbelief as I pulled back on his shirt to keep him in place. The more interactions I had with this man, the harder it was not to wipe him out of existence. Whether he liked me or not, he wasn’t going anywhere until I got some answers.

“Who has been to your house, Greene?” My tone was practically threatening.

He looked at me for a moment before he glanced away out of guilt. It only confirmed he knew of someone who might have been sending the messages from her husband’s phone.

“A lot of people have been to my house. I just lost my wife,” he tried to dismiss it, but I didn’t lighten my grip on his shirt from his poor excuse of an answer.

“And Laney lost her husband, but only three people have been here. Considering your house is the only real link to the creep who has been sending her pictures from outside her bedroom window, I suggest you give me some names,” I ordered as I tightened his collar around his throat.

He huffed in response to my threat as his hands shot up to give some slack between his shirt and his ability to breathe.

“Jeez, man! Alright, but you are going to need a freaking pen and paper. I wasn’t kidding that Caroline had a whole circus of family members in this state,” I loosened my grip slightly to reward him for coming to his senses.

“Start with people who are from Morley,” I followed, remembering the clue Laney had given me in her call.

Daniel blinked back his surprise. It had to be someone from our high school and Alderman's phone records proved our teacher wasn't involved. Most of the people on this base didn't even know the town was in Missouri let alone in driving distance. His immediate recognition of the name gave me hope at finding the answer.

"My wife's cousin lives there. He came by earlier today and asked about Laney," he replied to me as he rubbed his neck.

He must have thought that was all the answer I needed as we stood there, waiting for him to give me a name. When he didn't provide more after a few moments, I gave him a small shake to urge him along. Whoever it was seemed to have Daniel terrified to narc on him.

"Name. Now…" I hissed as I tightened my grip again on his shirt.

"Kevin, Kevin Gear. He's off his rocker, but I swear if I had known he would try to hurt her, I would have called the authorities," he finally sputtered, no longer filled with anger, but fear.

I dropped my hold on him the instant he said it. The nickname finally made sense and as hard as it was for me to grasp why he had been after Laney after all this time, in a way I kind of understood it. Laney had a way of getting under your skin and consuming your thoughts. I would know.

I pulled my phone out of my pocket with the full intention of calling in a favor to get Kevin's address. As I struggled on if I should have been calling the cops instead, I noticed the notifications that I had missed in my battle with Daniel for the answers.

Laney:

Meet me at the bench you found me at after the Spring Fling, but don't bother coming if you just plan on trying to talk me out of saying goodbye.

I stared at my phone as I realized she probably hadn't been the person who sent it. Doubling back to lock up her house, I reached for her set of keys on the shelf, my hand bumped into her purse, accidentally sending it flying across the floor. As my eyes fell to the source of the crash, they landed on the box that fell, blocking my clean exit.

Unable to breathe, I bent down to pick it up as her mother's words sounded off in my head. Laney hadn't caught a stomach bug. She was pregnant and any debate on calling the authorities went out the window. Kevin Gear had my entire world held captive and I'd be damned if he got away with that alive.

Chapter Twenty-Five

June 15, 2024

Delaney

I waited in the room alone as I doubted my plan to save Kendric. As much as I had hoped that Kevin hadn't wished Kendric harm, I knew that hope was almost as irrational as he was. I needed Kendric to heed the warning that I helped Kevin type out.

The longer I sat there, the more I realized I had been too caught up in saving my soldier and his child to remember who the text had been sent to. I hadn't accounted for the one thing I knew I could rely on when it came to Kendric. Even if he caught the message in between the words of the text, there wasn't a situation where he would pick saving his own life over mine.

Kendric's letter had made that overwhelmingly clear, but it took me being alone in my thoughts to realize it. All I could do was sit there and wait as I grasped at impossible plans to correct my mistake. If I hadn't second guessed everything between us, neither of us would have been in this situation.

When Kevin finally entered the room, I was prepared for anything I had to do in order to secure Kendric's safety. I watched as my captor moved through the room with scattered steps as if the nervousness of his plan had eaten away at his confidence.

"Is it time?" I asked coyly as he came to my side.

With a nervous smile, he nodded before he reached behind himself. Through the dresser mirror, I watched as he resituated the gun tucked between his jeans and his shirt. It wasn't going to be easy to grab it from him unless I was patient for the right time.

Forcing every muscle in my body to relax, I didn't react as he leaned over me to untie the hand furthest from his side of the bed. Fighting the urge to recoil became almost impossible, so I forced myself to look up at him to keep his chest from touching my face with every breath he took. I put my newly freed hand in my lap as he instinctively guarded his gun and readjusted to untie the other wrist.

"We could always just drive. His goodbye could be a suggestive selfie of the two of us. All it'd take is to see me happy with someone else," I tried once more, hoping he would take the out I was offering.

For a quick second, anger flashed behind his pupils as he eyed me suspiciously. Trying to keep up the act, I bit my lip and forced a blush to my cheeks. The shameless attempt to appear flirty worked better than I thought it had.

“I need more than that for reassurance. I think he needs to see it in person,” he grumbled under his breath as he freed my other hand.

I rubbed my wrists softly as I nodded and forced a soft smile to my face. Plan B it is.

“You are right, It’d send a stronger message,” I praised him, even though it made me sick to do so.

He shot me a look of approval as he extended his hand. Taking it with no hesitation, I silently forced down the repulsion of his skin against mine. The best thing about him being unable to see logic was the fact it was easy to convince him I was feeling a similar attraction.

Like a good captive, I let him guide me to the front of him and he pushed us toward the door. I spent every step through his grime covered house, coming to terms with what I needed to do. It wasn’t until we made it to his car that I figured out the flaw in my sleep deprived logic.

As he popped open his trunk, I knew he had no intention of letting me be seen. If only I had included that in my planning, I might have found a good reason to talk him out of it. He wasn't taking me on this field trip to use as bait; my text had secured that for him.

"Are you wanting me to climb in there?" I asked, pushing my luck.

He nodded, studying my face for any signs of betrayal. I knew I was running on borrowed time, but I couldn't make myself climb into that trunk willingly just yet.

"It'll be pretty hard to show me off if he can't see me...babe," I added but it felt disgusting to say it.

His brows pulled together as his irritation became clear. I had pushed a little too hard after being too eager to show my loyalty.

"But, if that's what you need me to do, I won't question it," I quickly backtracked before turning to face my mobile tomb.

Seeming satisfied by my answer, he didn't question my original defiance. By the time he shut the trunk over me, I had already moved on to plan C. All I needed to do was wait until we were on the move.

In all of his planning to take me prisoner and seek his revenge against Kendric, he hadn't cared enough to discard the extra rope he kept in his car in case his attempt to make me get in the car by gunpoint had failed yesterday. He didn't know his lack of preparation and ability to see reality would be his undoing.

The realization it could also be mine caused me to second guess my final plan to escape. I tried to focus my mind on the memories I had with Kendric and Adam when we were teenagers. More often than not, those had been the happier times I thought of when life got hard. It was thanks to them that I even had the plan to begin with.

When I first moved to Morley, one of the first things we did as a trio was go to a drive-in movie playing on the outskirts of town. We were barely old enough to drive, let alone hold down jobs, so Adam's mother had been the only one who provided any money to go. To save on the tickets, Kendric and I hid in the trunk of Adam's car.

As quietly as I could, I popped down the back seat, just like I had done all of those years ago with Kendric to watch that movie. Kevin had been too nervous to focus on anything other than the road in front of him. Rope in hand, I crawled out of the trunk without being noticed.

By the time he saw me in his rearview mirror, it had been too late. With the rope twisted in my fists, I wrapped it around his neck and pulled my makeshift garrote tight toward me. I closed my eyes shut as tight as I could as I felt the car speed up before swerving out of control as he tried to fight it. All the while, I was fighting flashbacks from the last car accident I had been in.

This time, I wasn't in the passenger seat and terrified. I hadn't been cramping and I wasn't trying to reach my husband overseas as my mother raced to get me to the hospital. I opened my eyes as a giant oak tree filled the view out the windshield.

Just before we slammed into it, he slacked against the rope. On impact, I flew upward, bouncing my head off the roof of the car as the yellow dust from the disturbed upholstery sprinkled down around us like tainted snow. My head bounced again off the headrest of his seat. I lost consciousness, but my very last thought was how grateful I was that I had kept Kendric safe.

June 15, 2024

Kendric

I must have waited in my truck across from Morley high for an hour before I realized Kevin wouldn't show. If he had expected me to be on the bench waiting for the ambush, he was kidding himself. Everything in me screamed I should have gone to the address my buddy had found for him instead of waiting.

When it was clear there was no sign of him, I gave into that impulse. The chances it had been sent as a distraction made me too anxious to stay there. The longer I waited, the longer Laney was at risk.

As I pulled out of my parking space, I dialed the number to Morley's police station. It hadn't been what I had wanted to do, but if I was driving right to my execution, I knew they wouldn't be far behind me. All I cared about was getting her away from him and I couldn't do that if I died trying.

According to my GPS, he lived on the outskirts of town. It wasn't until I got the address that I realized it matched the one Donaldson had found for Greene's package. It had been eerily similar to Adam's. Instead of 1285 Briar, where Adam's mother lived out her last days, Kevin's address was 1852 Blair only a few minutes away.

I had been too lost in my head to notice the smoke at first as I turned onto the poorly paved road a mile from his lair. Just as I passed a row of giant oak trees, I saw the wreckage. An older silver sedan was mangled and smoking as a bloodied man stepped in front of the open back door.

I had no intention to stop for him, but he looked at me while I passed by and I recognized him immediately. Slamming on my brakes, I threw the truck into park, and pulled my gun from its holster, carefully getting out of my truck.

He had been so focused on pulling Laney out of the vehicle that he didn't see me approach. If he had stuck around, it meant she might have survived that wreck. Forcing my fear for her life to guide my hand, I lined up my shot. I waited until he saw me. The moment his eyes met mine and he reached behind his back, I pulled the trigger.

Everything that happened after felt like a blur. I saw Laney. No sooner than I got to her side, sirens sounded in the distance. I watched them load her into the back of an ambulance as an overweight officer took my statement and asked me pointless questions. The moment they saw the rope and restraint marks on her wrists, any concerns about my shooting had been erased.

I barely remember the drive to the hospital or the way I had to plead with the nursing staff to let me into her hospital room. My first clear memory of being there was her big green eyes staring at me as I crashed through the door. It was the first time it felt like I had breathed in days.

Judging by the way she immediately teared up at my face, she must have felt the same. I stayed still as I remembered the pregnancy test that sat in my passenger seat. How would she react with the way we had left things?

“Oh, thank God…” she let out in a rushed whisper as I walked to her side.

I didn’t know how to ask her if she was okay or what it had all meant for our child. All I could do was stare at her in disbelief as the memory of her body laying half out of the car haunted me.

“Del…” I started, but the nickname felt foreign now.

I had only ever referred to her by that, when I wanted to put space between us, but that was the last thing I wanted right now. It only left my mouth because I wanted to respect the boundaries in place that she had set the last time I saw her.

“Don’t call me that…” She chided with a teary grin.

I let out a chuckle as I sank into the chair beside her bed as tears gathered in my eyes. To my surprise, she reached for my hand as I heard the most beautiful sound echo in our moment of quiet. It sounded like hoofbeats, and I lost all control of my emotions, my tears streaming down my face in relief.

“The baby is okay?” I glanced at the monitor containing a second heartbeat.

She nodded, stunned.

“We are going to be just fine. I was more worried about you. One of the nurses kept talking about how lucky I was to survive the shoot out and I didn’t know where you were…” she rattled through sobs of her own.

I squeezed her hand and gave her the moment to scan me over, knowing she’d realize it hadn’t been a fair fight for Gear. She squeezed mine back with a quiet, thankful expression.

“He didn’t get the chance to hurt me,” I reassured as I watched her process what I meant.

We sat there in silence for a while before I finally broke it.

“I’m sorry I didn’t tell you about the letters, but you should know I don’t think they were talking about an affair,” I admitted as she looked down at our hands to avoid my eyes.

“Kendric, it's fine. You don’t have to explain. I get it...” she tried, but I couldn’t let her keep thinking Adam hadn’t loved her enough to stay faithful.

“Daniel had been abusing his wife. Adam was trying to help her leave. I found medical records and her roommate confirmed the context behind the notes,” I explained and she finally looked back up at me.

Seeing her realize her husband was still the man she married wasn’t as hard as I imagined it would be. I felt no jealousy or guilt in seeing her mourn him and I knew if I had taken the letters to protect her, we never would have found out the truth behind them. Somehow even in his death, Adam had brought her and I closer and I loved him for that. He truly was my best friend.

“When we get home, I have another letter you should read,” I spoke softly, remembering his goodbye message.

Finding it had been part of the reason I spent so much time in that damn storage room. It was one last promise I could keep to him.

“Speaking of letters...Kevin read me one of yours,” Laney revealed. I stilled.

“On the last day of our last deployment, Adam and I had traded them. We wanted to make sure if anything happened to us before we got home, the other could deliver it to you…” I admitted as I wiped my face.

She studied me quietly, taking everything in.

“That's why I disappeared into my locked room. I was trying to find it for you after we...” I tried to finish, but I couldn’t out of shame.

She squeezed my hand as she glanced at our baby’s monitor.

“I get why he wrote me his, but I don’t understand why you wrote me one too. We didn’t even talk back then after the breakup. I’m not doubting your love for me, but you wrote it when you had no idea if I’d even open the envelope,” she whispered as if thinking her doubt out loud.

I followed her stare as I memorized the green jagged lines that ran along the screen.“Because I didn’t want to die knowing you thought I didn’t love you and to let you know I knew I messed up when I let you go the first time. I swear to you, I won’t make that mistake again,” I confessed honestly to the glorious hoofbeats sounds around us.

Epilogue

August 6, 2024

Delaney

It had been a year since my Adam died and yet felt like a lifetime ago. As I placed the sunflowers in the vase built into his headstone, I wondered what he would have thought of me. I didn't feel like the same person I had been when he boarded the plane for his last assignment.

Placing my engagement ring over my stomach, I pulled an old dirty envelope from my bag. I traced my name written in Adam's sloppy handwriting nervously as I tried to gather the courage to read it. Even though Kendric had urged me to when he gave it to me, it never felt like the right time to open that wound.

It took me a while to realize it had been my way of putting off the grief I knew I would feel the moment I broke the seal of that envelope. When I woke up this morning, I realized today was the day I needed to allow myself to feel it all. There wasn't going to be a perfect day to let the heartache swallow me whole and there was no better day to read it than the anniversary of his death.

As I pulled it out of the envelope, the tears immediately began to fall. He added insult to injury as the first thing written on that paper had been the date. He wrote me his final goodbye on my birthday.

October 18, 2020

Hey Sunflower,

If you are reading this, I never made it home like I had promised you I would try to do. I know you will hate me for joining and I don't blame you. You should know I had never meant to put you in the spot to compare our love to the Army.

You have always come first for me, and even though you may not understand it, you came first to Kendric too. So, please do not blame him for the choices that I made. We both enlisted for entirely different reasons and you know mine.

He joined to escape one of the few places I believe was close to being as messed up as it is over here. All I wanted to do was provide the future you and our children deserved and our first child came so quickly. This had been the only way I knew I could ensure you got that. I need you to know I died trying to come home to you and that future and above everything else, I want you to still find that.

I could write pages dedicated to all the reasons I am writing this letter, but I know you wouldn't understand most of them. As much as I hope you would come to love yourself the way that I do, I know the only way for that to happen is if someone is there to show you how much you deserve it, like I have failed to do. I am proud to be someone you let in enough to try and I will leave you with one more request, to help make up for you having to read this instead of hearing me tell you in person.

Before I ask this of you, you should know that I am the reason things with you and Kendric ended before graduation. He had planned to propose the day you broke up. I had told him this life that I have now forced you into wasn't fair. Where I regret the pain you felt because of me, I don't regret the chance I have had to love you.

My request is that you give him a second chance. As much of an asshole as I am sure he has been toward you, it's all a show for his impossible sense of honor. Him and I found each other again after so long apart. I never expected him to hold onto you, but he did. Through raining gunfire and psychological torture, the only time I ever saw him lose focus on a mission over here had been the moments where your name had been dropped.

When I picture what your life would be if I were to die tomorrow, he is who I imagine you growing old with. If I am being totally honest, it was hard not to see it even when you agreed to share my last name. For the longest time, I hated him for being meant for you in ways I never could be. I've come to peace with that now.

He told me something while he advised me to write this and I think it will forever stick with me. He said I should write to you because it could give me one last chance to tell you how much I love you. And that you may badly need to hear it. He explained that very few people get the chance to tell someone what they meant to them before it was too late. This was my chance and then he handed me his letter for you.

So as you read this and you question my sanity for urging you to get with my best friend in the event of my untimely demise, you should know this; I want you to grow old and difficult with the one person I know loves you more than I can ever dream of. You are our safe place and I swear on my soul, he can be yours.

If I have to say goodbye, know you are reading it as I hold our little boy. I hope that gives you as much peace as it does for me.

Waiting for you on the other side and loving you every second,

Adam

www.ingramcontent.com/pod-product-compliance
Lightning Source LLC
Chambersburg PA
CBHW060632310726
48982CB00003B/749

* 9 7 9 8 9 9 2 5 5 0 8 2 5 *